First published in Great Britain in 2023 by Boldwood Books Ltd.

A CIP catalogue record for this book is available from the British Library.

Paperback ISBN 978-1-80280-301-3

Large Print ISBN 978-1-80280-302-0

Hardback ISBN 978-1-80280-300-6

Ebook ISBN 978-1-80280-303-7

Kindle ISBN 978-1-80280-304-4

Audio CD ISBN 978-1-80280-295-5

MP3 CD ISBN 978-1-80280-296-2

Digital audio download ISBN 978-1-80280-299-3

Boldwood Books Ltd
23 Bowerdean Street
London SW6 3TN
www.boldwoodbooks.com

1

'This is a joke, right?' Leona Carson stared at Detective Sergeant Potter in abject disbelief, her eyes wide with accusation. 'He was here, posting dog shit through my front door like the cowardly bastard that he is. Yet you say that isn't enough to haul him in.'

The sergeant looked bored as he waved a placating hand. 'It isn't that straightforward.'

'It doesn't have to be complicated,' Leona shot back at him, seething with a blinding rage that threatened to bring on a headache.

'Look, I know you're upset—

'Really?' Leona rolled her eyes. 'What gave me away?'

'Upset and overwrought,' Potter continued, talking over Leona's sarcasm, 'and understandably so.'

'Don't you dare patronise me!'

Leona had an honours degree from Oxbridge and was damned if she'd let a smug misogynist with a limited IQ and warped view of the world tell her that she was being emotional. She hadn't met Potter before and would be perfectly happy if their paths never crossed again. He was about as much use in a crisis as non-alcoholic wine.

She got the impression that he'd drawn the short straw insofar as he'd been on duty when her call came in. He made little attempt to hide his boredom, or the fact that he wanted to get out of her cottage as soon as possible. Leona was equally keen to be rid of him, but not until she was satisfied that he'd taken her accusations seriously and intended to do something about them.

'I wasn't, love, but you have to see things from my perspective.' He lifted one skinny shoulder. 'My hands are tied.'

'Firstly,' Leona replied, striving to retain a modicum of composure, 'I am most definitely not your love. And secondly, this has nothing to do with you. It's all about Jessop and his fixation with me. If the restraining order that I'd tried to take out against him had been granted then he wouldn't be allowed to come within spitting distance of me and we wouldn't be having this conversation.' She picked up the documentation she'd cobbled together in a futile attempt to have the order in question granted and waved it in his face. 'And yet because the world and his wife think I'm overwrought, he can do what he damned well likes. And what he likes is to taunt me by demonstrating that he can get to me whenever he likes. And, trust me, *he was here.*'

'You saw him?'

Ah, so now they got down to it, Leona thought. Of course she hadn't bloody well seen him clearly enough to identify him! The conniving bastard was far too wily to get within camera range. But then, he didn't need to let her see him. His calling card in the form of dog shit had his name all over it.

Classy!

Spring was almost upon them but the clocks hadn't changed yet and he'd visited her after dark. But she had seen his car: his distinctive, penis-compensating, yellow Lamborghini. He'd even revved the sodding engine as he drove away, just to make sure that she knew he could get to her whenever he felt like it. His behaviour was designed to intimidate, and it damned well had. It had taken over an hour after his visit the previous night for her to stop shaking, and that had infuriated Leona. She didn't want to be a victim and most definitely didn't want Steve sodding Jessop to affect her in any way at all. She had put that episode in her life behind her, acknowledged to herself that she'd been an idiot to almost fall for his line and was now determined to look forward.

Never back.

No good could come from dwelling upon past errors of judgement. The only problem was, Steve would never let her win. Revenge would be his *raison d'être* now that she'd dared to defy him and he would procure it subtly, enjoying making her sweat. She had known it all along, which was one of the reasons why she'd held off from attempting to procure a restraining order, until his behaviour had grown so bizarre that it had forced her hand. His turning up wherever she went, or so it had seemed, just watching her. Coming to her cottage. Gaining access whilst she was away, going through her things and making sure he left enough clues behind for her to know that he'd been there. As if the lingering essence of his distinctive aftershave didn't do the job. She couldn't prove it, of course. Aromas weren't evidence apparently, which is one of the reasons why her application for a restraining order had failed.

Steve knew she'd made the application though and that had probably made matters even worse for her. He would have taken it as a personal affront. No one got away with challenging Steve. She'd seen for herself just how ruthless he could be in the business world when crossed. That mantra clearly spilled over into his personal affairs. What Steve wanted, Steve got, and nothing and no one stood in his way. Certainly not a female. He claimed to love women but he actually loved to control them. Leona wouldn't be controlled. By rejecting his advances and walking out on him, although she hadn't realised it at the time, she'd dented his ego and challenged his authority.

Given her first-hand experience of his vindictiveness, would she have done things differently given her time over?

Almost certainly not. Leona wasn't the passive type.

The man she had once worked for and admired was ruthless, cunning and very clever. Devious, dark and dangerous, he thought he could walk roughshod over the law and get away with it. Leona glanced at Potter in his rumpled suit, who was currently wiping his nose with the back of his hand. She turned away again, repulsed. If this was the best that the local constabulary could come up with to counter Steve's games, then he would run rings around them and she was definitely doomed.

Dead already.

She shuddered, wondering if Steve would hold short of committing actual murder if she continued to defy him. She couldn't be sure that a man with his arrogance and self-belief understood the need for boundaries. She'd heard him remark more than once that a man couldn't thrive if he obeyed the rules. Rules were for other people. That being the case, she had to accept that Steve had no boundaries, which terrified her.

He would probably get away with killing her, despite the fact that she had repeatedly told the local force that he was capable of extreme bouts of rage. Another prediction that had doubtless been put down to the ramblings of a delusional, overwrought female who, according to Steve's version of events, had come on to him and was now making accusations to salve her wounded pride. He had stopped short of publicly accusing her of manipulating company funds but that threat was never far from the surface. And infuriating. Leona had never stolen a penny in her entire life but she'd had plenty of opportunities to do so whilst working for Steve and knew that he wouldn't hesitate to make that suggestion to potential employers. Ergo, her career prospects were bleak since any prospective employer would apply to Steve for a reference: a reference that would not be favourable.

'Well?' Potter appeared to be having trouble holding back a sneer. 'Did you actually see him?'

'I saw his car,' Leona said with exaggerated patience. 'It's hard to miss, but that was the entire point.'

'A car isn't evidence.'

'Oh for the love of God!' Leona blew air through her lips. 'How many yellow Lamborghinis are there in this part of the world? And who, other than Jessop, owns one, has reason to come to this isolated spot and would put dog shit through my door? What other evidence do you need to take this seriously?'

'We take it very seriously.' Potter cleared his throat. 'But here's the thing. Jessop was interviewed as soon as we received your complaint.'

'He was?' Leona blinked at the annoying detective, wishing she could wipe the smug expression from his face, wondering why he hadn't mentioned that not insignificant point immediately. 'Presumably he denied everything.'

'More than that. He was in a restaurant with half a dozen business acquaintances at the time you say he was here. And he could prove it.' Potter's expression had turned condescending. 'I don't much like the man but even he can't be in two places at once. I'm afraid he has a cast-iron alibi.'

'He could have slipped out the restaurant for a while,' Leona said, recognising the weaknesses in her own suggestion the moment it left her lips. Still unable to accept that anyone other than Jessop had invaded her privacy. No one else had any reason to.

Potter shook his head. 'It's half an hour away from here. He would have been missed if he was away for that long. We spoke to two of the people at that meal who both swear that he didn't leave the table, other than to use the bathroom, for the entire evening.'

'They were women, I suppose,' Leona said scathingly, wishing after she'd spoken that she'd moderated her tone. She sounded like a jealous female, out to revenge herself on a man who'd jilted her, just as Steve had suggested. Not that she *had* been jilted but it would be a waste of breath to try and persuade Potter to believe her.

'Only one. The other was a long-standing business associate. An upstanding citizen with no criminal record and no obvious ties to Jessop. Goes by the name of Hugo Rossiter: a self-made man in the electronics business.'

Leona nodded. 'He's one of Jessop's suppliers. Provides him with components for Steve's computer repair empire. People have woken up to the futility of renewing laptops every few years just so that they can say they have the latest model, or latest phone for that matter. It's cheaper to have them repaired or upgraded. That's how Steve has made his money.'

Potter actually looked momentarily human when his gaze softened. But Leona resented his sympathy, to say nothing of his sloppy detective work. No wonder the ramshackle individual hadn't risen above the rank of sergeant. Getting out of bed in the mornings was clearly a challenge that he didn't always win. 'I don't disagree with what you're saying. You believe Jessop was behind the unpleasant incident and hate to think that he will get away with it.'

'I don't have any other enemies.' Leona wagged a finger at him. 'And don't forget all the other incidents I reported, which led to my attempting a restraining order against him.'

Potter nodded. 'I think he very well might have been responsible too but he didn't do it himself and we don't have the resources to delve any deeper. He's a clever sod and we'd finish up chasing our tails, amusing him no end in the process, and he might then be in a position to turn the tables and complain of police harassment.'

Leona took her turn to give a reluctant nod, aware that it was true, even though her own mind was whirling with possibilities. 'So that's it. You won't help me.'

'Can't help you. I know you have a justifiable grievance against Jessop. I've read the file but, as you've already been told, in order to get a restraining order, you have to catalogue actual evidence.' He waved towards her file. 'You did catalogue all the incidents of harassment but not once are you actually able to swear that Jessop was personally behind them. Your photographic evidence wasn't conclusive, nor could you produce anyone to back up your allegations of actual harassment, verbal or physical.' He waved a hand to prevent her interrupting him. 'There's no law against him turning up in the same places as you, given that those places were pubs and restaurants. Public facilities in other words.'

'He came here once. I found him inside the cottage.' She almost screamed the words as her frustration built.

'But have no evidence to prove it. It's a case of "he said, she said" I'm afraid.'

Leona's shoulders slumped. 'He knows the rules and is too clever to get caught. But he also doesn't want me to be in any doubt that it's him and that he can get to me whenever he likes.' Leona folded her arms defensively and tapped the fingers of one hand on her opposite forearm. Sensing her frustration presumably, Mulligan got up from his place in front of the fire and pushed his wet nose beneath her hand. Her expression softened as she glanced down at the large, ungainly mutt rescued from a local shelter and tugged at one of his ears. Mulligan made her feel much safer and was the only good thing to have come out of Steve's intimidation campaign.

'I'm sorry,' Potter said, sounding sincere. 'But the reality is that we have to work within budget limitations and make the best use of resources available to the police service. We've interviewed Jessop and can't prove that he left that restaurant so our hands are tied. It's not like before when a crime was a crime and the criminal was chased down, no matter what. But you didn't hear that from me.'

Leona offered the man a reluctant half-smile as she stood up. This was getting her nowhere, Jessop had won this particular skirmish, and she was ready to conduct Potter from her cottage.

'Look, you've followed our advice, have a state-of-the-art alarm system, you've changed your locks, got yourself a dog.' He glanced down at Mulligan, who was again stretched full length in front of the log fire, snoring. 'And have action-motivated external lighting.'

'Which is how I saw his car. Mulligan alerted me to its presence,' she added defensively, stroking her dog with her toe, astonished at how quickly she had become attached to the creature. 'He's a great early warning system.'

'But you didn't get sight of the car's number plate.'

'Even if I had, would you have believed me?' The bitterness had returned to Leona's voice. 'You already think I'm either paranoid, out for revenge, or an attention seeker.'

'I think you're afraid, and have good reason to be. You're safe here, even if it is an isolated spot, but don't hesitate to call us if anything else happens. Anything at all.'

Leona thanked the man, albeit ungraciously, double locking the door behind him the moment he'd walked through it. She leaned against the solid wood, tears of frustration tumbling down her cheeks.

'Well,' she said to Mulligan, who had trotted at her side when she moved to the front door but now, duty done, resumed his place in front of the fire and appeared to fall asleep again immediately. 'That went well, didn't it?' She padded into the kitchen, checked for the third time that night the back door was locked and bolted, and poured herself a substantial measure of wine. 'This is no way to live,' she said, returning to the lounge and addressing the comment to Mulligan, who flapped his tail but didn't open his eyes. 'Sergeant Sloth might have his hands tied but I don't.'

She sat down with her wine, mulling over what little she'd just learned. She recalled Hugo Rossiter from his visits to Jessop's offices. She doubted there was a female employee in the place who didn't remember his rather arresting presence. Rossiter and Jessop needed one another, supply and demand and all that. So, he would likely give Jessop a false alibi, if Jessop came up with a convincing enough reason for needing one. And no one knew better than Leona just how convincing he could be when the situation called for a little inventiveness.

Even so, would the other four people in attendance be equally willing? She had no way of knowing since Potter had only interviewed one other: a woman. And women were putty in Jessop's hands. He only had to turn on the charm and they would do or say anything he asked of them.

Leona allowed herself a wry smile. She should know because she'd once been one of them. An intelligent woman, she still found it hard to fathom that she'd fallen for her boss's – her *married* boss's – line. Her pride had been hurt when she'd discovered that despite his assurances to the contrary, Jessop's marriage was still solid. No question about that, his PA had told her when she'd found what she thought was a subtle way to raise the subject. She had felt so stupid then, thinking back to all the times when she had laughed at women who were so gullible. She had never imagined that she would join their ranks.

She had belatedly stopped an affair that never should have started, which was her second mistake. Jessop, she now knew, was never dumped. If there was any dumping to be done, he was the one who did it, and she had unintentionally released the monster lurking beneath an attractive, plausible exterior, one who was thirsting for revenge, if only to salve his wounded pride. One who lived a complicated private life dominated by his wife's powerful father, and probably relished the challenge that Leona's defection had unwittingly presented him with.

Even Leona hadn't anticipated the extreme lengths he would go to in order to exact that revenge though and she realised now that she hadn't known him at all. Not really. He'd kept the true nature of his character well hidden from her. From everyone who'd worked for him for a lot longer than she had; all of whom remained unswervingly loyal to their charismatic boss.

A successful local businessman, at least on the surface, a staunch family man who gave generously to good causes and encouraged his employees to reach their full potential, Jessop was bound to be a target for vindictive females, wasn't he? That was the way that the Potters of this world undoubtedly saw it. Because Leona had found the courage to fight back, she was now forced to live in a gilded cage, with locks on doors and windows, alarms, security lights... the whole nine yards. The only good thing to come out of it had been Mulligan.

Even so, unless she became a hermit, Jessop could get to her in lots of little ways the moment she set foot outside the door, and she was damned if she would hide away, scared of her own shadow. She would never know peace of mind again until she put a permanent stop to Jessop's game.

There had to be other victims, she reasoned, but like her, they were probably afraid of Jessop's penchant for revenge, unless she could convince them that they were more likely to be believed if they banded together. Finding out who they were though would be challenging. She had heard rumours that a former colleague at Jessop Electronics had left suddenly, walking out on a promising career and huge salary. Office gossip was rife as to the reasons for her sudden departure. Leona knew her name was Annie Blakely, that she was an attractive mother of two, married to a successful solicitor who worked from home.

'Hmm.' Leona got up, threw a log on the dwindling fire and sat down again to consider the possibility that Jessop had come on to her too. He certainly had wandering hands and a healthy disrespect for the rights of selective females working for his organisation. He paid above the odds and seemed to think that entitled him to do as he pleased.

The problem was that he was so plausible and charming, a master at not revealing his hand too soon, that he got away with it. Leona was a prime example of his success rate, or would have been but for the fact that she'd failed to climb into bed with him, sensing at the last moment that she was being played. He didn't take rejection well and that, Leona now knew, remarkable though it seemed to the Potters of this world, formed the basis for his harassment campaign. Well, that and the fact that Leona hadn't gone quietly when her position became untenable and she'd started to fight back by threatening to sue for unfair dismissal.

Especially when Steve threatened to publicly accuse her of mismanaging funds. That threat crossed a line and had changed everything.

Jessop meanwhile had upped the intimidation, secure in the knowledge that no one in positions of power would take her claims seriously, which was turning out to be the case. Jessop had a lot of influential friends, most likely including policemen, accounting for the lacklustre investigation into this latest example of threatening behaviour levelled against Leona.

'Well, Mulligan,' she said, taking a fortifying sip of her wine and feeling her depression and fear falling away as she resolved to go on the offensive. Not passive by nature, it felt good to have regained a modicum of determination. 'It looks as though we're going to have to unearth our own proof about the scumbag's methods and methinks that a little surveillance on Hugo Rossiter will be as good a place as any to start. Those two used to be mates, they were at university together, I happen to know, but there's definitely not much love lost between them now. So why would Rossiter give Steve an alibi?'

Leona tapped her fingers restlessly against her wine glass as she thought the matter through. Obviously, Rossiter and Steve needed one another; they were business associates but didn't have to be friends. But still, something must have happened to drive a wedge between them. Since she *knew* Jessop was responsible for the excrement being posted through her door, it seemed like Rossiter would be as good a place as any to start her fight back. Why would he give Jessop a false alibi? Was he as morally corrupt as Steve?

And, she added without bothering to articulate another possibility to the snoozing Mulligan, there was also Jessop's longstanding PA. A woman of fifty-something. Molly Fairfax was fiercely loyal, had worked for Jessop for years and missed little. She and Leona had become friendly and looking back, Leona could see that Molly had tried to steer Leona clear of Jessop's wandering hands in a number of subtle ways. Damn, she should have listened! But at the time Leona was full of ambition to succeed and was convinced that Jessop's interest in her represented a corresponding desire to see her make something of herself.

Foolish!

'Perhaps I should contact Molly,' she mused aloud. 'Away from the office, she might be willing to give me a few pointers. I'm betting she knows where all the bodies are buried, Mulligan.'

With that thought percolating through her brain, Leona drained her glass and called to Mulligan. Cautiously she unbolted the back door and watched the garden, now bathed in light from the motion detectors, as her dog sniffed the undergrowth and lifted his leg against an evergreen shrub. The moment he returned to the house, Leona relocked the door, put the guard in front of the fire and took herself off to bed. She now had three lines of enquiry to pursue, she reminded herself as she brushed her teeth: Annie Blakely, Molly Fairfax and significantly, Hugo Rossiter.

One of them would help her, she repeatedly tried to convince herself, as she climbed between the sheets and switched off the light.

2

Hugo Rossiter, in jeans and T-shirt, sweated over his latest 'baby' in the research and development department of his growing technology empire. His reading glasses had slipped to the end of his nose. He pushed them absently back into place and then ran a hand through his hair, frustrated by his company's lack of progress with the development of the advanced semiconductor his boffins were convinced they could produce in order to beat the Europeans, who were already racing ahead, at their own game. The common goal was, of course, to eclipse the west's dependency on imports from Asia, to say nothing of realising Hugo's long-held ambition to succeed in such a fiercely competitive field.

It seemed ridiculous to be working against Europe but ever since Brexit, cooperation between the UK and its former partners had ground to a halt. So be it. With an honours degree in computer science, Hugo had graduated with a fierce determination to make a difference, to say nothing of a reputation for himself. But nothing was ever that straightforward he now knew. Red tape had quadrupled, regulations were in danger of stifling creativity and burning ambition was, Hugo was obliged to concede, no substitute for reality.

Leaving aside the shifting political climate, the struggle to be taken seriously by investors when pitching for start-up funding and all the other hoops he'd had to jump through had been exhausting. It had taken several years to get his fledgling company off the ground. Looked at in that light, Hugo felt a certain satisfaction in having got as far as he had. The race was on to produce the ultimate semiconductor, and he was determined that his name would be up there with the legends of the industry.

'Welcome to the real world,' he muttered.

'You say something, boss?' A tousled head popped up over a partition. Brad, Hugo's lead researcher and close friend, worked even longer hours than Hugo did and never seemed to need any sleep.

'Just hallucinating.'

Brad chuckled. 'Goes with the territory. Seen any flying pigs yet?'

Hugo stretched his arms above his head. 'I'm going round in circles and getting nowhere. Time to call it a day. You should hit the sack too.'

'Shortly.' His head disappeared and Hugo knew their conversation would already have been forgotten as he applied all his attention to whatever programme had just pinged on his computer. 'I could be onto something here.'

'Ready to share?' Hugo asked optimistically, aware of his friend's reluctance to shout about his theories until they had been proven to his satisfaction.

'Nah! Could be nothing. Get off and get some beauty sleep. You could use it.'

Hugo laughed and shook his head. 'That ship has already sailed.'

He straitened up from the research document he'd been reading and massaged the small of his back to iron out the kinks that had accumulated there. He glanced up at the clock on the wall and blinked. Was it really past midnight? Very likely, he conceded, picking up his jacket and switching off his laptop. It wasn't the first time that he'd lost track of time and burned the midnight oil, but he knew that unlike Brad, he was getting too old for all-nighters. He needed to pace himself.

'Night, buddy.'

A hand waved airily above the partitioning but Brad's concentration remained focused on his screen. Competitors had tried all sorts of tricks, legitimate and otherwise, to tempt Brad away from Hugo's company but Brad refused to be cajoled, bribed or flattered into leaving. He was now as much invested in their research as Hugo himself was, fiercely determined to succeed and Hugo counted his blessings daily, at least in that regard.

Hugo climbed into his modest car, a five-year-old Jaguar, half-smiling and half-grimacing when he thought of his former friend and business associate Steve Jessop's mode of transportation. Flash had never been Hugo's style. He would prefer to plough his profits back into his research but appearances, he knew, were everything to Steve.

Steve and Hugo had met at school and followed one another to university, which is why Steve had chosen Hugo's company to supply the parts for his computer repair business. Hugo had good reason to dislike Steve but business was business and there was no room for sentimentality in that sphere. Despite his disapproval of Steve's behaviour, Hugo reluctantly gave credit where credit was due. Steve had anticipated a need for thriving, affordable repair companies long before the economy tanked and it became fashionable to recycle rather than replace. Steve had done well out of it. So too had Hugo. The income from the bread-and-butter side of his company paid for his precious research; just so long as Hugo himself wasn't fixated on eating at high-end restaurants.

As he drove the short distance home, Hugo's mind reverted to the business dinner he'd attended at Steve's instance the evening before. It had gone on for hours and Hugo had resented giving up time he could spend in his lab just so that Steve could flaunt his success in front of his adoring investors. Face it, he thought, he resented any time spent in a social environment with a man whose company he had once enjoyed but whom he now actively disliked. Steve, on the other hand, seemed determined to exploit Hugo's need for his business by involving him in his social activities at every opportunity.

The investors whom Steve had insisted would be interested in Hugo's research showed a marked lack of curiosity about it. In actual fact, the only interest he received was from one of the women, who came on to him quite blatantly.

If that was what it took to secure her backing then she could forget it, Hugo thought, shuddering. She'd been attractive enough, her fingers and wrists dripping with diamonds, but she was someone else's wife and Hugo didn't do married women. Where her husband was and why he didn't attend the dinner was a question that Hugo hadn't bothered to ask. It would have implied an interest he simply didn't feel. As it was, the woman had been persistent; her bejewelled fingers constantly creeping up Hugo's thigh beneath the table. When he showed no response, he could see that it at first confused and then irritated her. Clearly, she was unaccustomed to failure.

Hugo reluctantly conceded that he'd lost the opportunity for a much-needed cash influx. But still, some things simply came at too high a price. Unlike Steve, Hugo didn't have much time for the opposite sex; they were too high maintenance and Hugo could do without the distraction.

There had been something off about that dinner, he thought now as he continued to drive home through the deserted streets. It had felt as though Steve had an alternative agenda. When didn't he? he wondered, rolling his eyes. The entire evening had felt contrived but he couldn't for the life of him decide why it had seemed that way. Getting high flyers together in expensive eateries was Steve's way of doing things. His wife led her own life and seldom attended his business functions. That suited Steve, who preferred to keep her in the background. He certainly played away on a regular basis and liked to boast to Hugo about his conquests.

His wife Stella, from a wealthy family, behaved as far as Hugo was aware in a similar fashion. She always flirted outrageously with Hugo whenever the opportunity presented itself, even in front of her husband.

Especially then.

It seemed to work for the couple to have an open marriage. Stella ran a fashion design company, having her outrageously over-priced creations made in third world sweatshops, and was probably more successful in monetary terms than her husband. Her wealthy and politically ambitious father had at first balked at the idea of his precious only daughter marrying a westerner.

All three of Bizham Nawaz's sons had married women from their own background and seemed intent upon adding to their growing families. Nawaz supported them all and employed all three sons in his own business empire. Stella, his favourite child, continued to forge her own path but still received financial backing from her father as did Steve, Hugo suspected. But that was something he would never admit to, thereby implying a lack of financial guile.

Hugo didn't approve of Steve's tactics and certainly had reservations about Stella's willingness to add to her wealth through the exploitation of workers in Bangladesh. He recalled raising the subject once at the end of a dinner party when they'd all had too much to drink. Stella had pointed out that things were different in her native country; that there was no welfare system and if people didn't work then they didn't eat so ergo, she was doing them a favour. Everyone else at the table seemed to think that Stella was some sort of white knight, but Hugo thought she was taking advantage of desperate people in order to feather her own nest. He kept his mouth shut though, just as he kept his opinions regarding Steve's operating methods, both professional and personal, to himself.

Shaking off thoughts of the previous night's dinner, Hugo pulled onto the driveway of his modest semi on the outskirts of Chichester and cut the engine. The house looked dark and gloomy in what was now the early hours but Hugo didn't much care. It was cheap, somewhere to recharge his batteries and enjoy a modicum of solitude. Somewhere to take long walks in the surrounding countryside on the rare occasions when he wasn't in his lab; somewhere to appreciate the changing seasons and the beauty of rural England.

He threw off his clothes, shrugging off the thought of food, and headed for the shower. Ten minutes later, he was between the sheets and asleep in seconds.

He rose again six hours later, refreshed and ready to go. An hour after that, he pulled back into his space in the car park adjoining his offices. It was still before eight but the parking area was already almost full. Hugo had hand-picked every member of his team, paid them what they were worth, and knew they were a dedicated bunch, as motivated as he was to win the semi-conductor race.

'Morning,' Hugo said, addressing the remark to Marlon, a tough West African, his head of security.

'Morning, boss.'

'Any problems?' Industrial espionage was a constant worry, which was why Hugo spent a large sum on security. Every inch of his premises was covered by cameras, other than the bathrooms. No one could sneeze without it being caught on CCTV. Even so, Hugo still required Marlon and his team to present a forbidding physical presence. With his bulging muscles, shiny bald head and tough stance, no one got past Marlon.

'We have company,' Marlon replied casually, nodding towards a red Ford parked directly across from Hugo's premises. Premises that were on an industrial estate, well away from the local shops and housing estates, making visitors stand out. 'A woman. Been parked there for over an hour, not moving.' Marlon chuckled. 'You must be onto something, boss, if they're trying to distract you with *femme fatales*.'

Hugo glanced at the car and the woman seated behind the wheel and shrugged. 'She won't learn anything sitting there. Still, I know you'll keep an eye on her.'

Marlon grinned. 'Ain't no hardship.'

'You can't see her features. She could look like the back end of a bus.'

'Unlikely, if she's been sent here to distract you.'

'Ha!' Hugo gave a dismissive glance in the direction of the car. 'She's choosing an odd way to go about it if that's the case.' He gave Marlon's shoulder a slap. 'But still, I dare say she'll get round to telling us what she wants eventually. Most likely a reporter. But I know you'll watch her every move.'

'Count on it, boss.'

Hugo glanced over his shoulder one last time before walking away. They often had industrial spies lurking around the estate. This one was more blatant than most and probably imagined that sitting opposite his offices in plain sight would disconcert Hugo. He shrugged, already dismissing her from a mind that had more important problems to wrestle with. She would have to do something more original than loitering to concern him. Even so, the woman's presence bothered Hugo for reasons he was unable to rationalise and remained at the back of his mind, distracting him for the rest of the day.

When he left that evening at a modest ten p.m. she was nowhere in sight. According to Marlon's replacement, she'd left at the end of the lunchbreak and not returned. But nor had she approached the premises, asking for an interview, or whatever it was that she'd actually wanted.

'Odd,' Hugo muttered as he climbed into his car and fired up the engine.

* * *

Leona cursed her stupidity. What had she expected to achieve by sitting so conspicuously outside Hugo Rossiter's business premises? If that was the best she could do to fight back against Steve's intimidation campaign then she might as well pack it in now. She knew her presence had been clocked by his security team but they didn't seem unduly concerned and hadn't approached her, demanding to know what she wanted. Precisely what she would have done if they had, she had yet to decide.

'Way to go, Leona,' she muttered derisively.

She had watched Rossiter's arrival and observed him through binoculars as he spoke with his security man. They'd obviously been discussing her because they both looked in her direction. She assumed that someone would come and ask her what she wanted eventually and by the time that they did, she would have thought up a convincing reason to ask to speak with Rossiter. It was a testament to how rattled Jessop's calling card had made her that she'd come here blind. That wasn't ordinarily her way but the walls of her cottage had felt as though they were closing in on her and she'd had to get out for a while. At least she could tell herself that she was being proactive.

Fighting back.

The lunch break came and went but not many people left Rossiter's laboratory in order to feed themselves. Clearly, they were a dedicated bunch. Either that or Rossiter expected his pound of flesh.

Leona tried to remember all she knew about Rossiter, wondering again why it always felt as though there was a frosty atmosphere when they were in the same room. Steve had told her several times that they'd been joined at the hip during their university days but looking back, something didn't ring quite true about that assertion. Despite her closeness with Steve, they had never socialised with Rossiter, which supported Leona's growing conviction of a rift – a rift that wasn't of Steve's making. She wondered now if Steve had deliberately kept them apart for some reason. He wasn't big on competition and in terms of masculinity and attractiveness, Hugo could give it to him in spades.

She'd crossed paths with Rossiter in her role as head of PR for Steve's company. He had cooperated with her requirements. Well of course he had. His own company got free promo out of it. He'd always been professional and polite and yet slightly impatient; his mind on higher matters, she'd always thought.

She wondered if Steve was jealous of his reportedly fierce intellect. He had mentioned more than once that Rossiter had always been ambitiously determined to make his mark as a scientist. Steve had been equally determined to make a fortune and had already achieved that ambition, thanks in part to his father-in-law's generosity, so the slight resentment she'd noticed whenever Steve spoke of Rossiter's research seemed misplaced somehow. Besides, Steve had been to Oxbridge too so was no slouch in the intellect department. He simply chose to use that intellect for his own advancement.

'This is stupid,' Leona said aloud, when two in the afternoon came round and there were no further sightings of Rossiter. Her stomach rumbled, reminding her that she'd skipped breakfast and hadn't had the foresight to bring any lunch with her. Her bladder was also full. 'A fine spy I'd make,' she added, firing up the engine and moving away from the spot she'd been parked in for hours.

'There has to be a better way to get Rossiter's attention,' she told Mulligan as she walked him that afternoon, having devoured a sandwich and two coffees. Mulligan snuffled at the hedgerow and offered no opinion. 'I know where he lives. I recall him mentioning his humble abode when we chatted once at the office. Well, if the mountain won't come to Mohammed...'

The problem was, if Rossiter had given Steve a false alibi, he wasn't likely to make that confession to Leona. Even so, she had to start somewhere. Her business meetings with Rossiter had left her with the strong impression that the man had integrity. The slight disapproval he couldn't always hide regarding Steve's *modus operandi* reinforced that impression.

She shook her head. How could that be if he'd lied to the police for Steve's sake? She was working on the assumption that he hadn't wanted to but needed Steve's business too badly to let his mate down. Steve had remarked more than once that Rossiter was driven by the need to make a real name for himself by beating the opposition in the race to produce an advanced semiconductor that would invigorate the entire field of technology. Steve had laughed at his ambition, remarking that personal glory did not necessarily a rich man make. Leona wanted to point out that not all men were driven by the need to amass a personal fortune but knew her words would have fallen on deaf ears.

'He's definitely jealous of his friend's ambition,' she muttered, as Mulligan introduced himself to a spaniel, wagging furiously. 'I can quite see that since I removed Steve from the pedestal I'd placed him on.'

Leona smiled at the spaniel's owner, put Mulligan back on his lead and returned home in glorious spring weather. The trees were coming into leaf and the sun was doing its bit but the season failed to lift Leona's spirits. Nothing would, she knew, until the very real threat posed by Steve was eradicated. And that would never happen all the time the police failed to take that threat seriously. It wasn't only women who were dangerous when scorned, she wanted to scream, venting her frustration.

'Now, what shall we do next?' she asked Mulligan, watching him devour his dinner. 'I am absolutely not going to sit back and wait to see what moves Steve has in mind. Passivity doesn't sit well with me. But I suppose I ought to have more of a plan than simply sitting in plain sight outside his friend's laboratory.'

Mulligan chased his empty bowl round the kitchen floor with his nose, searching for stray morsels, took a noisy drink of water and then settled in his basket for a snooze.

'You know,' she said to her dog, 'our conversations can be a tad one-sided.'

Leona scrambled some eggs and added them to a plate of smoked salmon and avocado. She consumed her light supper without much enthusiasm, cleared away and then sat down to have a good think.

Hugo Rossiter was the key to discovering just how Steve had carried out his latest scare routine but if she appealed to him, she would be asking him to choose between her, a woman he barely knew, and the business Steve put Hugo's way. It would be asking a lot of him, no matter how much integrity he possessed. But still, she was desperate and had to start somewhere.

It was time to fight back.

Before she could decide how best to carry out that ambition, the sound of her doorbell had her jumping out of her skin. Mulligan stirred himself, growling and woofing, hackles raised. Her first thought was not to answer; she wasn't expecting anyone and anyway, it was too late for callers. Her second was defiance. If Steve had the temerity to call on her then she would welcome the opportunity to tell him precisely what she thought of him. With Mulligan to back her up, she would have the advantage.

With that thought in mind, she wrenched the front door open but the words she had prepared stalled on her tongue when instead of Steve, Hugo Rossiter filled the aperture with his musculature.

'You!' she stuttered, pointing an accusatory finger in his direction.

'I figured you were attempting to get my attention,' he said at the same time. 'So here I am.'

3

Hugo was taken aback by the combination of fear and defiance reflected in Leona Carson's admittedly attractive silver eyes. What precisely he had done to make her afraid of him he had yet to fathom.

'Do you want me to leave?' he asked when she continued to stand in the doorway but failed to respond to his rather dramatic introduction. 'I'm Hugo Rossiter,' he added, feeling a need to announce himself, even though she obviously knew who he was.

There was something about the woman that had caught Hugo's attention whenever their paths crossed at Steve's offices. Her friendly attitude and obvious efficiency sprang to mind, as did her attractiveness, and thoughts of her had lingered in Hugo's mind long after their brief encounters, which was unusual. Hugo was on a mission that precluded any sort of social life and left no time for dating.

When Marlon ran her numberplate through a friend at the DVLA and told him the identity of the female in the little red car sitting outside his offices for hours, he immediately recognised her name. Naturally, his curiosity had been piqued, as had his desire to see her again and find out what it was that she'd wanted but had decided against asking for. That surprised him since nothing and no one generally came between Hugo and his fierce desire to pursue his research. But thanks to Leona's odd behaviour, his concentration had been shot for the rest of the day and he had achieved precious little.

If she'd just got to the reason for her visit then Hugo would have been able to get on with his day. He had assumed that she'd come to see him on behalf of Steve and that she'd get around to driving up to the gates in due course. Perhaps she'd been on her phone, but phone conversations didn't last for hours. He wondered if she'd been waiting for something to come through before asking to see him. It was odd, but not unheard of for Steve to send someone over unannounced if there was a supply problem. But not ordinarily a woman who worked in PR. Besides, Hugo wouldn't trust Steve and his motives as far as he could throw him. He had no reason to jeopardise the mutually lucrative business arrangement they had going but it would be a mistake, he knew, to assume that Steve was motivated by a common goal. He had, Hugo sensed, always resented Hugo. Hugo straightened his shoulders, aware that he had every reason to.

Hugo had been kept informed of Leona's continued presence and felt disappointed when he was told that she'd finally driven away. Now Hugo needed to know what she'd been doing loitering with no obvious intent when she had to be aware that she would be seen in such an out of the way location. Hugo's research had reached a critical stage and he didn't entirely trust anyone and definitely not Steve, who was more than capable of indulging in a little subterfuge in order to steal a march on him.

'No, don't go.' Her soft voice jolted Hugo back to reality. She opened the door a little wider, clearly having reached a decision. 'Since you're here, you might as well come in.'

'Thanks.'

Hugo stepped inside and was almost bowled from his feet by the enthusiasm of his welcome from a large, multi-coloured dog. The same dog that had growled at him when Leona first opened the door but who appeared to have decided that he represented no threat to his mistress's security. Hugo laughed and scratched the creature's ears, sending it into a state of near delirium. He noticed Leona watching their interaction and sensed a little of the tension drain out of her.

'I think he likes me,' Hugo quipped when the dog stood on his hindlegs and placed his massive paws on Hugo's chest.

'Yes, so it would appear. He's supposed to be a guard dog.' She looked on pensively as Hugo continued to make a fuss of the creature. 'Mulligan isn't ordinarily so effusive with strangers. Clearly, he's forgotten his duties. His training, such as it is, is still a work in progress.'

Hugo wondered what she required guarding from. 'I like dogs,' he said instead, thinking it better not to probe. 'But I work long hours so it wouldn't be fair to have a dog of my own, unfortunately. Perhaps one day.'

Hugo raised a brow when she closed the front door behind him and double-locked it from the inside. He refrained from asking her why she was so paranoid about security. He thought about the motion detectors that had flooded her small front garden with light when he'd approached the door and about the guard dog. She was obviously a lady who took extreme precautions when it came to her safety; excessively so. He couldn't help wondering why.

'Come in.'

She opened the door to a small, cosy lounge with a log fire burning and classical music playing softly through hidden speakers. Hugo felt instantly at home. His mind drifted towards his own soulless abode, a little more than a place to crash and recharge his batteries, upon which he'd never felt the need to stamp his own personality. This homely atmosphere made him wonder about his priorities and he nodded his approval as his gaze took in his surroundings.

The overstuffed couches arranged on either side of the fire looked sinfully comfortable. There were shelves of books lining one wall and a desk in the corner, upon which Leona's laptop sat open, a neat pile of files next to it.

'I'm interrupting you,' he said, nodding towards her desk.

'You saw me,' she said at the same time, seating herself in one corner of a settee and gesturing towards its twin. She didn't offer him refreshment and still seemed wary of him. Hugo sank into the cushions and watched Mulligan turn in several tight circles before settling in front of the fire and appearing to fall instantly asleep. 'That, presumably, is why you're here, to warn me off on his behalf.'

Hugo allowed his confusion to show. 'I did see you but no one sent me here.' She fixed him with a sceptical look but refrained from comment. 'I couldn't help wondering what it was that you hoped to achieve by sitting outside my laboratory.'

She blew air through her lips and looked away from him. 'As though you don't know.'

'I don't, as it happens,' he replied.

'Then why are you here?' She kicked off her shoes and curled her feet beneath her. 'How did you find me? Well, obviously, I know the answer to that one.'

'I had my security man track your car registration.'

Her eyes widened. His response had clearly surprised her. 'He can do that?'

'It's part of his job description. We get a lot of spies lurking about but they aren't usually as conspicuous as you made yourself. When I realised who you are, naturally I wanted answers.'

'You didn't ask Steve?' A note of panic entered her voice which appeared to annoy her, causing Hugo to wonder.

'I prefer to ask you,' he replied, fixing her with a direct look.

She fell into a deep contemplation and Hugo saw no reason to break the heavy silence that ensued. Instead, he massaged the slumbering dog's back with his toe and waited for her to respond. He watched her as he did so, admiring the curve of her face, the waterfall of dark hair that fell over one shoulder, her svelte form and so much more about this complex and clearly troubled female. He sensed that she was wrestling with her inner demons and felt a ridiculous desire to right all her wrongs. Ye gods, what had gotten into him? Why was he even here, for that matter? There were a dozen more pressing matters awaiting his attention – when weren't there? – but something stronger than his own will had brought him to her isolated cottage with no clear purpose in mind.

'You had dinner with Steve and others a couple of nights ago,' she eventually said.

It wasn't a question and so Hugo simply nodded, attempting to hide his surprise. He'd had no idea what to expect from her but it certainly hadn't been a reference to that rather ostentatious dinner at a leading Chichester restaurant. A dinner that had gone on for far too long. Another Steve Jessop extravaganza. 'What about it?' he asked softly.

'The police spoke to you.'

Hugo frowned. 'They did, but if Steve's asked you to get me to tell you what I said to them... Well, he could have just picked up the phone.' He spread his hands, more bewildered than ever. 'Why all this cloak and dagger stuff?'

Leona responded with a question of her own. 'Did Steve really not leave the table other than to go to the bathroom?'

Still completely in the dark, Hugo again nodded. 'That's right. He left to take a few phone calls as well but wasn't gone for very long. You know how he can be when he's playing the congenial host,' Hugo added, a note of feint disapproval entering his tone, 'everything is about him and he'd never leave the stage for long.'

Leona tapped long fingers, nails painted a vibrant pink, on the arm of the sofa. 'Then how the hell did he...' Her words trailed off and she looked directly at Hugo through huge, luminous eyes that flooded with tears. His desire to comfort her increased exponentially and so he leaned down to scratch the dog's ears until the moment passed. 'It's hopeless!' she cried, throwing up her hands. 'He's won and you might as well tell him so. Then perhaps he'll back off.'

'What do you mean? Who's won?' Hugo shook his head. 'You're not making any sense.'

'Steve's won. He always has to have the last word.'

'Why don't you just talk to him if you have a problem? You see him every day.'

'Not for the past three months. I no longer work for him.'

'Ah, then why...' The pieces fell into place. What ought to have been obvious immediately now answered a lot of questions. Leona was exactly Steve's type. Of course he would have made a play for her. Did she have the good sense to reject his advances? That, Hugo knew, would not have gone down well with a man who always had to call the shots. 'You and he were involved?' he asked softly.

She blew air through her lips. 'I fell for the oldest line in the book.'

'My wife doesn't understand me,' Hugo said softly, nodding his understanding. He felt a great deal of sympathy for the lady, wondering if she regretted the break-up of the relationship or the loss of her job more. Either way, it was none of his business and he didn't have time to involve himself with her affairs. Especially if they were connected to Steve. 'If it's any consolation, you weren't the first,' he said abruptly.

'Not much, no.'

'You're in love with him?' Hugo was surprised at the extent of his disappointment. She seemed too intelligent to fall for Steve's line in bullshit.

'I hate him!'

She shuddered, speaking with enough venom behind her words to make Hugo think she was being honest rather than expressing the resentment of a woman who'd been used and then thrown over. He glanced at the files beside her laptop. 'You really don't work for him any more?'

'I'm freelancing from home at present.'

'What happened and what does it have to do with me and that dinner the other night?' Hugo leaned forward, resting his elbows on his splayed thighs, wanting to know. Wishing he hadn't asked. 'Why are police asking questions, come to that? I asked Steve, obviously, but he brushed the question aside. He just said that someone was trying to make unjust accusations.'

'And you bought that?'

She made the question sound like an accusation. 'I simply answered the questions that were put to me honestly. You don't seem too sure about that but I can assure you that I don't lie to the police. Or to anyone else, for that matter.'

'But you depend upon your contract with Steve, so I just thought...'

'You thought wrongly,' he snapped.

'You really don't know.' She tapped a long finger pensively against her teeth. 'Well, I don't suppose you do,' she added, not leaving time for Hugo to answer her question, 'but I dare say you've already formed opinions and think I'm irrational.'

'Don't presume to tell me what I think.' He allowed himself a long-suffering sigh. 'Just tell me what I've got dragged into and I'll leave you in peace.'

'Steve would never admit to being dumped. His ego would never recover.'

Hugo widened his eyes. 'You ended the affair?'

'It wasn't an affair in the traditional way. We worked long hours together, travelling and often staying in the same hotels overnight, which is how we became friends and how I learned that Steve was on the point of divorce.'

Hugo shook his head. 'Steve and Stella have an open marriage but he will never divorce,' he told her. 'They need one another too much. The ultimate power couple,' he added on a sour note.

'I found that out just before I agreed to sleep with Steve. Of course, once I realised that he was a player, there was absolutely no chance of our relationship becoming physical, which dented Steve's pride. I don't involve myself with married men and I made that point crystal clear to him.'

'I have no doubt that he was offended,' Hugo replied, feeling relieved that Leona hadn't become another of Steve's conquests. It would be cathartic for him to receive a dose of his own medicine for a change.

She offered up a mirthless laugh. 'That's one way of putting it. He didn't believe me, of course, and simply assumed I was playing hard to get.'

'When he found out that you weren't, I imagine he didn't take rejection well? It's not something he's accustomed to.'

'He pursued me relentlessly, to the point where I felt that I had no option but to resign from a position that I enjoyed and found challenging. That way, he could save face but it still wasn't enough for him. Not that I had much choice.' She paused, plucking at her lower lip as she hesitated to speak her mind.

'Go on,' he encouraged.

'When he couldn't persuade me to change my mind and I told him that I definitely intended to leave, he told me that an internal audit had uncovered financial irregularities that I would have to explain.'

'Irregularities?'

'I had control of the PR budget. It was part of my job to arrange hospitality. Most of it was billed and accounts dealt with the payments but I had a hefty cash float that I used to... well, to deal with the smaller stuff. Gratuities mostly that oiled the wheels and bought us cooperation from the people who mattered. Obviously, there were no receipts and honesty on my part was taken for granted.'

'And he challenged your honesty?' Hugo felt his own anger erupting, even as he wondered why he was so surprised. He of all people knew how manipulative, how determined to get his way no matter what, Steve could be.

'Not only that but he told our HR manager of his suspicions. The implication was that if I decided not to leave and if I continued with the affair then the mix-up would be resolved.' Hugo could see that she was seething and wondered if this was the first time she'd talked openly about Steve's underhand tactics. 'But I called his bluff and handed in my resignation anyway.'

'HR didn't try to escalate the myth of the missing funds?'

She sent him a look. 'Thanks for believing that I'm not a thief. And to answer your question, no they didn't. I gambled on them not doing so. There was absolutely no proof and not even Steve could manufacture any. Besides, he wouldn't want the adverse publicity. What I didn't count on though was him ruining my chances of getting other employment. I have to say where I'd been working whenever I apply for a position and obviously he's applied to for a reference.'

'And he casts doubts upon your honesty?'

'Yep.' She gestured towards her laptop. 'So I have to settle for what I do now. Freelance PR, which is not well paid but at least he can't badmouth me to my clients.'

'I'm sorry,' Hugo said, meaning it.

She sent him an arch look. 'Why? None of this is your fault, is it?'

'No, but Steve and I go way back. And for the record, I have never approved of the way that he operates, either in business or his personal life. Cutting corners and having the last word has always been his way and he doesn't care who he tramples on provided he comes out on top.' He glanced at his watch. 'But really, I still don't see what all this has to do with me.'

'Yes, well...' She picked up a throw cushion and hugged it against her belly in a defensive gesture. This lady was hurting and hurting bad, Hugo sensed. Not because she was still attracted to Steve but because she was afraid of him. Hugo thought about his history with Steve, about the way he operated and what he was capable of, and felt sorry for her. She'd inadvertently made herself a formidable enemy. Even so, he didn't have the time or the inclination to get involved.

'I still don't get why the police have been asking questions.'

'Steve wanted me back in the fold, working for him, beneath his control, and like you said earlier, he's not accustomed to rejection. When I defied him by going freelance, he began stalking me.'

'Stalking?' Hugo probably looked as shock as he felt. 'Seriously?'

'Seriously. I don't know how he found out what I was doing or where I was going, but he did because he kept turning up in the same places.'

'Easy enough to bug someone's phone or car in our line of work.'

She nodded. 'That's what I figured and it freaked me out.'

'I can well imagine.' Hugo wasn't having a hard time imagining

Steve resorting to such tactics. Like most narcissists, he kept his failures quiet; either that or, it seemed, took extreme forms of revenge to assuage his wounded pride. Leona's security measures now seemed necessary rather than excessive. 'What did you do to deter him?' he asked.

'I decided not to be a victim and fought back,' she said casually, as though it was the most natural thing in the world. But Hugo knew just how formidable, how well connected, Steve actually was, and reckoned it must have taken either courage or desperation on Leona's part to follow that route. 'I took pictures of him, date and time stamped whenever he turned up at the same place as me. I kept a log of all the late-night phone calls, when no one was on the line. He was even in this room once, waiting for me when I got home. But he'd never been here before and didn't have a key, which meant he could only have broken in. That's when I increased my security, got a dog and...' She paused to look up at Hugo, stark determination forming the bedrock of her expression. 'And, when I applied for a restraining order.'

'Fucking hell!' Hugo breathed.

'Well, of course you would take that attitude. You're his business partner.'

'I wasn't disapproving. Far from it; I admire your courage, but you've now made him even more determined to have the last word. You do realise that?'

'Er... thanks for pointing out the obvious,' she replied, her voice laced with sarcasm. 'But my application was unsuccessful.' She blew air through her lips. 'Not enough concrete evidence, apparently. I didn't take a picture of him in this room, which was a mistake, but even if I had, he could have argued that I'd invited him in. The odds were stacked against me, I can quite see that now.'

'I still don't get why the police spoke to me, or why you were parked outside my workplace for a big chunk of the day.'

'Presumably Steve warned you that they'd be in touch?' she replied, answering his question with one of her own.

'He called me. Told me to expect them. Said someone had accused him of something he hadn't done and that he needed to have his whereabouts verified.' Hugo lifted one shoulder. 'I didn't ask for specifics since I was being asked to confirm that he'd been in that restaurant all the evening and, I'm sorry, Leona, but he was.'

She let out a long sigh of defeat. 'I know,' she replied. 'It's what I wanted to ask you about today but I hadn't really thought it through when I drove to your place. I would have sounded like a mad woman and your first call after I left would have been to Steve. Fortunately, I eventually came to my senses and didn't ask to see you. I figured Steve pointed the police in your direction because he knew he could depend upon you and if he had left the restaurant for a length of time, you wouldn't have told the police.' She paused. 'Or me.'

'Wrong,' he said, his voice silk on steel. 'I told you just now that I wouldn't lie to the police for anyone, nor would I perjure myself, not even for Steve, whose business keeps my research project going. I think you need to understand that I have my standards and won't compromise them for anyone.'

'Sorry,' she said meekly. 'I just don't know what to think, who to trust, but I do believe what you just said.'

'Well, thanks for that.' He smiled across at her. 'I think.'

She didn't respond to his smile. 'The other person interviewed was a woman, I'm told.' Leona rolled her eyes. 'Stands to reason that she would vouch for him but still, if he didn't leave the restaurant for long enough to...'

'To what?' Hugo sat forward on the edge of his seat. 'What did he do to get you to involve the police?'

'With the benefit of hindsight, I'm in a position to know that it was a massive mistake to apply for the restraining order.' She absently bit her lower lip. 'It has only made him more determined to break me, and he's getting nasty.' She had been staring into the fire as she spoke but she now turned her full attention towards Hugo. 'On the night of that dinner someone drove his car here, posted dog shit through the letterbox and made sure I saw the car before driving it away again.'

'Fuck,' Hugo muttered beneath his breath.

4

Leona watched her visitor's expression closely as he absorbed the implications behind all she'd just told him. She was still conducting an inner battle to project calm in the face of all the questions his appearance had raised. What was he really doing here? Had he told Steve that she'd been hanging around outside his laboratory and did Steve send him here to find out what it was that she thought she knew? Good luck with that one. She'd be happy to know the answer herself.

Hugo didn't strike her as anyone's errand boy but what did she know? Why the hell had she let him in *and* then opened up to him? Was she losing her mind? He and Steve went way back, she reminded herself, and despite the fact that there now appeared to be a coolness between them, she wasn't stupid enough to suppose that their loyalties didn't still run deep. Her problems were inconsequential in comparison to their lucrative business dealings. Besides, waning friendships notwithstanding, would Hugo, a fierce intellectual, really want to mire himself in the murky world of Steve's love life? Surely, it would be beneath him.

All that aside, did he believe her?

Leona took a deep breath as she tried to quell the multitude of questions that continued to jostle for position in her overcrowded mind. She was surprised just how much she wanted Hugo to accept her version of events, unlikely as they would seem to him, without looking upon her as an overwrought female, scorned and out for revenge. God alone knew why she cared about his opinion. She had learned through bitter experience to trust no one other than herself and yet she had spilled her guts at the first opportunity because a good-looking guy had been willing to listen.

Geez!

A small part of her worried about her lousy judgement. A much larger part continued to wonder why she had allowed Hugo to cross her threshold. She was glad though that she had in many respects. He was easy to talk to and she'd been bottling things up for way too long. If he had come on a fishing expedition at Steve's behest then he would be able to tell him that she was far from defeated, she assured herself, sitting a little straighter, determined not to wilt in front of Hugo. She justified her willingness to lean on him, just a little, by reminding herself that Mulligan had taken a liking to him and she had learned to trust her dog's judgement. Be that as it may, she would reserve her own judgement regarding Hugo until he had proved himself to be trustworthy.

She sensed his agitation, the barriers he'd erected to keep a distance between them. Now that he knew she hadn't been sent to spy on Steve's behalf, he didn't really want to hear what she'd had to say. He didn't even want to be in her cottage, and yet he made no effort to leave.

Strange!

'Thank you for not asking if I was sure it was his car,' she said, plucking absently at the arm of the sofa, feeling the need to fill the deafening silence that had stretched between them for too long.

Hugo chuckled, a deep, throaty sound that Leona reacted to

somewhere deep within her core; the sort of distraction she could well do without. The type of reaction that she hadn't expected since it implied a narrowing of the distance that he'd put between them. Even so, she had learned her lesson with Steve and wasn't about to be influenced by a handsome face or coercive charm for a second time. The pain simply wasn't worth the pleasure.

'That gas-guzzler of his is hard to miss, or mistake,' he said. 'That's kind of the point with Steve. Everything has to make a statement, to prove to the world that he's made it. Nothing has ever mattered to him more.' Hugo leaned back in his chair and stretched his arms above his head, stifling a yawn. Leona wondered what to make of the criticism he'd just voiced. 'Even so, he couldn't have been driving his car. We left the restaurant together and I watched him get into a cab.'

'I never supposed he'd do his own dirty work.' Leona leaned her elbow on her thigh and her chin on her clenched fist. 'He was sending me a message; letting me know he could get to me whenever he feels like it. I walked away from him, then tried to take out a restraining order. That's not the sort of slight that an ambitious man will ever forget. He *has* to have the final word, but right now, he's enjoying keeping me rattled. He's your friend, though,' she added, keen to see if he would refute that assertion. 'Excuse me, but I can't help wondering why you seem so ready to believe what I've told you about him?'

'Friends with different agendas, but I'm not blind to his faults.' Hugo fixed her with a direct look, his features taut. 'Let's just say for now that I've seen him operate.'

Leona nodded, sensing there was a lot more to it but aware that Hugo had probably already said more than he'd intended to. 'Fair enough,' she said.

'Has he asked you to return to your old position?'

'Several times early on but I turned him down.' Leona blew air through her lips. 'He accused me of being a thief, scuppered my chances of getting another job in a similar capacity that was nearly so well paid and then blithely assumed that I'd run back to him with my tail between my legs. Honestly, the arrogance of the man! But he isn't the only stubborn one, driven by pride. I'd rather starve than...' Mulligan looked up and whined. 'Not you, baby,' she assured him, sharing a spontaneous smile with Hugo as she tugged at one of her dog's ears. 'I swear he understands every word I say, especially if it has anything to do with food.'

'So it would seem. Is he a rescue?'

'Yes. I'm not sure if the police believed my version of events or Steve's but they did advise me to tighten up my security if I felt threatened and to get a dog. Mulligan had been in the rescue place for a while but was bigger than most people could handle so got passed over.' She smiled. 'For me, it was love at first sight. A male upon whom I can depend absolutely.'

'I can quite see why. Rescue dogs have usually had a tough time of it and have often gone hungry. Mulligan obviously falls into that category and hasn't forgotten those days.'

'You're making excuses for him. You can't possibly know for sure...'

Hugo winked at her. 'You're right, I can't, but us guys have to stick together.'

'Would you like a drink?' she surprised herself by asking. 'I have beer.'

'Beer would be good. Thanks.'

Leona went to her kitchen, opened a beer for Hugo, poured herself a glass of wine and took a moment to wonder how to make use of Hugo's apparent willingness to believe her version of events. Why not? she decided. What did it matter if she couldn't trust him? Thus far, she hadn't told him anything that Steve himself didn't know but she doubted whether he had shared that knowledge with

Hugo, at least insofar as her application for a restraining order was concerned. That she could prove and Steve wouldn't want Hugo to know that he had done anything to precipitate her actions, which made her doubt that Steve had sent him here on a fishing expedition.

Even if Hugo did believe her, how could she use that belief to her advantage? she wondered as she returned to the lounge with their drinks.

'Thanks,' he said, taking his beer from her hand. Their fingers clashed and Leona felt a frisson of awareness streak through her. But if Hugo noticed it too, he gave no sign. His expression had turned formally polite and Leona suspected that they were again about to walk on eggshells around one another.

He still doesn't trust me.

'Cheers.' She snatched her hand back and took a hasty sip of her own drink. She swallowed it too fast, which resulted in a coughing fit.

'You okay?' he asked.

'Sorry. I gulped.'

He smiled a lazy smile that didn't trouble his eyes. 'Happens all the time.'

She didn't know how to respond and so remained silent. All the time she'd been talking about Steve's treatment of her, she had been fuelled by a sense of injustice that eradicated the awkwardness she felt at being alone with a man whom she liked but was still unsure if she could trust.

'Okay,' he said, putting his drink aside, leaning back in his chair and crossing one foot over his opposite thigh. 'What do you plan to do now?'

'So you can tell Steve,' she shot back at him.

Hugo looked mildly offended. 'For what it's worth, I believe you,' he said softly.

Leona let out a long breath. 'Sorry. I'm a mess.'

'Understandably.' His feet returned to the floor and he leaned towards her. 'Look, I get why you don't trust me, I really do, but you came to me, remember. In a manner of speaking.'

Leona acknowledged the point with a tilt of her head. 'I suppose I just thought...' Her words trailed off. What the hell had she thought?

'That Steve sent me to sound you out?' He smiled but didn't pause so that she could respond. 'I have a strong personal and business association with the man but it doesn't follow that I approve of his behaviour.'

'You don't?' Leona blinked at her guest. 'What has he done to earn your disapproval?'

'Our friendship transmuted into a business arrangement years ago.' Leona sensed there was more to it than that but also knew that he wouldn't enlighten her. He was clearly a very private individual. 'We mix socially on business occasions, like the other night, but I can't remember the last time the two of us just went out for a beer.'

'Steve doesn't drink beer.'

Hugo smiled at her. 'Designer lager or premier cru wine is more his style nowadays. Me?' He held up his beer. 'I have simple tastes. But my point is, we've grown in different directions. I'm all for my research. I want to make a difference. Steve is all about the bottom line.'

'At least we agree about that much.' Leona leaned towards him. 'I understand about life getting in the way of friendships but I sense there's more to it in this case. From what you've told me, it seems a distance has grown between you and Steve that's personal.' When he sent her a speculative look but didn't immediately respond, Leona felt the need to justify her conclusion. 'I don't mean to pry but you must see how it looks from my perspective. On all the occasions that you came to Steve's offices, I never once suspected that you were anything other than friends. That being the case, naturally I assumed you'd have his back.'

'And yet you opened up to me.'

She shrugged. 'I haven't told you anything that Steve doesn't already know,' she pointed out, articulating her earlier thought.

'Nor have you told me how you intend to fight back,' he replied softly. 'Perhaps I can help you.' He blinked as the words left his mouth and she wondered if he'd actually intended to make the offer or whether it had been spontaneous.

'Thanks, but I'm not sure there's much point in even trying.' She held up a hand. 'No offence, but Steve holds all the aces and is halfway to convincing anyone who will listen that I'm a hysterical female obsessed with him, out for revenge because he rejected me when, in fact, the opposite is true. It's madness, really. If he just left me alone, we could both get on with our lives but... well, I think his brain is wired wrong because he just can't seem to let go.' She looked up at Hugo, feeling defeated, all out of options. 'I don't expect you to believe me.'

'Actually, I do.'

Leona sent Hugo a wary look. 'You do? You're not just saying that?'

'I never say anything I don't mean.' He paused to rub the side of his index finger against his lips, leaving Leona with the impression that he was using the gesture as an opportunity to choose his words with care. 'The fact of the matter is that during our final year at university, Steve was heavily involved with a very pretty fellow student. She was brilliant but fragile and had no self-confidence. Steve dumped her and she... well, she took her own life over it.'

Leona gasped. 'I had absolutely no idea.'

'No reason why you should have. Steve never accepted any blame, even though she left a long note expressing her feelings for him, proclaiming that she couldn't face a life without him in it.' Hugo shook his head. 'Like I say, she was very clever, even by Oxford's standards, but academic brilliance and worldly wisdom seldom go hand in hand. Steve didn't treat her well. She didn't understand that to him, it was a game, a young man enjoying the freedom of youth, if you like. She took it all far too seriously and couldn't get past the fact that Steve ran out of patience with her when she clung too tenaciously.'

'That's awful.' Leona sighed. 'What was her name?'

'Sophia. Sophia Granger.'

'Didn't Steve feel any responsibility?'

'Not an ounce, as far as I could see. He never referred to the incident once the police had done their work. He wouldn't even face the girl's parents, or attend her funeral.'

'But still you do business with him.' A note of censure had entered Leona's voice.

'Business is business. Everyone has a past. I just happen to know what's in Steve's. I also know he won't have changed and so yes, I believe everything you just told me and his reaction to being the one who was dumped doesn't surprise me. He's an arrogant, self-entitled individual who uses people to get ahead but I'm probably not telling you something you don't already know.'

And yet there was more, something he was still holding back, she sensed.

Leona felt the tension leave her shoulders. What Hugo had just told her about that poor girl killing herself at Oxford had a ring of truth about it. There would be a record; Leona could check it out, she assumed, but didn't feel the need. It simply wasn't the sort of thing that anyone would make up.

'I used to think I was the luckiest woman alive because he made me feel so special,' she said wistfully.

'He's good at that. I've seen him operate.'

'You probably think I'm an idiot for falling for his line.'

'Don't assume to know what I think.' He smiled to take the sting out of the mild reprimand. 'Sophia had a mind as sharp as a razor but she was no match for Steve when he turned on the charm.' Hugo paused. 'And you know what's worse: he only took up with her for a dare. She was a pretty girl but studious and none of the guys could hold her attention. She never dated and the guys told Steve that even he wouldn't break through her defences. Naturally, Steve accepted the challenge and it was a doddle for him.'

Leona shook her head. 'That's horrible,' she said softly.

'We none of us tried to stop him, so we should all take our share of the blame.' Hugo spread his hands.

'You couldn't have known how the girl would react.'

'Even so, it plays on my conscience. Perhaps I'd be able to get past it if I thought that Steve felt remorse, but he's just pretended it didn't happen and got on with his life.'

'Yeah, he's perfected compartmentalising.' Leona allowed a momentary pause. 'Do he and his wife really lead separate lives?'

'Oh, they do. She plays away as much as he does, but I some-times wonder if she does so because she knows that feigning disinterest in him is the best way to... well, to hold his interest. I also think that Steve resents needing her more than she needs him.'

'How so?'

'She's a lot better off than he is, at least her family are, and money as we both know is Steve's god. Much as he can't let you have the last word, so he needs to eclipse his wife financially. Only then would he consider ditching her. Her father is Bizham Nawaz, who's made a name for himself in this country in business circles. He also has political ambitions. When Stella insisted upon marrying Steve, Nawaz got Steve on side by subsidising his business.'

'That would explain where his start-up funds came from.'

'Nawaz is as much of a control freak as Steve himself is but Steve told me once that he knows exactly how to play him. He holds the ace because Stella is dedicated to Steve and Nawaz adores his only daughter.'

Leona wrinkled her nose. 'Sounds to me as though Steve and Nawaz deserve one another.'

'They are kindred spirits. Probably recognise the ruthless streak in each other. Anyway, now perhaps you understand why I believe you.'

Leona nodded. 'The girl at Oxford has always been on your mind.'

'In a way, I guess she has.'

'Don't worry. I have no intention of topping myself over the bastard, if that's what you're thinking. I just want to be left alone.'

'How can I help?'

Leona shrugged. 'I don't see how you can. You may not think well of Steve but you do need his business if you want to pursue your research. If he finds out you've thrown in with me then you might get some unwanted late-night calls too.'

Hugo chuckled. 'Don't worry, I'm a big boy and can take care of myself. Besides, Steve needs me as much as I need him. When it comes to business, he won't shoot himself in the foot simply to prove a point.'

'But you will make yourself a formidable enemy.'

'So too will he.'

His icy, uncompromising expression made Leona's mind up for her. 'Well, I now know that no one is taking me seriously and has me down as an overwrought female obsessed with her ex-boss. God alone knows what story he gave the police about the reason for my leaving but I won't bet against him having implied that I was totally smitten, the arrogant sod. Steve can be charming and persuasive, as we both know. He keeps his misogynistic side well hidden.'

'Agreed.'

'But you've confirmed for me that I am not his first victim. I think the others were paid off in return for their silence and I wondered about trying to track down some of them. If I can persuade them to speak out then... well, *Sergeant Don't-Give-A-Damn* will have to listen. Then perhaps I will be taken seriously, I'll get my restraining order and I will have won.'

Hugo shook his head before she even stopped speaking. 'Do you really believe he'd let it go, even if you could achieve all of those things?'

'What else would you suggest?' she shot back at him. 'I should sit here and wait for his next assault?'

'No such thing.' His easy smile failed to settle Leona's skittish nerves. He was right, damn him: Steve would never let up until he broke her, rather as he'd broken that poor woman at Oxford. He looked upon it as a participation sport. 'Do you have any idea who else he might have targeted?'

'There was a woman called Annie Blakely, who worked for Steve when I first joined. Our paths briefly crossed. Then she left suddenly. Rumours were rife about the reasons for that. The official line was that she'd taken a position closer to her home, so she'd have more time with her children, but her husband works from home and is there for them, so it doesn't stack up.'

'Even so.'

'Steve's PA has been with him for years. She is totally loyal, never speaks out of turn, but I don't think she misses much. She was the only person who noticed Steve's interest in me, I think. She recognised the signs, I guess, and tried to warn me off in subtle ways. Either or both might speak to me off the record.'

'Annie is married so her first thought will be the protection of her marriage,' Hugo replied thoughtfully. 'But the PA, what's her name?'

'Molly Fairfax.'

'She might be worth a try, given that she attempted to steer you clear of danger.'

Leona waggled a hand from side to side. 'I very much doubt if either of them will speak out publicly. Like you just pointed out, Annie has to protect her marriage and Molly probably needs her job. It's hopeless.' Leona let out a long, frustrated sigh. 'He's won.'

'Not necessarily. Don't forget that I've known him forever. I've watched the way he uses women and then dumps them, scattering hearts in his wake.'

'Anyone recent who might be willing to speak on the record?' Leona asked, more in hope than expectation.

'Absolutely.' That slow, lazy smile again. 'Jane Gibson, my research assistant.'

5

Steve was in the very best of moods. He whistled as he dressed for the evening ahead, unable to prevent himself from smiling each time he considered Leona's reaction to his latest little reminder of his abiding affection. It would have freaked her out, especially when the police told her that he couldn't possibly have had anything to do with it. Even he couldn't be in two places at once.

It would teach the silly bitch a lesson. Trying to take out a restraining order against him, indeed. How fucking dare she! Who the hell did she think she was? Even so, just the thought of her shapely body gave him a massive hard-on, even now when he ought to be furious with her. Her willingness to fight her corner rather than to simply curl up and surrender to his terms, as they usually did, also earned her his admiration. Oh yes, this one was worth going that extra mile for.

He *was* infuriated by her actions but that didn't stop him from wanting her. If she'd been a good girl and fallen into bed with him on their last visit to potential customers that heralded a night in a fancy hotel then he would have gotten her out of his system. Eventually. As things stood, she was still very much unfinished business and he fully intended to do the finishing, when he judged the time to be right. She was proving to be a challenge that he found stimulating. None of his women stood their ground for long; they were too predictable and the game had lost its allure. But Leona... well, she was a class apart and he fully intended to play her on his own terms, slowly breach her defences until he decided the time was right to make his move. Nothing like a little anticipation to sharpen the senses.

'What are you so cheerful about?'

Stella's voice jolted Steve back to the here and now and he returned his attention to adjusting his black tie. It refused to sit exactly right.

'Here, let me.'

With deft fingers, Stella resolved the problem. She was so fucking capable that Steve sometimes felt like a spare part. That was why he needed a regular supply of women to bolster his ego. Stella pretended not to give a toss about him but Steve knew differently. She had pursued him quite relentlessly and made it clear just how helpful her family could be regarding his ambitions if they married.

Stella wasn't prepared to settle for anything less than marriage. Steve had seen the wisdom behind her argument and agreed, provided that they both had flexibility within the marriage itself. He had always known that monogamy wouldn't suit him. Nawaz had fought his daughter tooth and nail when she introduced Steve as her intended but she prevailed, and so Nawaz had taken Steve under his wing. *Look after my daughter, keep her happy, give her babies and I will take care of you.*

So far, everything but the babies had been forthcoming and the fault in that respect lay with Stella. She either couldn't have them or took precautions to ensure that she didn't fall pregnant. Steve didn't know which and didn't much care. But Nawaz did. Public image was everything to him but Stella refused to talk about her inability to conceive. Since all three of her brothers toed the parental line and obeyed every dictate issued by their widowed father, Steve secretly admired Stella's determination to stand up to him and live her life on her own terms.

He sometimes thought that Nawaz did too. Her character more closely resembled her father's than any of her brothers did.

'Thanks,' he said, taking a final glance at his reflection and liking what he saw. He happened to know that the pretty little wife of a financier would be at the function they were attending tonight. She'd been giving off all the signals of neglect that Steve had learned to recognise and he fully intended to take advantage of her boredom. 'I'm in for good news this evening,' he added, aware that his father-in-law had called this dinner in order to announce the appointment a non-executive director to his board. The position had Steve's name all over it; he'd earned the privilege. This would be a shoe-in.

'I won't be home tonight,' Stella said casually, making no reference to Steve's expectations.

Steve sucked air through his teeth. 'Who is it this time?' he asked casually, pretending not to know. He always knew who Stella was screwing and how long the liaisons lasted. Knowledge was power.

'As if you care.' She sent him a look that Steve found hard to interpret. 'What about you? Who do you have your eye on?'

'It's all business for me tonight. Can't afford to screw this one up.'

Stella laughed aloud. 'Darling, it's never all business with you. You've turned multitasking into an art form.' She gave her hair a final pat, tore her gaze away from her own reflection and fixed it upon Steve. 'You're a selfish, ambitious bastard, much the same as me.' She placed a light kiss on his cheek. 'It's one of the traits that

I most admire about you. You know what you want and aren't afraid to go after it, not caring who you trample on in the process.'

Steve laughed. 'That's one of the nicest compliments you've ever paid me.'

'My pleasure.'

'What would we do if one of our conquests attempted to go public?' he asked on a whim.

She swung round to face him, a frown creasing her brow. 'Why, we'd crush the irritant like an inconsequential fly, of course. We are invincible, Steve: the ultimate power couple. The envy of all our friends. Appearances are everything. Never forget it.'

'Sure, but ...' Steve fixed her with a penetrating look, wondering why she'd chosen to make such an odd statement. There was something different about her tonight; an excitement, a gleam in her eye that he didn't think had anything to do with her latest conquest. Her attitude made him uneasy. For once he couldn't guess at the nature of his wife's thoughts.

'Come on.' She picked up her bag. 'The car's here. We've left it late enough to make an entrance. I promised Daddy we'd be there to help receive his guests.' She slipped her hand through the crook of his arm. 'It's game time.'

* * *

Hugo had promised Jane that he would never reveal the true reason for her breakdown. It wasn't the sort of promise he'd break without reason but time had elapsed and he now did have a very pressing reason. He knew she had never got past the way Steve had used and then dumped her and likely never would if she didn't get some sort of closure. He saw an opportunity here to help both women. If anyone would be able to empathise with Jane, it was

Leona, who had found the strength to resist Steve's charms and was now bearing the brunt of a scorned man's spite.

The two ladies ought to find a great deal to talk about, Hugo reasoned. Hopefully, the experience would prove to be cathartic and Jane would forgive Hugo for breaking his promise.

'I recruited Jane straight out of university,' he said. 'One look at her CV and before I even interviewed her, I sensed that she had the type of creative mind, the determination to get to the truth through solid research rather than cutting corners and bending results to suit her own purposes. I'd almost given up hope of finding someone with those qualities and so I snapped her up.'

'Steve gets turned on by intelligence,' Leona said softly. 'He looks upon it as a challenge. If a woman has brains then he feels duty bound to outsmart her, to put her in her place which if he had his way would probably still be in the kitchen. Anyway, I assume he recognised the trait in Jane.'

'Oh, big time. But he was subtle about it. He only saw her once in my laboratory. I got called away and wasn't aware that he'd asked for her number. He's a fast worker, I've always known that, but even so...'

'It wouldn't have done you any good if you had known and warned her off. She probably wouldn't have listened. Take it from one who knows.'

'Perhaps.' Hugo took a deep breath. 'Their affair got underway, five years ago now, and I knew absolutely nothing about it until it was too late to warn her. When it ended, Jane fell apart. She was totally smitten, completely under Steve's spell and convinced that they were destined to be together. Steve had made her all sorts of obscure promises in that regard.'

'Steve kept their relationship from you?'

'Yep. He knew I would have warned her off. He told her it was their secret, he wanted her to himself, and all that crap.'

'How did you find out?'

'Jane came to me with a few casual questions about Steve and the state of his marriage when the affair was nearing an end and she was getting desperate to hold on to him. I realised then what was different about her. Blamed myself for not having noticed before.'

'Back up a bit. Was Jane married, or in a relationship?'

Mulligan grunted in his sleep and rolled onto his back, paws pointing skywards. Leona absently massaged his belly with her toe.

'She was married to her work but that all changed a bit before she started asking questions about Steve. She wasn't putting in as many hours, her clothing changed, she wore more make up, the usual signs...'

'In case Steve called at the laboratory.'

Hugo nodded. 'That's the way I saw it. It was... I don't know, like she'd been lit up from within. She glowed and seemed to glide around the lab without her feet actually touching the ground.'

'But the house of cards came tumbling down once she was completely invested in Steve? It's the way he operates,' Leona added in response to Hugo's raised eyebrow. 'He enjoys the chase but once he wins it, he loses interest and is ready to move on.'

'How do you know, if you didn't give in to him?'

'I don't, not for sure, but I don't have a hard time believing it.' Leona tapped the fingers of one hand against her lips, wondering herself now how she could be so sure. How did she explain feminine intuition? 'I've read up on misogynists in positions of powers and all the books agree that once they've dominated a woman, the sport is at an end.'

'You're surprisingly intuitive.'

'I wanted to understand his need to... well, to behave in the way that he does. After the event, of course, once he started stalking me.'

'Well, in Jane's case, it was textbook. It all unravelled big time. Jane was naïve, believed every word that spewed from Steve's mouth and so when he turned his back on her, she had a massive breakdown and was institutionalised for a while.'

Leona touched his arm. 'I'm sorry,' she said softly.

'Yeah, well, she got through it, discharged herself from residential care and came back to work. But she's lost her sparkle.' Hugo scratched his ear. 'I was never able to properly talk to her about it in the aftermath of her breakdown. She acted like nothing had happened and that it was business as usual but I figure she's still got it all bottled up inside and I don't know how to help her. I feel responsible. I should have tried to warn her.'

'She wouldn't have listened.'

Hugo shrugged. 'Even so... I didn't want to push her to talk about it and so I haven't.'

'Sometimes it's better not to bottle things up but she probably felt like a gullible idiot for being taken in. I know I did, and I didn't actually end up in bed with him. Does she have any family members to support her?'

'No. Her father's dead, her mother remarried and moved to Australia and she has no siblings. Because she lived for her work, she doesn't have any close friends either.'

'I assume she's attractive.'

'Very.'

'Well then, she would be just Steve's type. He either goes for the married ones who won't rock the boat for fear of causing a marital rift, or those like Jane and me, who have no one to fight our respective corners.'

'Except you didn't buckle.'

'I am not as clever as Jane, or Sophia, and significantly more worldly. Even so, he almost had me fooled. But because I worked fairly closely with Steve, it wasn't hard to see through the "my-wife-doesn't-understand-me" bullshit, even if I was briefly besotted and wanted it to be true.' Leona threw back her head, tossing her hair over her shoulder. 'What an idiot! I still can't believe that I...' She let out a long sigh. 'Anyway, it sounds as though Jane has pulled herself together... if she's functioning properly at work.'

'She is but she's not the same. Her work's as brilliant as ever, and she's putting in ridiculously long hours again, but I feel as though her emotions are locked down. I've thought for a while that someone needs to find the key and release them so that she can embrace life again, get her sparkle back.'

Leona nodded her understanding. 'You're not wrong,' she said softly.

'I have felt that way for a while but haven't known how to broach the subject or what to do to help her, so I've done nothing up until now. She's refused counselling, which implies that she doesn't want to talk about it and I have no idea how to open that particular door without risking her mental health.'

'You want me to meet Jane, chat with her?'

'I think it would be a good place to start. Jane and I are colleagues and friends. I drag her away from the lab, or vice-versa, from time to time and we go out for a drink, a meal. Do normal things and ban shop talk for the duration. I steer the conversation towards art, literature, places we'd like to visit, interests we have in common, safe subjects because I know she has no social life to speak of. Well, that goes for us both; we're workaholics. I have often been tempted to raise the subject of Steve but...'

'But you're a man and don't know how,' Leona finished for him, smiling. 'Men famously don't do emotion.'

'I do have a softer side, I'll have you know!'

Leona smiled. 'I'm willing, but how will you bring the meeting about, given that the subject of Steve is taboo?'

He winked at her. 'I'll think of something.'

'Okay but given her fragile mental health, I don't suppose she'll be willing to go on record. And even if she, or any of the others are, I'm not sure how much help that will be to my cause, now that I've had time to think about it. I mean, Jane was dumped, and I suspect anyone else I can find will have suffered the same fate. So I might be able to prove that Steve is a serial womaniser but since he hasn't, as far as I know, targeted any of the others in the way that he has me with his petty forms of intimidation, I will be no nearer to getting a restraining order, or even being taken seriously.'

She sent him a wry smile and simultaneously sighed. Even with Hugo willing to help her, it felt as though she would never prevail. Steve was simply too powerful, too determined to set the rules for the game. 'I told you I hadn't really thought this through,' she said weakly. 'All I do know is that I want the harassment to stop and to get my life back but I have absolutely no idea how to make that happen.'

'What is the one thing that scares Steve the most?'

He watched Leona as she threw back her head, closed her eyes and took a moment to consider. 'Poverty? Being ordinary? Failure?'

'All of the above,' Hugo agreed, nodding his approval. 'But you have missed something vital.'

'His marriage,' Leona replied slowly, her mind reverting to her earlier speculation. 'He depends upon his father-in-law's backing and if there was any public scandal insofar as Steve's behaviour is concerned...' She offered Hugo a beaming smile and the defeat, the despondency, left her expression. 'But, Hugo, that's brilliant! Don't get mad, get even by hitting him where it hurts the most.' She bounced excitedly on the edge of her chair, a bit like a child on a sugar rush. 'And if we save some other poor, misguided female from being the recipient of his questionable charm offensive then we will have provided a public service.'

'Are you sure you want to do this?' Hugo asked. 'Steve won't take it lying down; nor will his father-in-law, and that man's money buys him the sort of power that you or I can only dream about. It could get ugly.'

Leona raised a brow. 'Nawaz would take his side?'

'Certainly he would, at least in public. His image is everything to him. If he's aware of the true nature of Stella and Steve's open marriage then he won't approve, but he won't chance raising it with either of them. He knows how stubborn Stella can be, but she's his only daughter and he won't risk losing her.'

'Stella has a successful fashion empire. Even I've heard her name. Isn't that enough to make him proud of her? I mean, an indulged daughter didn't need to work at all and yet she's made a huge impact in a highly competitive world.'

'Stella has daddy issues. Not surprising really, given that her mother died giving birth to her and that all three of her older brothers are almost as protective of her as Nawaz himself is.'

'No wonder she rebelled and insisted upon marrying Steve. Do you think she really loves him? I can't see how if she goes with other men, but stranger things have been known to happen.'

'I actually think that she does love him, but she knows that Steve would never commit to one woman so plays him at his own game. That way, she's sure to hang on to him.'

A thought clearly struck Leona, as evidenced up the widening of her eyes. 'What do we know about the husbands of the women Steve goes for? Perhaps they'd be willing to add their weight to our campaign? It's not only women scorned who thirst for revenge.'

'Hmm, possibly. I suspect that none of them would want to get embroiled in a scandal though and in all probability, they'll be beholden to Nawaz in some way so won't want to rock the boat.'

Leona twitched her nose. 'That makes sense. Steve chooses his victims with safety in mind.'

'Well anyway, let's put that possibility of the back burner for now.'

'Steve covers all the bases.' She pouted. 'I'm starting to see what you mean about taking him on.'

'You don't have to do this.'

'I do though, you must see that.' She paused. 'But I'm at a loss to understand why you'd want to get involved. I've been backed against a wall and having nothing to lose. You, on the other hand...'

'I have my reasons.'

He appeared tight-lipped on the subject and Leona knew he wouldn't explain what those reasons were. 'Steve won't let up until he's convinced that he's crushed my spirit,' she said, frustrated, 'and I'm damned if I'll allow that to happen. I don't care how powerful they are. I didn't start this war but I intend to do what I can to finish it. I want my life back.'

Hugo leaned towards her and reached out to briefly touched her hand. 'Then I'll help you, if you'll let me.' She nodded mutely. 'Why don't I attempt to arrange for you and Jane to meet socially? That way we can test the waters. It's as good a place as any to start. Would tomorrow evening be too soon?'

6

Leona found it hard to concentrate on her work the following day. Eventually, she abandoned it and took a delighted Mulligan for a longer ramble than usual in the woods. She did her best thinking outside and Hugo had certainly given her a great deal to think about. Part of her still suspected his motives. After all, his research was dependent upon his lucrative business arrangement with Steve. He clearly cared about his employees and was upset about the damage done to Jane, not to mention the girl from Oxford who'd supposedly killed herself over Steve. Even so, would he really risk his funding for the sake of Leona, whom he didn't even know?

Or did he have reasons for wanting to help her that he had decided against sharing? It had seemed that way yesterday but the man gave little away about himself and she had no way of knowing for sure.

She picked up a stick and threw it for Mulligan, her mind in overdrive. The dog barked, wagged his entire body and then bounded after the missile with an ungainly gait, paws flying in opposing directions. She smiled at the sight, wishing her life could be that uncomplicated.

'You know, Mulligan,' she said as she reattached his lead and they walked home together, 'this business doesn't need to be complicated. If Jane's willing to speak about her experiences, I will soon know if she's being honest and, more to the point, if she's as keen as I am to put the episode behind her. Perhaps she already has and won't thank us for stirring it all up again. Then again, perhaps she'll never get closure until she's exacted some form of revenge and if I can persuade her that she doesn't have to fight him alone then it might make a difference. We'll see.'

Leona dragged her way through the rest of the day, trying to think about something, anything else, but she achieved little. Eventually, she closed her laptop down with a heavy sigh and took herself off to enjoy a long soak in the bath.

She dressed carefully yet casually in jeans and a favourite top. She washed her hair, let it dry on its own and brushed the resulting riot of curls into some sort of loose order. Wearing minimal makeup, she examined her reflection and was pleased to see a determination, a new energy, in her expression that had been lacking for too long. She hated that Steve had drained the life out of her but was now ready to fight her corner, with or without Hugo's help.

'Well,' she told Mulligan, who flapped his tail at the sound of her voice but failed to open his eyes, 'my visitor has given me a new sense of purpose and if nothing comes from tonight, at least I'll feel as though I've been proactive.'

She kissed her dog's shaggy head, gave him a rawhide bone to compensate for the fact that he couldn't come with her, picked up her bag and car keys and left her cottage.

The drive to the pub where she'd agreed to 'bump' into Hugo on the outskirts of Chichester was relatively short, too short for her nerves to get the better of her. It was a fine evening, spring was in the air and she welcomed the lengthening days. The lingering light helped to buoy her flailing nerves. Not that she had any reason to be nervous, she reminded herself, but she couldn't entirely eradicate her feelings of apprehension.

She sensed that this confrontation would be harder for Jane than it would be for her and that she needed to be at her most sympathetically persuasive. Perhaps by talking openly about Steve's techniques and the manner in which he had almost won someone as streetwise as Leona over would help to convince Jane that she had been the victim of a smooth-talking Lothario who needed putting in his place before he pulled the same stunt on another vulnerable victim.

'Don't get mad, get even,' she muttered as she pulled into the pub's car park and cut the Kia's engine. 'Right,' she added, flipping down the visor and examining her appearance. 'Game time!'

Leona entered the half-full bar with a purposeful stride. A few heads turned in her direction but she didn't recognise anyone. The doors to the terrace were open and several of the outside tables were occupied with optimistic drinkers huddled around space heaters who seemed to think that summer had already arrived. Leona wasn't so sure about that but did think the fresh air would be a better place to hold the delicate conversation she hoped to instigate, always assuming that Jane didn't simply get up and leave when she realised Hugo had coerced her into a situation that she might not be comfortable with.

She glanced around the bar and it took a moment for her to notice Hugo sitting at a corner table, deep in conversation with a woman of about Leona's age. She smiled, suspecting that they were discussing their precious research and felt a moment's gratitude to Hugo for dragging himself away from it for an entire evening. Steve had told her that he regularly put in sixteen-hour days, was married to his work and survived on a just a few hours' sleep. Only now did it occur to her that Steve had spoken scathingly, almost as though he resented his friend's dedication.

Hugo must have sensed her presence because he looked up, caught her eye and sent her a smile that melted her insides in an entirely inappropriate manner. What the hell?

Hugo stood up to beckon her over.

'Leona.' He kissed each of her cheeks in turn. 'Glad you could make it.'

'Wouldn't have missed it,' she said, returning his smile.

'This is my research assistant, Jane Gibson. Jane, meet Leona Carson, a friend.'

Jane's smile was guarded as she extended a slender hand. 'Please to meet you,' she said, sounding unsure about that assertion. She frowned as her glance flitted between Leona and Hugo, her curiosity clearly piqued.

'Let me get us a drink,' Hugo said, patting his pockets. 'What are we all having?'

He took their orders and sauntered across to the bar watched, Leona noticed, by just about every female in the place.

Leona took a seat at the table and a moment to study the woman across from her. She was shorter than Leona and considerably thinner, almost painfully so. Leona wondered if she had always been that slender or whether her weight loss was a result of her dealings with Steve. That thought brought fresh anger and determination to the forefront of Leona's mind. Jane had huge, intelligent eyes and features that complimented one another. She gave the appearance of being delicate and malleable as well as clever, and therefore definitely Steve's type, she thought with a wry smile.

'How do I know your name?' Jane asked frowning. 'I'm sure we've never met.'

'We have an acquaintance in common,' Leona replied, experiencing a surge of guilt because she knew she was about to seriously upset this likeable but clearly vulnerable young woman.

Unsure whether she should dive straight in, Leona was grateful when Hugo returned to the table at that precise moment, his large hands clasped around three drinks.

'Here we go,' he said, handing both ladies their wine and taking the top off his beer with a healthy sip. 'Cheers!'

'What's going on here?' Jane asked, her earlier frown returning with fresh intensity.

Hugo glanced at Leona, clearly wanting to know if he should explain. Leona gave a tiny shake of her head. This was her party. Hugo had got Jane here. It was up to Leona now to persuade her to stay.

'Steve Jessop,' she said, fixing her entire attention upon Jane.

Jane's face flushed as she sent Hugo a look of deep betrayal. 'What have you said?' she asked. 'You promised me that...'

Hugo held up a hand. 'I had a very good reason, Jane. You know I wouldn't betray a confidence lightly.'

'I don't know what to think any more,' she replied sullenly.

'Hear Leona out. I think you will be glad that you did. If you listen to Leona's story but don't want to have anything more to do with her, that will be the end of it. You have my word.'

'You work for Steve.' Jane snapped her fingers at Leona. 'That's how I know your name. I've seen your signature on documents.'

'I did work for him, but not any more and, just for the record, I hate the scumbag with a passion.'

Jane snorted. 'Join the club.'

'Would you like me to leave you ladies to talk in private?' Hugo asked. 'You've never told me the intimate details, Jane. All I've seen is the consequences of his bad behaviour, in you and now in Leona. I don't want to pry.'

'You've already done enough damage so you might as well stay and hear all the gory details, if I decide to speak. I've done my best to put it behind me and this isn't exactly helping.'

'Except you can't put it behind you, can you?' Leona asked. 'Not completely. You've lost the ability to judge people and no longer trust your instincts.'

Jane's head snapped up. Her eyes were fiery yet rimmed with tears that she didn't permit to fall. She was stronger than she looked, Leona decided, and Hugo had been right to suggest that she might be willing to open up to someone who understood her ordeal. 'You've been there?' she asked.

'Oh yes!' Leona knew that she would have to tell the complete, unbridled truth if she expected Jane to reciprocate and so she did precisely that, explaining about her career and how she'd been obliged to sacrifice it because she saw through Steve at the eleventh hour. How he had persecuted her, implied that she was dishonest and spoiled her chances of getting the employment she deserved elsewhere. She explained too that she was determined to fight back.

'Well, at least you saw through him before he got inside your knickers,' Jane said, but there was sympathy in her tone now rather than aggression. 'But I'm not sure what you expect by coming to me, or why Hugo even suggested it. Steve used and abused me, then discarded me like trash. He made grandiose promises about leaving his wife and us being together.' She waved a hand. 'I know. Stupid me for falling for something so obvious.'

'He can be very convincing. I almost believed him myself. I probably would have if I hadn't worked alongside him and observed him in unguarded moments.'

'He gave himself away?'

'Not precisely.' Leona waggled a hand from side to side. 'There was just something that rang warning bells which I couldn't ignore indefinitely.'

'Well, I've put the past behind me.' Jane expelled a long sigh. 'Dwelling on it was bad for my mental health. Besides, people like Steve win in the end. They always do.'

'Only if we let them.'

Jane remained silent for a protracted moment. Leona glanced at Hugo, wondering whether she should try to persuade Jane to express herself. He shook his head and Leona knew that was the right call. This was a defining moment. Jane would decide to tell her story only on her own terms. Leona wasn't about to put pressure on her even though it was screamingly obvious that she needed to get it off her chest if she wanted to regain her self-confidence and get her life back together.

'He swept me off my feet with his charm,' she eventually said. 'I was flattered and completely taken in by him, more fool me. Like I just said, he promised me that his marriage was over in everything but name and that we would be together once he'd finalised his divorce.' She offered up a rueful smile. 'How can an intelligent woman fall for the oldest line in the book?'

'You weren't the first,' Leona said, reaching out to touch Jane's hand. 'If I hadn't actually worked alongside Steve then I would likely have believed him too. He can be very convincing. He has a way of making a woman feel like she's the most fascinating creature on God's earth. Trust me, I've been there.'

'I've never had time for romantic entanglements. My work has always consumed me. Or it did until Steve came along and showed me another side to life.' She frowned. 'Why does he do it? What does he get out of it?'

Hugo explained about Steve's wife's hold over him. Leona got the impression that Jane was hearing it for the first time. She thought it had been a mistake for Hugo to hold out on her out of concern for her wellbeing. It was always better to know the truth in such situations, otherwise a part of Jane would remain convinced that Steve really had wanted only her, as opposed to his being a serial womaniser.

A raucous bark of laugher from a group of lads coming in from the garden when a light rain began to fall failed to distract Jane, who seemed intrigued by Hugo's explanation. The doors to the terrace banged shut behind the drinkers who now crowded the bar, filling it with noise and laughter.

Jane's attention was drawn to their horsing around, carefree, enjoying themselves. Leona had taken an instinctive liking to the damaged, far too serious young woman and cursed Steve anew for targeting her, robbing her of her self-confidence. She was more determined than ever to recruit Jane's assistance in the fight back, not for her own sake but for Jane's. Quite what form that fightback would take she had yet to decide but she did know that there was strength in numbers. She was also fully aware of the power of social media.

There was more than one way to expose a dangerous narcissist.

Most importantly, when she heard Jane's description of Steve's seduction technique, proof if any was necessary that it was a tried and tested routine, it reinforced Leona's resolve to stop him in his tracks and prevent him from using it on his next helpless victim. It might be too late to repair the damage done to Jane but Leona was pretty sure that if she knew he was no longer a player, it would help her recovery enormously.

'I can understand why you want to bring Steve down,' Jane said thoughtfully when Hugo ran out of words. 'He ruined your career because you had the temerity to reject him, Leona, and now he's making life hard for you because he realises you really don't intend to go back to him. He's a misogynist, must always have the last word and he can't bear for a woman to get the better of him. I can quite see now what ought to have been obvious to me at the time.' She turned to face Hugo. 'I'm less sure why you want to get involved, Hugo. You need Steve's business in order to fund your research. Why would you risk losing that?'

'I need his business, it's true, but not at any price.' He went on to explain about the girl at uni who'd killed herself over Steve. Jane's face paled, causing Leona to suspect that Jane herself had considered suicide during her lowest period.

'I see,' she said, swallowing. 'I wish I'd known,' she added so quietly that Leona barely caught the words.

'Would it have made any difference?' Hugo asked.

Jane flapped a hand. 'Probably not. I was groomed at the hand of a master and had absolutely no idea that it was happening until I was in too deep to extricate myself.'

'It's what he does best,' Leona assured her. 'It amuses him to manipulate women because he looks upon us as the weaker sex.'

'Even if I had told you that I disapproved of his methods, Steve would have come up with a plausible explanation for his past indiscretions. Besides, I didn't know he'd gotten his claws into you until it was too late for me to do anything about it. He was clever that way. Making it your secret: something special just between the two of you.'

'Perhaps.' Jane conceded the point with a thoughtful nod. 'I'm surprised he went after you though, Leona. You are clearly far more worldly than me and you saw through him.'

'Only just and look where that's gotten me.' She fixed Jane with a direct look. 'Will you help me to get my life back as well as your own and, more to the point, save his next victim from what we've been through?'

Jane's pause was gratifyingly short. 'What do you need from me?' she asked, straightening her shoulders, an inner strength that she was probably unaware she possessed and which had doubtless brought her back from the brink of despair shining through.

'I hope to get enough of his former victims as possible to speak out, just so that the police will have to reconsider my account and take it seriously. If they do that then Steve will have to back off and stop badmouthing me to prospective employers. That's all I want.'

Jane pulled a dubious face. 'Can't see it myself but yes, if it comes to it, I'll speak out. But – and it's a big but – I don't have any physical evidence: letters, or anything like that to back up my assertion. It could look as though I'm just being spiteful, or that I'm your friend, backing your account out of a sense of loyalty.'

Leona pulled a glum face. 'I know, but we have to try,' she said. 'Besides, if word leaked back to Nawaz and threatened his reputation, or that of his precious daughter, that would really put the cat amongst the pigeons.'

Hugo smiled. 'Remind me never to get on the wrong side of you,' he said.

* * *

Steve ordinarily excelled in social situations, especially when his father-in-law was present and he could use the opportunity to reinforce their bond. Tonight though, Steve was about to be publicly endorsed when the announcement was made regarding his appointment to the non-executive board position: the pinnacle of his ambitions. A public sign that he had finally won the old man's trust. They didn't always see eye to eye but it suited their interests to present a united front. Public perception was everything to Bizham Nawaz.

On the surface, Steve and Bizham's daughter were a match made in heaven. Stella was Bizham's weak link. He adored her, and all the time Steve kept her happy, Bizham would help Steve to achieve his own ambitions, as evidenced by the accolade he was about to receive. Stella's brothers and their wives were all in attendance. Steve got on well with the boys and chatted affably with them prior to their taking their places for dinner.

Stella, the wily little bitch, played the part of the golden daughter every step of the way. Steve sometimes amused himself by considering Bizham's reaction if he knew about the extent of Stella's sexual exploits. Steve kept a close eye on her liaisons and could name names, places and dates if it became necessary. That would take the blinkers off, he thought with a modicum of satisfaction. Except Bizham would probably blame Steve for not keeping his precious daughter satisfied since what other reasons could she possibly have for breaking her wedding vows?

Keeping on Bizham's good side was an ongoing battle that Steve couldn't afford to lose. A challenge like no other, with the possible exception of that posed by that traitorous bitch Leona: the one who'd escaped. At least for now. Steve wasn't unduly worried about her bid for independence. She wanted him and they both knew it. Besides, he never failed. Leona would eventually see the error of her ways and come crawling back to him.

With an effort, Steve returned his attention to Bizham, annoyed that thoughts of Leona had distracted him at such a vital moment. Steve would be unwise to lose sight of just how much he still needed his father-in-law's approval. If he removed his financial backing for Steve's company then Steve's luxurious lifestyle would be seriously curtailed and both men knew it. So Steve continued to play the game, pandered to Bizham's ego and publicly toed the line.

His gaze fell upon the lady he had in his sights for the night. She wore a dress so tight-fitting that Steve marvelled at her ability to breathe. It showcased all her curves and given the way that she kept sending Steve coy looks, it was clear that she knew precisely what an enticing little package she presented.

'Have some sense,' he muttered beneath his breath. He was tempted, sorely tempted, just as he was supposed to be, but this one was no wilting violet. She knew her own worth and although she would keep her trap shut to preserve her marriage, she would likely try to run the show – Steve knew the type – and that was unthinkable. Steve always had to be the one in charge.

Shame, he thought, smiling at the old trout whom he was seated next to and who had been banging on endlessly about the benefits of cruising. Steve didn't hear one word in ten, especially when the woman in the tight dress sitting directly across the table from him worked her toes up his shin. Steve glanced at her and gently disentangled his leg. By making the first move, any lingering doubts about her suitability had taken a nosedive.

He turned to watch his wife, seated beside Daddy dearest at the head of the table, looking lethally gorgeous in emerald-green, shimmering silk. Beautiful but she did absolutely nothing to arouse Steve any more and he wondered, not for the first time, if gaining Bizham's support had been too high a price to pay for his success.

But then again, he mused, Bizham wasn't as squeaky clean as he would have the world believe. Steve knew more about his underhand tactics in his business empire than Bizham realised. He was keeping his powder dry, knowing that when the time was right, he would turn the tables on the bastard and finally have the upper hand.

He watched his wife sending covert little signals to the admittedly handsome man seated across from her, close to her father's right hand. He was a damned sight closer than Steve had been seated, he thought resentfully, wondering what dangerous game his wife thought she was playing and what she hoped to achieve by it. He wondered how Daddy would react if he knew that she planned to take the guy home with her, using him as a replacement for the desserts she never ate. God, this was all such a bore! When was Bizham going to make his damned announcement so that they could all sing Steve's praises and bugger off home?

Leona's defection had affected him badly; there was no denying that fact, Steve privately conceded. He had seriously misjudged her; moved too fast because he was unaccustomed to failure. If he'd been able to get her into bed then he would have recovered and moved on but his unexpected failure had dented his self-esteem.

Ergo, she couldn't be allowed to get away with it.

Bizham stood, tapped a spoon against a glass and the room instantly fell silent. He already had Steve's full attention. There was a big announcement in the offing, some sort of merger between Bizham's retail empire and... and what precisely? The man fixed Steve with a prolonged look and all Steve's resentments fell away. Clearly, he was about to be publicly recognised and not before time. The carrot had been dangled often enough.

Steve affected a relaxed pose, even though he felt more tightly coiled than a spring. Why he hadn't been asked to sit closer to the top of the table, he was still at a loss to know. Bizham so enjoyed his little games, but that was okay, Steve was a player too. He pretended to pay attention to Bizham as he droned on about the hard work it had taken his dedicated team to reach the pinnacle of success, but in actual fact his mind had drifted once again to the subject of unfinished business.

To Leona.

He wondered where she was at that moment, what she was doing and how soon he could send her another little reminder of his dedication. He was having to become more creative in that regard. How dare the bitch report him to the police! But still, she was the one who'd come out of it with egg on her face, looking like a resentful woman scorned, especially when Steve had implied to Sergeant whatever his name was that she'd been stealing from him. The detective had suggested pressing charges but Steve implied that he would personally absorb the loss rather than risk adverse publicity for his company. Two men bonding over thoughts of a manipulative woman. Nothing she said to the police would be believed.

Steve had made sure of that.

Everyone was applauding. Lost in a reverie, Steve had missed the vital announcement. He pushed his chair back, only to realise that the praise was being heaped on the guy that Stella had in her sights for the night. Worse still, Stella had fixed him, Steve, with a spiteful little look.

She knew this was going to happen!

Now her earlier behaviour when they'd been getting ready for the night made sense. What the hell had he done to piss her off so badly that she felt the need for revenge? Her new squeeze was the one being offered a non-executive position of Bizham's board and Bizham himself was looking directly at Steve as he shook the man's hand, a mocking expression gracing his fucking features.

Steve applauded along with everyone else, pretending for all the world that he'd known what was coming and that it was no big deal, even though it was a massive disappointment. A humiliation. This position would have been the pinnacle of Steve's achievements. A guarantee of respect and acceptance and Steve had been depending upon it. He'd anticipated the financial benefits too. What a fucking mess!

To be so publicly scorned burned like acid. He tilted his head towards Bizham, silently acknowledging that he'd been outplayed but none the wiser as to what he'd done to deserve such public degradation. Bizham's three sons looked staggered. He knew that Bizham liked to play them off against one another and one would find himself out of parental favour for no apparent reason.

Steve had never imagined he would be the recipient of Bizham's petty spite, though. He glanced at Stella. He could tell that she was enjoying his humiliation. A bad mistake, lady, he thought malevolently. The gloves were off. If Bizham wasn't prepared to give him the leg-up that had been agreed upon in return for tolerating his spoiled and indulged daughter then he was surplus to requirements.

And so too was his wife.

This time, when the woman's toes repeated their journey up his shin, he didn't move away. Instead, he smiled at her, all the while thinking about murder. How easy would it be to kill a man in Bizham's position along with his daughter and get away with it?

7

Hugo had mixed feelings about the meeting with Leona and Jane that he'd orchestrated. In retrospect, he ought to have run it past Jane first rather than sandbagging her but hadn't because... well, because she was likely to be more receptive, he'd hoped, if she heard Leona's story first-hand. He'd sensed Jane's feelings of betrayal and confusion now when Steve's name was mentioned and felt bad for stirring up memories that she'd worked hard to put behind her.

'Much as I'm willing to help, much as I want to bring the bastard down,' Jane said, twisting the stem of her wine glass through her fingers when Leona ran out of words and Jane paused to consider what she'd just learned, 'I'm still not sure what you have in mind or how I can help you to achieve your aims. Wanting revenge is all well and good but Steve is well-protected. We'll never get at him.' She waved a hand. 'It's a bit nebulous to say there's safety in numbers.'

'He thinks he's untouchable, mainly because no one's ever tried to bring him down. I'd say that a little subtlety is called for,' Leona replied pensively. 'I've tried the legal route and it's got me precisely nowhere.' She leaned towards Jane. 'My point is, anything I try to do to expose Steve's methods will only be viewed as the spiteful actions of a woman who doesn't take rejection well.'

'You mentioned the possibility of tracking down other women,' Hugo reminded her.

'And I will find as many as I can,' Leona said, sounding resolute, 'and hopefully persuade them to talk. The more people willing to speak out, the more chance we have of being believed.'

'Even if those women have marriages and families to protect?' Jane asked.

'Well, there is that and I certainly won't try to disrupt their domestic arrangements, which is one of the reasons why I'm thinking about attacking his power base.'

Jane and Hugo shared a glance. 'I'm listening,' she said, a defiant spark glistening in her eye. Hugo sensed a little of her strength and self-confidence slowly returning. She was ready to fight back. She *needed* to fight back and Hugo would do all in his power to ensure that these two ladies combined forces to do precisely that.

He had his own reasons for wanting to bring Steve down that he hadn't yet shared with Leona or Jane and perhaps never would.

'Steve's god is power and money, to say nothing of a burning desire to impress his father-in-law,' Leona said, nodding slowly. 'Destroy the trust between the two men by showing Bizham Nawaz that Steve has betrayed Stella and the entire house of cards will come crumbling down. Bizham has the power to crush Steve like the irritant that he is, which is much more likely to succeed than any dents we can make in his armour,' Leona pointed out.

'He's about to be appointed to a non-executive position of Nawaz's board, so Steve has confidentially told me,' Hugo pointed out.

'He's been angling after that position for years,' Leona replied, 'but the time has never been quite right. Presumably he's fairly sure of his facts now or he wouldn't have mentioned it to you, Hugo.' She rubbed her chin between the thumb and forefinger of her left hand. 'Hmm. That might put a spanner in our plans.'

'It will certainly increase his influence,' Hugo agreed. 'If Nawaz believes the rumours about his infidelities, it will be in his best interests to suppress them. He depends on his image as a man in control of his family to give him the edge. It's vitally important to him.'

'Well then, I wonder if Daddy knows what his precious little girl gets up to behind closed doors.' Leona tapped her fingers against the surface of the table. 'Not that I have any axe to grind with her. *She* is not the problem. Steve assured me that they had an open marriage and I actually believe that. But they also depend on one another because they both need her father's support. That's why his marriage would never have broken up, despite all the promises he made to us both.'

'You can't destroy Steve's reputation without risking Stella's,' Hugo said. 'If he goes down then you can be sure that he'll take her with him.'

'It might be a lucky escape for her,' Jane said. 'If she plays away from home as well then she will have to accept the consequences. Had she been the faithful little wife, oblivious to Steve's shenanigans, I would have thought twice. As it is, she's as much to blame as he is. I don't know what game the two of them think they're playing, but they shouldn't have involved others and destroyed lives.'

Leona grinned. 'I know how Steve's business operates: every little twist and shortcut. Every little detail that he hasn't bothered to share with the taxman. Post questions about his operating methods online, raise red flags and it will reduce the value of his share price.' Leona's smile widened. 'That will give him something to think about.'

'You can really do that?' Jane asked.

Leona smiled. 'I really can. Not that I'd previously considered anything quite so devious but I know Steve won't give up on goading me, or preventing me from procuring gainful employment by casting aspersions on my honesty, so I intend to fight my corner.' Determination coursed through her expression. 'And if fighting dirty is the only way to go about it, then so be it. I am tired of being a victim.'

'I hear you,' Jane said softly.

'So, how do you intend to go about this campaign?' Hugo asked.

'I am going to sound Molly Fairfax, Steve's PA, out first,' Leona replied. 'She knows where all the bodies are buried. She and I were friends and she did try to warn me about Steve... I just chose not to hear her.'

'She's been with him for a long time and will want to protect her own interests,' Hugo pointed out. 'Tread carefully. She's loyal.'

'She's more conflicted, I think,' Leona replied pensively. 'She's been married to the same man for thirty years and is a regular church goer. She will have seen Steve's expense claims, put two and two together and not approved. Whether she will want to do anything to redress the balance is another matter. She did tell me once, without actually spelling it out, that Steve had destroyed the life of a young woman, a friend of Molly's, who came to work for the firm as an intern.'

'Sounds like Steve.' Jane wrinkled her nose.

'Molly took a maternal interest in the young woman. Bear in mind that Molly is approaching fifty. Her husband has a very well-paid job so perhaps Molly is thinking about early retirement. She reckons the world of big business is a young person's game.'

Hugo nodded as he drained his glass and stretched his arms above his head. 'Anyway, ladies.' He glanced at his watch. 'If there's nothing more, I'd best be getting along.'

'Thank you.' Jane paused. 'I think.'

Hugo watched the two women embrace, bonding over a common cause. He left the pub ahead of them, satisfied that something good had come out of the evening.

Wondering too what he had set in motion and how much of a hit his own business would take as a consequence.

He'd take his chances.

* * *

The dinner party broke up into smaller groups, all the glad-handers keen to congratulate Bizham's new blue-eyed boy. Several sympathetic glances were cast Steve's way but he ignored them, put his game face on and pretended that he'd known all along what was coming.

'Embarrassing,' one guy said to him, less than convincingly.

Steve shrugged. 'Bizham has his reasons. Everything's cool.'

'Glad to hear it.' The man's glance fell upon Stella, up close and personal with the new board member; a man with whom Steve was acquainted but whom he'd dismissed as non-threatening to his own ambitions. 'Something to do with Stella's business, I imagine. Farmer is a massively successful importer of silk.'

Since Steve had seriously underestimated Farmer, despite the fact that he'd known he was Stella's latest squeeze, he merely gave off a disinterested vibe. This was all Stella's doing, Steve belatedly realised, struggling to contain his volatile temper. How he'd love to issue the backhander that the disloyal little cow so richly deserved but he knew better than to lay a finger on her. Daddy would hear about it before the bruises had faded and Steve would bear the consequences of a protective father's formidable wrath, to say nothing of that of her brothers. So, Steve was obliged to accept that

Stella had persuaded Bizham to honour not her husband, but her friend, her lover.

Well, that changed everything. He'd stuck by his side of the bargain. She was the one to step out of line.

This was war!

He excused himself and went to the gents. Ensuring that all the cubicles were empty, he extracted his mobile and called the investigator he had on speed dial.

'I have a job for you tonight,' he said as soon as the call was answered. 'Follow my wife from the Grand Hotel. I want to know where she goes, who with, how long she stays, the full nine yards. Pictures too. Got that?'

'Got it.'

The connection was cut without further need for words and Steve know the job would be done, efficiently and unobtrusively. He and Stella had an agreement, but by allowing him to be so publicly humiliated and not even giving him the heads-up beforehand, she had crossed a line.

Her behaviour couldn't go unpunished. Actions had consequences, as Leona had already discovered to her cost and Stella very soon would too. The plans he had for Leona, his latest little reminder of his devotion intended for the wee small hours, would have to wait. He now had other priorities.

Feeling slightly better about the world now that a way to fight back had formed in his head, Steve straightened his jacket and returned to the fray.

* * *

Leona's phone rang when she was half-way home. She checked the display, smiled, gave a little whoop and took the call.

'You're back!'

A chuckle echoed down the line. 'And I have *so* much to tell you, girlfriend.'

'Where are you?'

'Hovering outside your door with a bottle. There's something that sounds like the hound of the Baskervilles creating a hell of a racket inside. What's that all about?'

'I'm ten minutes away. Hang fire and I'll explain all.'

Her mood lifted considerably at the thought of a reconciliation with her oldest friend. She and Patsy Clinton had gone through school and university together, joined at the hip, working and playing equally hard. But Patsy had gone into the corporate entertainment game and finished up being whisked around the world in first class luxury by her various wealthy clients who couldn't seem to manage without her exemplary management skills and her ability to make anything happen, no matter how impossible.

She had been in Monaco for six months, helping some high flyers to impress investors and pull off a multi-million-pound deal. Leona didn't need to ask if Patsy had been successful.

Patsy never failed.

Leona was still grinning when she pulled up outside her cottage. The moment she stepped from her car, a whirlwind that was all five foot four of Patsy hurled herself into her arms.

'You look astonishing, damn you!' Patsy cried.

Leona smiled, aware that she felt and probably looked anything but, even though she appreciated the compliment. 'It's so good to see you!' Leona returned her friend's hug. 'It's been too long. You've been jetting off around the world in style, forgetting all about your old roots and older friends.'

'Never!'

Mulligan's barking had turned to excited whines at the sound of Leona's voice. She extracted her keys from her bag, noticing Patsy's frown when she used three different ones to unlock.

'What the devil...'

Before Patsy could say more, Mulligan was upon them both. He gave Patsy a brief sniff and, appearing to find her non-threatening, jumped up to place his paws on her chest. Patsy laughed and ruffled his ears.

'Come on,' she said when Mulligan finally got down and ran outside to lift his leg against a bush, 'let's get this bottle open, then you can tell me what the hell's going on and why you're living in a what appears to be a gilded cage.'

'Tell me first about your adventures.' Leona smiled, aware that Patsy had a way about her which made her an instant hit with everyone she charmed. She waited for Mulligan to come wagging back to them and relocked the door behind him. 'Which rich entrepreneur wanted to whisk you away to paradise this time?'

'Bah! I've given up on men. More trouble than they're worth.' She took a long slug of her drink and frowned with genuine-seeming concern. 'So come on, tell me. Why the dog, the keys, the security lights I saw outside? Are you and Steve still playing footsie?' she asked, her frown intensifying.

Patsy had never liked Steve and had warned Leona against getting involved with a married man, especially one whom she worked with. But, Leona knew, she would never say *I told you so*. Her support and understanding now it had all gone pear-shaped would be absolute. Only now did Leona realise just how much she appreciated her as a sounding board and how much she'd actually missed her. Several times, she had almost phoned and told all but doing so long distance would have made her feel even more of a needy, pathetic idiot than she knew herself to be. Besides, Patsy would probably have dropped everything and run home, but there was nothing she could have done and Leona would then have had the loss of her friend's career on her conscience.

In dribs and drabs, Leona's story spilled out. She explained that

Patsy had been right about Steve the entire time and how she'd had a lucky escape.

'But he won't let it go,' she finished up by saying. 'He has to have the last word and won't ever forgive me for attempting to take out a restraining order, which his erratic behaviour forced me to do, or for dumping him.' She frowned and spread her hands. 'I just don't understand why I matter so much to him. Why can't he just put the past behind him and move on to his next victim?'

'Doesn't surprise me.' Patsy screwed up her features. 'The guy's a misogynist. And as to why he's trying to get back at you... well, that's an easy one. His pride is hurt, darling. He isn't used to rejection. He takes it as a personal slight.' Patsy took a healthy swig of her drink. 'From what you've told me, his father-in-law has him by the short and curlies so it stands to reason that he feels less of a man as a consequence. That's why he needs an attractive bit on the side. Someone to stroke his ego and... other things.'

Leona tilted her head in a considering fashion. 'Perhaps. I know you always suspected his motives.'

'Well, in my line of work, a lot of which requires socialising, you soon get to recognise the self-entitled type and Steve Jessop was right up there with the best, or the worst, of them. But I knew you had to find out for yourself. You were never going to take my word for it. He played you like a Stradivarius, darling.' Patsy reached across to squeeze Leona's hand. 'But now that your eyes have been opened, how do you intend to fight back?'

Leona explained what she knew, or suspected, about some of Steve's other victims and went on to describe her meeting with Jane.

'Hmm.' Patsy screwed up her nose.

'What does "hmm" mean?'

'I think your alternative suggestion of destroying his relationship with his father-in-law is more realistic, especially if Steve depends upon his financial support. You and the others might come across as women scorned who've joined forces, exaggerating in order to be taken seriously, which you won't be. Well, not seriously enough to do any long-term damage or restore your career prospects. Besides, Jane sounds fragile. Is it fair to involve her?'

'Perhaps not but she wants to play her part. Besides, what else...' Leona's voice trailed off as she struggled to articulate her opinion.

'I've actually met Bizham Nawaz a couple of times. He has business dealings with some of the enterprises I support. Not that he will remember me.'

Leona gave a disbelieving laugh. 'Darling, everyone you meet remembers you. You make that sort of impression.'

'I also happen to know that the non-executive directorship Steve was depending upon being appointed to in a glittering announcement tonight didn't take place.'

Leona slammed her glass down, feeling her spirits lifting. 'How do you know that? Steve told me it was his for the taking and would be the making of him. I never doubted... I mean, his own father-in-law wouldn't humiliate him, would he?'

'Seemingly so.' Patsy pulled out her phone and googled a business site. 'Here you go,' she said, handing the phone to Leona.

Leona absorbed the basic facts: the directorship had gone to an importer, an obvious friend of Stella's. 'I wonder if Steve had advance warning,' she mused, biting back a smile. She would be less than human if she didn't feel a modicum of satisfaction at his public put down. 'I also wonder what he'll do to get his revenge.'

'Well, my lovely, it seems to me that his relationship with Bizham has hit rock bottom and there's no time like the present to exploit that fact. Hit him where it hurts, that's what I say.'

'We'll be had up for libel – or is it slander? – if we attempt to slate him in public without anything to back up our assertions.

Steve might be temporarily down but I very much doubt if he's out. When cornered, he's at his most dangerous and will fight back with everything he has.'

'Which means he will put his campaign against you on hold.'

'He probably wishes I was still in his employ. I would have had his back and thought of a way for him to regain the upper hand; he knows that.'

Mulligan got up, turned in several tight circles and flopped down again across Patsy's feet. Patsy bent to tug at his ears. Leona knew that her friend would lose all feeling in her toes if her dog got too comfy, but for now, the arrangement appeared to suit them both.

'Well, darling, he doesn't deserve you.'

'I still intend to speak with Steve's PA. What's the worst that can happen? If I'm wrong about her then she will run to Steve, telling tales about my vindictive determination to get revenge, but that won't be telling him anything he doesn't already know.'

'But it will put him on his guard and threaten Molly's position.'

'Only if she decides not to tattle and he finds out that I've spoken to her, which I don't think he will.' Leona lifted one shoulder. 'I have to start somewhere. What do I have to lose, other than my sanity? If I sit here wondering what he's going to do to spook me next, I will definitely go out of my tiny mind.'

'True, so perhaps a two-pronged attack. His powerbase, which is Bizham and his womanising. Mud sticks if it's thrown from enough directions.' Patsy drained her glass, yawned, collected her belongings and stood up. 'I only got back today and am feeling pooped. I need to get some sleep. But I'll think about this and get back to you soon.'

'Well, thanks for making me your first port of call.' Leona threw her arms around her friend. 'I've missed you.'

'I will do a little delving. Bend the ears of a few contacts and see what I can find out about the real state of Bizham's business, as well as Steve's.' She tapped her forefinger against her lips. 'Can't help wondering why Bizham gave that directorship to an outsider. There must be more to it than a deliberate attempt to humiliate Steve. Family appearances are everything to that man.'

'Do you suppose he's found out about Steve's womanising?'

'Well, darling, it's one possibility.' A slow smile spread across Patsy's face. 'But if he doesn't know, perhaps we should be the ones to enlighten him. Subtly, of course.' Patsy paused with her hand on the door and turned to blow Leona a kiss. 'Laters,' she said.

8

Hugo reached home for once before the witching hour. He switched on a few lights and sat on the terrace with a beer in hand, thinking the events of the night through, listening to the sounds of the countryside settling down for the night that he was seldom there to appreciate.

If his interference caused Steve's business to fail then Hugo knew that it would have a knock-on effect for his own research funding, a very detrimental effect, so why was he even contemplating shooting himself in the foot to help a woman he barely knew? Some things, he supposed, not many but a few, were more important than his life's work. That was the downside of having a conscience and something that would never cause Steve sleepless nights.

Besides, rumours had reached him about Steve potentially having cashflow problems. He'd expanded too fast, spread himself too thin. Steve would never admit to his failings but Leona had made one or two off-the-cuff remarks about his cutting corners that reinforced Hugo's impression. Steve was contracted to purchase a minimum number of components from Hugo on a quarterly basis.

Up until six months ago, he'd significantly exceeded the contractual requirement to the extent that Hugo's team sometimes struggled to meet his demand. Not so for the past two quarters, which had set alarm bells ringing. But Hugo hadn't asked Steve if there had been a downturn in the demand for his repair service. Steve, Hugo knew as a result of their long friendship, never admitted to his own failures, preferring to bury his head in the sand. Hugo had often wondered if Steve's extravagant lifestyle would one day be his downfall, even though he had a wealthy father-in-law who wouldn't permit him to fail.

Well, probably not.

Hugo glanced at his watch. It was still before ten o'clock. On an impulse, he dialled the care home and was greeted warmly by the nurse on duty. Everyone in the establishment knew Hugo; he was a regular visitor.

'Hugo!' His mother's voice sang down the line, bright and alert. Clearly, she was having a good day. 'What a lovely surprise. I haven't seen you for so long.'

Hugo didn't bother to remind her that he'd been in two days previously and spent over an hour with her.

'How are you, Mother?'

'Oh, busy just like always. Margaret and I are having tea at the Royal tomorrow. I can't decide what to wear. My sister is such a snappy dresser and I don't want to feel like a dowd by comparison.'

Hugo sighed. His aunt Margaret had been dead for twenty years but lived on in his mother's fragmented memory, dating back to a time when they had been teenagers. 'That will be nice for you.'

'It's time you settled down with a nice girl, my dear, and gave me grandchildren. Margaret and I both agree about that.'

He allowed his mother to ramble on. She didn't seem to notice that Hugo wasn't making any contributions to the conversation. She lived in her own fantasy world and Hugo had been told to enjoy it whilst it lasted. The day would soon arrive when she became aggressive. It was a phase that most Alzheimer patients went through but he refused to believe that it would happen to someone as gentle and compassionate as his own mother. After that, she wouldn't even remember who he was.

He felt so frustrated. It was such a cruel disease and research to find a cure was frustratingly slow. As things stood, all the money in the world couldn't resolve her particular problem, a problem that burgeoned along with an aging population.

Cutting the connection, he glanced at his watch and saw that it was still before eleven. Feeling a curious lack of guilt for playing hooky, he fetched himself another beer and returned to the terrace. He looked up at the clear night sky, attempting to recognise the constellations. His knowledge of astronomy was patchy at best, but he was pretty sure that he could make out Orion, albeit one of the most prominent and easily recognisable formations. When he had more time, it was a subject that he would like to explore in depth. If he ever had any spare time. The thought was laughable and not one that had troubled him before. He lived for his work and was fine with that.

Wasn't he?

He enjoyed the solitude, allowing his thoughts to ramble. As a general rule, he always had the latest hitch with his research at the forefront of his mind but right now, Leona's problems seemed determined to take precedence. That concerned him. He had done what he could for her tonight and owed her nothing. Perhaps he regretted being so helpful because if she succeeded in regaining her professional reputation and freeing herself from the attentions of a sexual leach then he would be destroying his business relationship with his former friend. But there were other people jumping on the electronic repair bandwagon nowadays and Hugo already had representatives out there looking for new customers.

He had known and understood what drove Steve for years and it had never sat comfortably with him. It was far too late to save Sophia, the girl who'd taken her own life at Oxford. In retrospect, Hugo should have tried harder to convince the besotted girl that Steve was bad news. His failure in that regard would always trouble his conscience. It seemed like another life in many respects and yet the impact had never entirely left Hugo. Perhaps his work, into which he'd thrown himself relentlessly since graduation, was an excuse to avoid personal entanglements. The one serious affair he'd entered into had ended disastrously and Hugo still wore the emotional scars.

The sound of a car screeching erratically to a halt outside his cottage jerked him out of his reverie. This was a quiet lane, it was late at night and he seldom had visitors. Before he could reach the front door, someone pressed the bell. And kept their finger on it.

'What the hell? Okay, okay, I'm coming.'

He wrenched the door open and was confronted by the last person he'd expected to see. The same person towards whom his thoughts had drifted for the first time in ages just a few moments ago. What were the chances?

'Cleo?' Hugo blinked to make sure his eyes weren't deceiving him. 'What on earth are you doing here?'

'Can I come in?'

She pushed past Hugo without waiting for a response. Of course she did. Cleo had always been able to wind Hugo around her little finger and clearly supposed that the passage of more than a decade had changed nothing.

'Be my guest,' he muttered, glancing outside before closing the door and noticing her car parked at a dangerous angle across his drive, the lights still on, engine running. He ran outside switched the car off and locked it.

Hugo returned to his cottage, threw her keys onto the hall table and found Cleo standing in the middle of his lounge, taking in her surroundings, clearly unimpressed by what she saw. He could see her face more clearly now and was surprised by the changes in her appearance. She had been stunningly beautiful in her twenties. Now in her mid-thirties, she looked harrowed, her eyes haunted. She had obviously been crying.

Cleo's face and svelte figure had always been her fortune. It had certainly caught the attention of the wealthy man she'd ditched Hugo for without a backward glance. As far as he was aware, they had never married but the man was often in the news, announcing his latest multi-million-pound deal, Cleo looking stunning on his arm.

'What are you doing here?' Hugo asked. 'How did you know where to find me?' *And why would you want to?*

She turned to look at him, smiled, and Hugo saw a brief glimpse of the woman he'd fallen so hard for all those years ago. The woman who had so callously ditched him for a richer alternative, causing damage to Hugo's heart in the process.

Damage, he now knew, that had not been terminal but more of a timely warning. In some respects, he supposed he ought to be grateful to her. He had certainly found it easy enough to resist the appeal of the various attractive women who'd crossed his path since then. He dated, but he never let anyone get close.

'Have you got anything to drink?' She sat down in her graceful manner and crossed her long legs at the ankle. Hugo had forgotten about her ability to answer a question with one of her own, especially when she wanted to prevaricate. A drink would give her an excuse to linger, he supposed. Even so, he went into the kitchen, extracted a bottle of white wine from the fridge and poured her a glass. He opened another beer for himself, feeling he was likely to need it. Cleo's dramas had never been short in duration and he doubted if that situation had changed over the intervening years.

He handed her the wine and sat across from her, saying nothing, watching her. Her distress, he quickly decided, was genuine. Why she had brought it to his door, especially at this time of night though, was less obvious.

She took several delicate sips of her drink, her morose gaze occasionally resting upon his face. The silence appeared to unsettle her but Hugo did nothing to ease her discomfort. Perhaps he was supposed to fawn over her, as he once would have done, but those days were behind him. Looking at her now, he acknowledged that she was still a lovely woman, despite her distress, but he felt absolutely nothing for her. In a way, it was a relief to see her again. Now, when her face occasionally had the temerity to intrude upon his subconscious, it would be a doddle to dismiss thoughts of what would have been a disastrous alliance. He recalled going down on one knee, proposing and fully expecting her to accept him.

She had not. His pride had been hurt but he could see now that she'd done him a favour. He'd had ambitions but no money and that, he understood, had been the deciding factor for Cleo.

'You're looking good,' she eventually said.

Hugo was unsure how to respond so simply shrugged. 'You still haven't told me what you're doing here,' he said.

She put her glass aside and leaned forward, elbows resting on her knees. 'I'm in trouble, Hugo, and need your help.'

'What sort of trouble and why turn to me in your hour of need? We haven't seen one another for years and didn't part on the best of terms anyway.'

'You were always there for me.' She pouted, then pulled her lower lip between her teeth – a gesture that used to fascinate Hugo. But it was out of place on the older woman's face and did nothing for him.

'The same cannot be said for you,' he replied without rancour.

'I know, I'm sorry.' She looked down and plucked at the fabric of her skirt. 'I didn't behave well. I have always regretted that.'

She did appear to regret it now that she needed his help – help that she seemed to think would be forthcoming. Years ago, before she'd rejected his proposal almost insolently, it would have been, but Hugo was no longer that man.

'Just tell me what it is that you think I can help you with,' he said wearily. 'It's late and I have to be up early.'

'Always such a hard worker,' she said softly. 'I knew you'd make a success of yourself. You were always so driven, so determined to make a difference, even as a young man. You had no time to devote to me.'

'You're prevaricating,' he pointed out, refusing to be softened up by a few meaningless platitudes.

'It's James,' she eventually said into the ensuing silence. 'He's having an affair. I'm losing him.'

'I'm sorry to hear that but people stray from relationships all the time,' Hugo replied, fixing her with a speaking look that caused her to look away from him. 'What do you expect me to do about it?'

'I've suspected that he was playing away for a while but he always denied it.' She drew in a long, ragged breath. Cleo Addison was vain. Hardly surprising given that she'd been a sensation as a teenage model and her face had been her fortune. Hugo knew it must have taken a huge effort of will to admit that the tables had been turned and she was now the one being cheated on. 'But tonight my worst fears were confirmed.'

'Tonight?'

'We attended Bizham Nawaz's bash.'

Nawaz? Hugo leaned forward and she was now assured of his full attention. She was wearing a sleek evening gown that clung to her slender curves. Curves that would be enhanced by the addition of a few extra pounds, he absently thought, his mind briefly drifting in the direction of Leona's slightly fuller and far more impressive figure.

'Go on,' he said softly. 'This was to announce Steve's appointment as a non-exec director to Bizham's board, wasn't it?'

Cleo nodded. 'That's what we all assumed. I had hoped I might see you there.'

Their paths had crossed occasionally in the past decade but Hugo had made a point of avoiding her whenever they did. He had absolutely nothing to say to her that she would want to hear. 'Not my scene,' he said shortly.

'Well, you should have been there because Steve was publicly humiliated.'

Hugo's body jerked upright. 'He was?'

'Yep.' Cleo moistened her lips. 'Steve didn't get the directorship.' She paused. 'James did.'

'Fucking hell!' A dozen questions whirled through Hugo's mind. 'Was Steve forewarned? He told me just a couple of days ago that he was looking forward to the public acclamation he deserved.'

Cleo shook her head. 'I'm pretty sure that he had no idea. I watched for his reaction. He hid it well but I could see he'd been blindsided.'

'Stella didn't prepare him?'

Cleo's expression turned dark and forbidding at the mention of Stella's name, which is when the pieces fell into place and the real reason for Cleo's visit became clear. James Farmer was a major importer of silk, which Nawaz bought from him. Farmer's father was English, his mother Indian, from the same area of India as Nawaz. James's mother had provided the family contacts that enabled James to get his business off the ground. Nawaz and Farmer needed one another, they had a mutually profitable arrangement as well as cultural links, but it didn't explain why Nawaz would punish Steve so publicly.

'Stella was the reason why James got the appointment,' she said, a bitter edge to her voice.

'Stella and James are...'

'Right.' Cleo drained her glass and rippled her shoulders indignantly. 'They didn't even try that hard to hide it this evening. I have never felt so mortified...' She held out her empty glass, assuming that Hugo would refill it for her.

'You're driving,' he said, taking the glass from her and putting it aside. 'And that wasn't your first this evening. Losing your licence won't solve anything.'

'Always so practical,' she replied in an accusatory tone.

'You came to me with your problems, Cleo,' Hugo replied, remaining calm in the light of her growing ire and obvious desire to pick a fight. 'Not that I know what you expect me to do about them. Stella and Steve have an open marriage. I will confess to being surprised that Stella chose to persuade Nawaz to acknowledge James quite so publicly but there's bugger all I can do about it.' He put his beer aside and absently rubbed his chin. 'It will have infuriated Steve but Steve always bounces back.'

Except that he'll find it harder without Nawaz's backing, especially if Hugo's suspicions were founded and Steve had frittered away his profits, assuming that the lucrative directorship would make up the short fall. Nawaz definitely wouldn't approve of financial irresponsibility. Was that why he'd punished Steve?

Steve wouldn't take this lying down, Hugo knew, and he had the upper hand insofar as he was married to Stella. He thought about Steve's assault on Leona when she abandoned him and shuddered. How much worse would his retribution be against his wife? And father-in-law. Was there anything he could do to attack such a powerful man?

'Yes, but what about me?' Cleo's voice had taken on a whine.

'Have you spoken to James about the situation?'

'I tried to when we left the do this evening but he said I was being paranoid. That instead of whinging, I ought to be proud of him. We had a terrible row, he stormed out of the house, no doubt to go to *her* and I... well, I couldn't think of anywhere else to go. No one else I could depend on to help me.'

'Help you how, Cleo?' Hugo spread his hands. 'How am I supposed to resolve your domestic differences and what makes you suppose that I would even want to?'

His intransigence clearly rattled her. She seemed to have overlooked the fact that he was considerably older and a lot wiser than when she had held him in her thrall. He made his decisions with his head rather than his heart nowadays. She hadn't expected him to turn her away and the inevitable tears now leaked from the corners of her eyes. Hugo watched the display impassively, unmoved by it. She always had been able to turn on the tears when it suited her purpose.

'I hoped you might talk to Steve. Explain why he was humiliated and make him force his wife to give James up.'

Hugo threw back his head and laughed. 'You really do live in a different universe to the rest of us mere mortals. Steve and Stella play by their own rules and won't thank me for interfering. Not that I have any intention of getting involved.'

'Well of course I know that they're players!' she snapped. 'But as far as I'm aware, she has never so publicly supported one of her lovers before and that changes everything. I can't lose him, Hugo, I just can't! It isn't as though we're legally married. We never saw a need for that.' But Hugo could tell from her furtive look that she'd been pushing for marriage. It was obviously James who didn't want to take things that far.

The tears went into freefall but Hugo knew that she would

lament the loss of Farmer's money and the lifestyle it afforded her more than the loss of his actual affections. The scathing look she'd given his small, cosy sitting room had not been lost on Hugo. It was definitely not the type of accommodation that she was accustomed to, nor had any desire to acquaint herself with. How she would stand financially if James threw her out, he had no idea. Nor did he intend to open that particular can of worms.

'Then talk to him, not me.' Hugo knew it was the time to tell her a few brutal facts of life. 'Your relationship can't be that solid—'

'It is.' She drummed the fingers of one hand against her thigh. 'Or rather it was, until she infatuated him, drawing him in with promises of what Daddy dearest could do for him. But he doesn't need that sort of help. He's doing really well on his own.'

'You have never strayed?'

'No, of course not.' But she couldn't meet his gaze and Hugo knew she was lying.

'Stella and Steve will never separate,' he said. 'You're aware of Nawaz's firm views on that subject: his insistence upon a display of family unity in public.' He didn't give her an opportunity to respond, instead driving his point home. 'Stella's affair with James will run its course and if you play along then James will come back to you eventually.'

She twitched her nose, seemingly unimpressed with that advice. 'I feel totally humiliated. I need to fight back. To remind James of what he already has.'

Hugo thought of the manner in which Cleo had so carelessly rejected his proposal, then dumped him once she'd gotten her claws into James Farmer and wondered if she appreciated the irony of her last statement.

'Even so, there's nothing I can do to help you,' he said, finality in his tone.

'I thought you could tell Steve, get him to... well, do something to break them up.' She threw her hands in the air, the refracted light sparkling off the diamonds on her fingers. 'He must be feeling pretty pissed right now and could use your advice.'

Hugo laughed. 'That isn't Steve's way. And even if it was, I wouldn't get involved.' He fixed her with a look of firm resolve. 'I already offered you some advice but you took precious little notice because it wasn't what you wanted to hear. Not everything is about you, Cleo, and you need to wake up to that fact.'

'I had no idea you were still so bitter about our breakup,' she shot back at him, malice briefly flashing through her eyes.

'Darling, I'd forgotten all about it and about you until you turned up here uninvited, expecting me to right all the world's wrongs.'

Her face flushed with anger and she seemed temporarily lost for words. This was clearly not the reaction she'd been expecting.

'You'd best be going,' he said, standing.

'I thought I could stay.' She sent him a suggestive smile. 'I've had a lot to drink.'

Hugo shook his head emphatically. 'Not happening,' he replied. 'You're in a loving relationship, or so you would have me believe, and you won't be using me as a means of revenge because your feelings are hurt, if that's what you're thinking.'

'Yes, but...'

'I wish you luck with James and advise you to think about what you have to lose before you throw accusations his way.'

He walked towards the front door but she was slow to get up and follow him. 'You've changed,' she said. 'You're harder.'

'Good night,' he said, opening the door wider and handing her the car keys he'd left on his hall stand. 'Drive carefully.'

He watched from the doorway as she got into her car, fired up the engine and made a ragged five-point turn. He hoped she made it home without mishap. He also wondered, as he closed and bolted the door, when she had last been rebuffed. A bit like Steve, he supposed, turning off the lights and heading for the stairs, it was an alien feeling. Both narcissists, neither of them took rejection well. Despite that, her supposition that she could simply rekindle their affair and get him to do all her dirty work took his breath away, even though it ought not to have surprised him.

What was significant, he thought as he stripped off and crawled beneath the sheets, was this latest very major hitch in Steve's ambitions. He had been depending upon that directorship to enhance his own standing in a fiercely competitive business world, and to resolve any financial hiccups he'd encountered, to say nothing of cementing his relationship with an often-judgemental Nawaz. Instead, it implied a significant cooling of relations between him and Bizham.

Why?

Whatever the reason, Hugo knew that Steve wouldn't take the humiliation lying down.

As he drifted off to sleep, Hugo wondered what form Steve's retribution would take and how he and Leona could use it to their advantage.

9

Leona was woken early by the sound of her ringing phone accompanied by a dog's hot breath and cool nose pressed against her ear. She groaned, opened one eye and was greeted with the sight of Mulligan panting at the side of her bed, wagging his entire rear end, eager for his morning walk.

'Who the devil would call me at such an ungodly hour?' she asked her dog, thinking that calls at antisocial hours usually only equated to bad news. She sat up, feeling groggy and apprehensive as she pushed the hair away from her eyes and picked up her phone. 'Hugo? What on earth does he want?' she wondered aloud as she took the call. 'Good morning. Bed caught fire?' she asked.

Hugo's rich laugh echoed down the line. 'This is the middle of the morning from my perspective.'

Leona glanced at the bedside clock. 'But it's only six-thirty,' she wailed. 'Even Mulligan isn't *that* serious about getting up yet.' Or wouldn't have been if the phone hadn't woken us both, she thought but did not add.

'Sorry. I didn't stop to think.'

'Yeah.' It was Leona's turn to smile. 'I got that part.'

'Time's money.' His tone sobered. 'More to the point. There have been unexpected developments that you need to be aware of. I can't talk about it over the phone. Besides, I'm in the middle of something.' Leona could hear sounds in the background and someone calling his name, confirming her suspicions that he was already hard at work. 'Can we meet later today?'

'Don't you ever need to sleep?' she asked.

'Sleep's overrated.'

'I'll have to take your word for that. I need a solid eight hours. Anyway, I'm intrigued. I also have news of my own to impart,' she added, thinking of Steve's disappointment over the directorship and failing to summon up one iota of sympathy. Couldn't have happened to a more deserving person.

'Can we do lunch? Then we can update one another.'

'If you can afford to take the time away from your precious work.'

'I'm sure that can be arranged. I'm on friendly terms with the boss.'

'Well, good luck with that one.' Leona had got her fingers badly burned over the Steve business. She'd come out of it deciding that she could no longer trust her own judgement when it came to men and so had sworn off them. And yet, here she was flirting with a man she barely knew at some ungodly hour and enjoying herself immensely. *Steady, girl!* 'I hear he's a bit of a slavedriver who demands his pound of flesh.'

Hugo chuckled. 'I've heard that about him too.'

They agreed on a time and place and Leona ended the call.

'What was that all about, baby?' she asked Mulligan, who was now wide awake and turning in anticipatory circles, his mind obviously focused on a morning ramble that would require him to keep the local rabbit population under control. 'Come on then. I won't get back to sleep now. I'm far too intrigued by Hugo's call,' she said, throwing back the covers.

It was a lovely morning and so Leona took her time, allowing the dog the freedom to run where he liked, chasing anything that moved with more enthusiasm than killer instinct.

She watched the dawn breaking over the horizon and let her mind wander as erratically as her feet, wondering what was so important that Hugo felt the need to ring her so early.

The dog's morning ablutions attended to and a long ramble in the woods completed, Leona made herself a light breakfast. She scanned the news on her phone and found scant details of Farmer's position on Nawaz's board reported, with the inevitable speculation about Steve being passed over. The news cheered her considerably.

After attending to some of her online work, making calls and arranging an appointment to see a new potential client the following day, she shut down her laptop and thought about what to wear to meet Hugo.

'What the hell?' she asked Mulligan. 'This isn't a date.'

Defiantly, she pulled on her favourite jeans and a light sweatshirt, determined not to appear to have made an effort for his sake. She ran a brush through her tangled hair, applied makeup sparingly and was good to go.

'Sorry, baby, you can't come,' she told Mulligan who, aware that she was going out, stood wagging expectantly at the door. 'Your job is to guard the house and stop any scumbags from invading our privacy. Got that?'

Mulligan's wagging intensified, which she took as an affirmative. The increased excitement could, of course, have been attributable to the rawhide bone she presented him with before she slipped through the door and triple-locked it behind her.

A short drive, which gave her little time to dwell upon her feelings about Hugo and the avid interest he appeared to be taking in her affairs, delivered her to the pub where they had agreed to meet. Her instincts told her that he was on her side, despite all he had to lose if he and Steve parted on bad terms. He really must still harbour a lot of resentment about the girl from uni who killed herself, she thought as she checked her appearance in the rear-view mirror and exited the car. After all, nothing could change the past or bring the poor girl back, so why risk his all to help her?

'Hold that thought, Leona,' she muttered aloud, 'and don't be swayed by a pretty face and convincing argument. You went down that route before and it did not end well.'

She walked into a bar half full of lunchtime diners and her gaze was drawn to Hugo leaning against it, looking far too lethally hand-some for Leona's comfort. His appearance already threatened her resolve to question his motives, a testament to just how shallow she actually must be, she thought with a wry smile as she continued to enjoy the view.

He wore jeans with a dress shirt open at the neck, the tails not tucked in. Clearly his company believed in dressing for comfort and it made Leona feel disadvantaged simply because he could rock a humble pair of jeans so effectively.

Hugo was chatting to the barmaid, who appeared to find what-ever he'd just said to her amusing, and totally absorbing. Several customers were waiting to be served but she ignored them all. Hugo glanced over his shoulder, as though sensing Leona's pres-ence, and a broad smile graced his features.

'You made it,' he said unnecessarily, leaning forward to kiss her cheek.

'How could I refuse such a clarion wake-up call,' she quipped.

The barmaid overheard the comment, clearly misinterpreted and stomped off to serve one of the waiting customers.

'Is it something I said?' she asked Hugo, smiling at the rigid set to the barmaid's shoulders.

Hugo smiled that easy smile of his, asked her what she'd like to drink and managed to catch the attention of another member of staff.

With soft drinks in hand and food ordered, they retreated to a quiet table.

'Cheers.' Leona clinked her glass of tonic water against that containing Hugo's coke. 'Okay, give,' she demanded, determined to be all business. 'What's so important that it required such an early call?'

'You've heard about Steve's disappointment by now, I'm guessing,' he replied.

'Yes, before seeing it in the news this morning. I'll explain how in a moment.' Leona frowned. 'But I still don't see why that should require an emergency wake-up call.'

He paused, the long fingers of one hand resting against his cheek as he observed her with unnerving stillness. Whatever he was about to tell her, she sensed, would be a game-changer. 'Perhaps that's because you're not aware that Stella is romantically involved with James Farmer,' he said casually.

'Ah, I see.' Leona nodded as she thought that information through, somehow not surprised to hear it. She knew from what Steve had told her that his wife always went for the high-flyers. Men who could help her own ambitions. 'It's a departure from her norm. She's always been so discreet about her affairs and as far as I'm aware, she never sought to favour any of them through her father's influence. Steve must be fuming.'

Hugo chuckled. 'That's a safe bet.'

'Anyway, how did you find out about Stella and Farmer? Presumably Steve cried on your shoulder, just as he sometimes does when he hits a bump in the road. He used to say that he could depend upon you, no matter how tough the going got.'

'That's not precisely what happened this time.'

Their food was delivered by the barmaid who had so pointedly ignored Leona earlier. She placed Hugo's in front of him with a coy smile, before slapping Leona's plate down and not even looking at her.

'I think she's warming to me,' Leona said as the girl walked away.

They fell silent as they ate their lunch but Leona felt on edge and had little appetite for hers. She pushed her food away, half finished. Hugo consumed all of his own without appearing to notice what he put in his mouth and returned his attention to Leona.

'The one and only woman I've had a serious relationship with called upon me unexpectedly last night,' he said, looking away from her again.

'Go on,' Leona said persuasively. 'I'm all ears.' *And ridiculously jealous*, she conceded, which was plain stupid. *Get a grip, girl!*

'She dumped me for someone with better prospects. I thought I was heartbroken at the time, but it didn't take me long to realise that no permanent damage had been incurred and that she'd actually done me a favour. The experience taught me a valuable lesson and I decided that I was better off putting my private life on hold in favour of furthering my ambitions. Women are too time consuming. All I wanted to do was to get on with my research.'

'Understandable. You'd had your fingers burned.' She paused. 'But why are you telling me this, Hugo? We barely know one another. It's a little soon for soul-baring, isn't it?'

'I'm telling you because the woman who failed to break my heart is James Farmer's significant other.'

Leona let out a slow breath. 'Ah, I see.'

'I had no idea she knew where I live but she turned up late last night, spitting tacks and wanting me to resolve her relationship problems for her.' He shook his head. 'I've no idea how I was supposed to do so. It's hard for me to believe that she'd imagine I'd give her the time of day, or do anything to help her, even if I could.'

'Have you seen her since your split?'

'At a few functions but I've always managed to avoid her.'

'Well, she obviously kept tabs on you, if she knows where you live.'

He gave a careless shrug. 'The reason why I'm telling you all this is because she's convinced Steve had no advance warning that the directorship wasn't going to him. He will be not only fuming but also feeling publicly humiliated. Mind you, the majority of the people there probably enjoyed seeing him cut down to size, much as they might have pretended otherwise. He's trodden on a few toes on the way up the greasy pole and isn't that popular. People stick with him though because of his connection to Nawaz. Now that Nawaz has so publicly side-lined him, Steve will be in damage control mode and, as we both know, when his back is against the wall, he doesn't fight fair.'

'He will be devastated.' Leona was unable to suppress a smile.

'Quite. He's kept his side of the bargain with Stella but she's now reneged on that deal. Cleo said she wasn't at pains to hide her affection for Farmer from Nawaz last night and that Nawaz didn't react to her provocation.'

'He did react insofar as he rewarded Farmer with that directorship.' Leona tapped her fingers on the edge of the table. 'Why? We both know just how jealously Nawaz guards his family image. He would never ordinarily countenance a public display of adultery. What can have changed?'

'That's what I would very much like to know.' Hugo paused. 'I did wonder if you were right to suggest that Steve's overspent. Nawaz would not approve of financial imprudence.'

Leona nodded. 'Possibly, but it seems extreme.'

'I agree.'

'How do you suppose Steve will react?' Leona asked, leaning her elbow on the table and the side of her face on her fisted hand. 'He won't take it lying down.'

'That we can also agree upon.'

'What did Cleo expect you to do about it, just as a matter of interest?'

Hugo shrugged. 'Hell if I know. I think she just needed a shoulder to cry on.' Hugo's expression hardened. 'Unfortunately for her, I was in no mood to oblige. She isn't married to Farmer and I don't know where she'll stand financially if they split, which will be her main concern. I advised her to keep shtum and let the affair run its course.'

'If it does,' Leona said pensively. 'You're right insofar as both Steve and Stella have been discreet. If she's prepared to risk Daddy's wrath by showing her true colours in public and, as I just said, if Nawaz is prepared to support her association with the man then there must be a compelling reason that we haven't thought of.'

'Perhaps her own company is doing well enough now that she doesn't need Nawaz's support.' Hugo spread his hands. 'I mean, she's an adult, well past the parental control stage and has always fought her father's old-fashioned stance.'

'Doesn't sound good for your friend Cleo's prospects then, to say nothing of Steve's.'

'Which is what I wanted to talk to you about. I can't help thinking that he'll stop harassing you now. He has bigger problems than a bruised ego so you'll have nothing more to fear from him. You can get on with your life.'

'Perhaps he'll back off for a while but there are no guarantees. Besides, the damage is done insofar as he's implied to a couple of potential employers that I'm not trustworthy. Word will spread and I'm not prepared to live with the stigma. I know him well enough to realise that he'll get back to me eventually and I'll never know a moment's peace, always wondering how and when he'll strike again.' She leaned forward, her expression intense. 'We should seize the opportunity to gain the upper hand.' She frowned across at him. 'But how?'

'What brought the fiasco with the directorship to your attention?' Hugo answered her question with one of his own.

'I had an unexpected visitor yesterday too, but mine was considerably more welcome than yours, by the sounds of things.'

She went on to explain about her long friendship with Patsy and the line of work she was in that brought her into direct contact with a lot of high rollers. 'She brought the directorship thing to my attention. Patsy never approved of my relationship with Steve and tried to warn me that it would end in tears but, of course, I knew better.' Leona rolled her eyes at her own naivety. 'She was the only person I confided in about it, by the way. Steve was paranoid about people finding out. Said he wanted me to be his secret pleasure, or some such crap, and he was so convincing that I almost fell for it.' Leona flapped a hand in disgust. 'Anyway, Patsy has promised to do some delving into Nawaz's personal affairs. She seems to think that he's distracted about something and that not all is well in paradise.'

'Well, that would make sense if Stella's found the moxie to flaunt her lover in front of him.' Hugo paused, presumably to think the matter through. 'Perhaps Stella and Nawaz have had a private falling out and this was her way of fighting back. She knows just how important her father's image is to him, so it would be the best place to attack him, leaving Nawaz with no choice but to show solidarity with her behaviour, at least in public. She's always been a feisty individual and Nawaz has only ever been able to control her by controlling the purse strings.'

Leona nodded. 'That jibes with what Steve used to say about her. I only met her a couple of times when she called in to see Steve. We were introduced but she made it very clear that I was beneath her notice, as my old Mum would have said. The hired help didn't register on her radar.' Leona snorted. 'I hate stuck-up people who think that just because they have a bit of dosh, it makes them better than anyone else. I think perhaps that her attitude, so different to the image of himself that Steve made sure I saw, was one of the reasons why I fell for Steve. I felt sorry for him, if you can believe it.'

'I can,' he replied softly. 'I've seen the way he operates.'

'Thanks for trying to make me feel better about myself.'

'My pleasure.' He flashed that sexy smile again. 'Can your friend really dig that deep? Nawaz is a very private individual. You will only find what he wants the world to know about him.'

'Nothing would surprise me. In her line of work, Patsy picks up all sorts of useful information. Discretion is her byword; it has to be. Even so, I wouldn't bet against her coming up with the goods.'

Leona allowed a significant pause as she tried to decide how best to exploit the advantage that had fallen into their laps.

'You know,' she eventually said, 'perhaps I should contact Steve.'

'What the hell...' Hugo's loud voice caused the bar to fall quiet and its inhabitants to glance in their direction. 'Why?' he added in a more moderate tone. 'Surely he's the last person you would want to come within a mile of?'

'Damage limitation,' Leona replied briskly. 'Steve's reputation will be his first priority; we both agree on that. He will consider that before he murders his wife for breaking their agreement,' she added flippantly, 'or, at the very least, not giving him the heads-up with regard to the directorship.'

'Even Steve wouldn't revert to murder.'

'I wouldn't put anything past him.' Leona screwed up her features. 'Look at the aggressive manner in which he's tried to get revenge on me, just because I wouldn't sleep with him. How much more seriously will be look upon public humiliation and his wife's betrayal?'

Hugo nodded. 'Cleo said he hid it well but she was watching him as the announcement was made and could see that he'd been blindsided.'

'I excelled at having his back and portraying a positive public image of the man, if I do say so myself,' Leona replied. 'He will need me more than ever right now. If I pretend to regret our breakup, it will help to salve his wounded pride and I'm absolutely sure he'll welcome me back with open arms. Only my arms will remain firmly by my side, of course.'

'The situation has changed with this directorship business. He will be fighting mad and it will be his sole priority. Even so, it's not safe for you to offer yourself up and I won't be able to protect you if you're on the inside.'

She gaped at him. 'Protect me?'

'We're a team, or I thought we were.'

'Think about it, Hugo. My suggestion is inspired. It will give me a natural opportunity to speak with Steve's PA too.'

'It's a bad idea, Leona.'

'I'm trying to save your professional relationship with Steve,' she replied, 'precious thanks I appear to be getting for it.'

Hugo turned sideways on his chair and crossed one foot across his opposite thigh as he studied Leona's face with an intensity that made her look away first. It was a casual pose but Leona sensed that he was anything other than relaxed. Why her very sensible suggestion to get up close and personal with Steve – the *only* way, in her opinion, to discover what he was plotting to revenge himself against his wife and father-in-law – should bother him so much, she had yet to fathom. Her plan *did* seem rather nebulous, but still, her senses told her this was the best opportunity that she'd have to beat Steve once and for all and she had no intention of letting it slip out of her grasp.

Use whatever means necessary to destroy Steve before he could destroy her, in other words.

Part of her accepted that Hugo was right to suggest letting things be, but Leona wasn't in the mood to listen to common sense. She was tired of being afraid and it was beyond time that she took the initiative. This opportunity had fallen into her lap; it seemed like providence and she was damned if she'd let it slide.

She wanted her life back.

'He will smell a rat,' Hugo said, his voice casual but his expression set in stone. 'You tried to take out a restraining order against him, for God's sake. Why would you go running back?'

'To help him in his hour of need. He's too self-obsessed to assume it's a ruse and will imagine that I'd never recovered from my infatuation.' She blew air through her lips. 'Take it from one who knows. The man is a narcissist, thinks he's irresistible.'

'Even so...'

Hugo broke off when his friendly barmaid came to clear their plates and asked them if they required anything else. Sent on her way, Leona continued to rationalise her thinking.

'Besides, in case it's escaped your notice, it will save you from coming up with a scheme that would almost certainly put you at odds with the man who provides the bread-and-butter funding for your research.' She threw up her hands when he looked unmoved. 'For the love of God, Hugo, use the sense you were born with!' she cried, exasperated by his moody frown. His intransigence. 'You don't have any solid reason for risking your lucrative business with Steve. You and I are strangers. Why should you care about what he did to me? Besides, I was the one who accused you of giving him a false alibi and yet you want to help me.' She shook her head. 'It makes no sense and I won't let you self-destruct out of some warped sense of responsibility.'

'I have my reasons and they are far from being warped.' His stubborn stance showed no signs of abating. 'Steve didn't leave that restaurant but I have no difficulty in believing that he had someone else drive his car to your place and frighten the life out of you. That sort of behaviour goes against the grain. Besides, I don't like being used, Leona.' His expression hardened. 'Steve has been using me all our adult life in one way or another and I've been too preoccupied to do anything about it.'

'You look very fierce. What did he do to you?'

Hugo shrugged. 'Youthful indiscretions, competitiveness. He won our various challenges by cheating, which ought to have told me all I needed to know about his moral compass. And... well, other things.'

Leona could see that the other things were eating away at him. She also knew that he wouldn't elucidate.

'Well,' he added, 'all that's about to change and if it costs me my funding then I'll find another outlet for my components. It's a competitive business but demand is growing and I will find a way to exploit that demand. In fact, I already have people looking for alternative markets.'

'That's as may be but my idea is the better one and you're just too stubborn to admit it,' she replied, moved by his obvious desire to help her as well as exacting revenge upon his user friend, but she was damned if she would show it. 'There's nothing you can do to prevent me.'

'Perhaps not.' His voice lowered and his expression softened. 'Even so, promise me that you'll leave it a day or two before jumping into the lion's den. Can you do that?'

Leona nodded reluctantly. 'Okay, a couple of days.'

'Thank you. Let the dust settle, see if Steve does anything

publicly. See if your friend can dish the dirt of Nawaz and Stella. I get the impression that something's going on there and that it would be wise to go in, if you still insist upon it, once we know more, armed with as much information as possible.'

'Fair enough. I guess a few days won't hurt.'

'Thank you.' His meltingly gentle smile did serious damage to Leona's equilibrium. If he kept looking at her that way, it wouldn't be hard for him to talk her out of her resolve. With that thought in mind, she gathered up her bag and looked for her keys.

'Thanks for lunch, and for the chat,' she said, as he stood to join her and they left the pub together. 'I'll let you get back to your research.'

'Keep in touch and let me know as soon as you find out anything.' He paused beside her car and took her arm in a light grasp. 'And don't forget your promise. You're not going to do anything rash.' He rolled his eyes. 'At least not yet.'

'Rash? Me?'

Hugo laughed as he gave her a chaste kiss on the cheek. 'Just don't forget what we agreed,' he said, wagging a finger beneath her nose. 'Or there will be consequences.'

She wanted to ask who'd appointed him as her minder but recalled all the sacrifices he was prepared to make for her and so bit back the words. 'I'll remember,' she said instead as she unlocked her car and climbed behind the wheel.

On the day following his humiliation, Steve's blood pressure was still off the scale. The desire to commit a few violent murders hadn't abated either but that desire was tempered by his concerns regarding Bizham's unexpected actions. Damn it, he knew how flaky his daughter was! How determined she was to press the boundaries at every opportunity. The two men had an agreement. Steve would keep her in line and in return, Bizham would look after Steve.

Not fucking publicly mortify him.

The pictures of his wife and Farmer that his investigator had come up with, showing them arriving at a top end hotel within minutes of each other the previous night, displaying a worrying lack of discretion, only added to Steve's feelings of deep misgiving. Why was she going out of her way to burn her bridges with both her father and her husband by being caught in an affair?

What the hell was Stella's game? Steve wondered.

'What the fuck?' Steve kicked at a footstool, sending it spiralling across the room.

A slow smile spread across his face, partially restoring his self-respect, when he glanced at the pictures again and thought just how much damage he could do with them, were he the vindictive type.

Which, of course, he was.

One possibility was that she'd fallen for Farmer and intended to set up home with him. Farmer was rich enough to keep her business solvent but would she really cause a permanent rift with her father just because she fancied the guy? There was a possibility of her being in love that Steve dismissed with a careless wave of one hand. In order to love, one must first possess a heart: an organ that was missing from his cold wife's anatomy. Besides, she had strong family roots too, much as she fought against them, and wouldn't walk away from Bizham, no matter how great the temptation.

Would she?

She had yet to return home, a clear sign that she intended to provoke a reaction from Steve.

'Bring it on,' he muttered, thinking she ought to know by now just how ruthless he could be when backed against a wall. Or into a financial corner that hadn't concerned him because the directorship would have bailed him out of trouble.

He closed down the images on his laptop, feeling moody and unsettled. He hated it when the people in his life developed independent ideas. Images of a defiant Leona flashed through his mind, reinforcing the feeling that right now he'd have trouble controlling a go-cart.

He glanced at the online business section of the papers, unsurprised to see his humiliation reported in all its spiteful glory. His face flushed with renewed anger. His so-called business associates had lost no time in dishing the dirt, but then what else could he have expected? There was no such thing as loyalty in the business world. He'd trampled on a few egos, cut a few corners on his way up, he conceded, and it seemed his rivals were the types to bear grudges. He thought he had covered his disappointment well, pretending that he'd known what was coming.

Clearly not well enough.

The sound of a key turning in the lock alerted him to Stella's return. He glanced at the clock. It was almost ten.

'Oh,' she said, walking into their drawing room and feigning surprise at the sight of him. 'I thought you would be long gone by now.'

There was a malicious light in her eye that troubled Steve. They were fond of one another, in their way, and their open marriage arrangement had always worked well. They sometimes discussed their respective conquests as a substitute for foreplay on the rare occasions when they shared the same bed. He had even confided in her about Leona, making her out to be a deranged groupie who didn't take rejection well, just in case she took it into her spiteful head to contact Stella with exaggerated stories about their non-affair. He'd neglected to mention that she had dumped him. She had only done so, he reasoned, in order to force him into leaving Stella for her.

Yeah, like that was gonna happen!

God forbid that Leona *had* actually contacted Stella and put her straight. His blood ran cold as that very real possibility belatedly occurred to him. Could that account for Stella's public form of revenge?

Despite living separate lives, he knew that Stella was possessive and wouldn't countenance serious rivalry, or any action by a third party that would bring Steve's activities to her father's ears. Her vindictive expression now frightened Steve. The fact that she was willing to flaunt Farmer in front of Bizham and now take Steve on as well was decidedly ominous. Even so, surely she wouldn't throw everything away just because she'd believed Leona and decided that Steve had deep feelings for the little tramp?

Even though he did.

Steve knew better than to let his uncertainty about Stella show. He had forgotten more rules pertaining to their marital game of cat and mouse than he'd ever bothered to acquaint her with. She might have made a success of her business empire, but she would never be a match for Steve's cunning.

'Just about to leave.' He shut down his laptop, got up and kissed her cheek. 'Good night?' he asked.

She blinked at him, clearly blindsided by his casual approach.

'Splendid, thanks.' She sighed and stretched her arms above her head. 'Very satisfactory.'

'Then I'm glad for you.'

'I'm sorry the directorship didn't go your way,' she said with a marked lack of sincerity after a pregnant pause that Steve saw no reason to break. If she wanted to provoke a reaction from him then she would have to try a lot harder than that. 'I know how much you were depending upon it. Not sure why Daddy didn't give it to you. He never said anything to me or I would have warned you, obviously. I dare say he had strong business reasons though and that he will explain when you next meet. But still,' she added, 'your business is flourishing so perhaps he did you a favour. You don't need the distraction.'

'Don't give it another thought.' Steve somehow managed to suppress his blinding rage at her provocativeness. 'Anyway, best be getting along. I have a meeting at eleven. Perhaps see you this evening?'

'Hmm, possibly. I don't have plans right now.'

Steve left the house, patting his pockets for his car keys, calmer because he'd come out on top of that particular skirmish, after a fashion. The throaty roar of the Lamborghini's engine further soothed his turbulent emotions. The envious glances directed towards his car as he negotiated his way through light traffic were a further reminder of how far he had come, how much he had achieved, since his less than stellar university days, where no one had taken him seriously.

He had been consistently underestimated because he gave the impression of preferring to play rather than work, which was just the way he liked it. He had gotten into Oxford through his own endeavours. People tended to forget that and to overlook the fact that only the sharpest of minds were admitted to one of England's premier seats of learning.

'I'm down but most definitely not out,' he said aloud, giving the steering wheel an affectionate pat.

His thoughts drifted towards Cleo Addison, Farmer's significant other. Steve had always had an eye for her but knew better than to poach on Farmer's territory. Besides, Hugo had been there before him and his one golden rule was never to play catchup behind his charismatic friend, if that's what they were still pretending to be. It riled him that the women in their youth had made a beeline for Hugo in the first instance rather than for him. Even so, he mused, Cleo might be useful to him now. There was nothing easier than to get a woman whose comfortable lifestyle was under threat, to fall into line.

Cleo was a selfish little madam and Steve figured there wasn't much she wouldn't be prepared to do in order to cling on to what she felt was hers by right. Farmer clearly didn't see things the same way, Steve mused, as he waited for a red light to change, or he would have married her long since. Even so, they were still living beneath the same roof. Cleo was clinging on by her fingertips. She would have noticed Stella and Farmer getting up close and personal the night before and would not have enjoyed the visual threat to her security.

Steve had been aware of Cleo's gaze fixed on him when the directorship had been announced. She hadn't been fooled by his relaxed response, as so many others hadn't been – ergo the speculation in the press that morning had to have come from one or more of the people present. The difference was that for the majority, it was simply a scandal to rub their hands over gleefully. For Cleo though, her entire future was at stake.

He used his hands-free device to call up another investigator, one who lived in a cyber world rather than the real one.

'Get me a mobile number for Cleo Addison,' he said when his call was answered, giving her address.

'On it. Anything else?'

'Plenty but start with that.'

'You're the boss. How soon do you want it?'

'Yesterday.'

'It'll cost you.'

Steve rolled his eyes. 'Doesn't it always. Oh, and here's the thing. I want to know what new irons Bizham Nawaz has in the fire.'

His contact's voice went up an octave. 'I keep you informed about his movements the entire time.'

'Not well enough,' Steve snapped. 'He's up to something and I want to know what it is. Focus on his dealings with James Farmer.' He stopped short of asking his contact to look more closely at his own wife's activities. He would do that himself. When he'd left her to stew for long enough. And after he'd spoken with Cleo. 'Capiche?'

'On it.'

Steve cut the connection, aware that his investigator's professional pride had taken a denting and that he would be all over

Bizham's affairs as a result. Consequently, Steve felt better about life when he pulled into his parking space outside his business premises. He had a plan forming in the back of his mind.

And if that didn't work, there was always Plan B. The desire to commit a few murders had not yet lost its appeal.

* * *

Hugo left his lunch with Leona, deeply disturbed by her determination to stick her head back into the lion's den. It was none of his business, of course. She was a grown woman, who understood Steve's *modus operandi* and could do as she pleased. Be that as it may, he felt responsible for her, partly he supposed because he knew Steve had been behind the invasion of her privacy a few nights previously and had used Hugo to cover his back.

Hugo did not like being used.

He returned to his office and dealt with all the little niggles that had sprung up since he'd left it for not much more than an hour. He attended to these matters with less than half the attention he would ordinarily deem necessary, returning calls, answering queries raised by his team.

Alone in his office and with a momentarily clear desk, he took the opportunity to sit back and think things through. Leona was right to say that Steve wouldn't countenance disloyalty and that he would lose his custom if he took sides against him.

'So why am I so determined to shoot myself in the foot?' he wondered aloud. He made a mental note to meet with his marketing manager, who was actively seeking alternative markets for Hugo's computer components. Hugo had been diversifying, trying not to depend so heavily on just one client's business, for a while now.

Nawaz's influx of cash into Steve's fledgling business, just after he married Stella, had always satisfied Hugo's curiosity regarding the source of Steve's massive start-up funds. But could there be another explanation? As opposed to being in financial straits, was Steve into dodgier areas and had Nawaz found out about it? That would explain the directorship. Except the Nawaz Hugo knew would have confronted his son-in-law face-to-face regarding his nefarious activities. He wasn't one to sweep unpleasantness under the rug and ruled his family with a rod of iron, despite the fact that they were adults in their own right.

Steve had a very close business associate by the name of Dave Marden. They'd known one another since childhood but Hugo had never taken to him. He was a chancer, into a little bit of everything – most of it on the dodgy side of legal. He was street wise and a tough nut, an associate of Steve's criminal father. A man whom Hugo had made a point of having as little as possible to do with.

But significantly, Marden was always there with Steve on important occasions, watching his back whilst gladhanding with the movers and shakers. He'd been around with a classy woman on his arm on the night that the police were interested in. And Hugo could well imagine Dave driving Steve's Lamborghini and frightening the crap out of a lone female. It was just the sort of cowardly behaviour that he'd get a kick out of. Hugo tried to recall if he'd left the gathering for any specific period of time but failed to come up with an answer simply because Hugo had made an art form out of blanking the man.

Even if he had been the driver, Hugo conceded that he didn't have a cat in hell's chance of proving it. Nor would it be good for his professional and personal future if he started digging. He wasn't afraid but saw no point in stirring the pot if there was little chance of discovering anything worthwhile. Even so, the thought of Marden being the guilty party had lodged itself in Hugo's brain. He'd taken one hell of a risk. The yellow Lamborghini wasn't exactly low-profile. If the police chose to do their job properly and checked the cameras on the route to Leona's cottage then the chances were that it would have been spotted. Not that they would spare the manpower for such a petty complaint, which is what Steve would have been counting on.

What the hell!

Hugo threw his hands in the air, wondering if there was another way to come at the problem. He couldn't recall the name of the woman who'd been with Marden but did know that she was friendly with Gale Bower, a lady who'd been at the gathering with her husband and with whom Hugo had business dealings. Gale had been at university with Hugo and Steve but had never crossed the friendship line with either of them. He wondered how much more she knew about Dave Marden's friendship with Steve and the reason why it had endured. Gale and Peter socialised with Steve and Stella far more frequently than Hugo did and Gale was a wonderful and surprisingly accurate source of gossip.

On a whim, he picked up the phone and called her.

'Hello stranger.' Her warm voice echoed down the line. 'To what do I owe the pleasure? Or was it Peter you're after, although I suppose if you'd wanted him, you'd have called his mobile not mine, so now I'm intrigued. Are you hoping to lure me into an indiscretion? If so, I think I should tell you that you won't have to try too hard.'

Hugo smiled. Gale was an outrageous flirt, totally dedicated to her husband, and had never been one to use two words when ten would suffice. 'I was thinking it's been too long since we got together.'

'Ah, and I suppose you'll make excuses not to bring a date with you, just like always, in which case I shall just have to fix you up and you'll have to take your chances. It's a criminal waste for a gorgeous specimen like you to remain single. You owe it to the women of this world to put yourself out there.'

Hugo laughed. 'You're good for my ego, Gale. But actually, there is someone I'd like you to meet,' he said.

'Ah, at last!' Gale sighed down the line. 'I suppose she's a gorgeous young thing and so I shall attempt not to be jealous, or to feel the passage of the years.'

Hugo knew it would be a waste of time to explain so allowed Gale to draw her own conclusions. 'I don't suppose the two of you would be available for an early drink this evening,' he remarked on a whim.

'Early? But darling, you work until the witching hour.'

'Not always.'

'Well then, by all means, but you will have to make do with me. Peter's away on business for a few days. Anyway, it doesn't matter. I'm the one that needs to give the seal of approval to your latest squeeze. I shall know at once if she's a gold-digger.'

Laughing, they agreed a place and time and Hugo cut the connection. He then called Leona, hoping that his makeshift plans wouldn't interfere with her own arrangements.

'Drinks twice in one day,' Leona replied when Hugo picked her up that evening. 'I must be doing something right.'

'I think I know who might have been responsible for your late-night visit and the person we're going to meet could help to prove it.'

'Then I'm definitely ready to meet him or her,' Leona replied without hesitation. 'Can you tell me anything more now?'

'Don't get your hopes up. It might be nothing and even if I'm right, it will be impossible to prove.' Hugo slowed for a red light. 'The lady we're going to meet was at the dinner the other night and may have noticed an absence that would account for your visitation. But we'll have to tread carefully. Her husband and Steve do business together.'

'Then I'll know his name.'

'Probably. Peter Bower.'

Leona nodded. 'Yeah, I recognise it but I don't think I ever met him.'

'Gale, his wife and the lady we're going to meet, was at university with us.'

Hugo went on to explain about Dave Marden and his constant presence in Steve's life.

'That's another familiar name,' Leona replied, screwing up her lips, 'and I have seen him once or twice lurking about the offices. Steve mentioned in passing that he was an associate of his father's but when I asked about the father in question, he clammed up on me.'

'He would do. His father was in and out of prison during Steve's younger years, then disappeared from the scene all together. Steve wouldn't speak about his disappearance. He just said that he was better off without his disruptive influence in his life.'

'He was ashamed of him?'

'Probably. His mother wasn't much better. She scarpered too the moment Steve finished his A levels. He never speaks about either of them but I do think that his humble origins and admittedly strong intellect were the driving force behind his determination to improve himself. And his need to flash the cash.'

'I would imagine so.' Leona nodded. 'It makes sense. But if that's the case, why keep this Marden person about?'

'He's useful to Steve. He'll do just about anything and, I guess, Steve is used to having him around.'

'If you think that he drove Steve's car to mine then I can well believe it. Frankly, he gave me the shivers. It was the way he looked at me whenever I saw him in the office, like he was picturing me naked. There was definitely something creepy about him.'

Hugo pulled in the car park adjoining the pub where he'd agreed to meet Gale. She was already there, sitting at the bar and sipping at a glass of wine. She gave a whoop of delight when she saw Hugo and launched herself into his arms. Laughing, Hugo kissed her on each cheek and disentangled her arms from around his neck.

'This is Leona,' he said, indicating her. 'Leona, my old friend, Gale.'

'It's a pleasure,' Leona said.

The ladies shook hands, covertly sizing one another up. Gale, ever the extrovert, gave a nod of approval as Hugo bought drinks for them all and they retreated to a corner table. They made small talk for a short time, or more to the point, Gale quizzed Leona about her background. She was careful what she said, making no mention of Steve.

'Now then.' Gale leaned towards Hugo, her eyes sparkling. 'What's this really all about? Much as I enjoy your company, and yours, Leona, there has to be more to it than a sudden desire to acquaint the two of us.' She waved a hand towards Leona. 'So come on, Hugo, out with it. What is it that you think I can help you with?'

'Dave Marden.' Leona leaned towards Gale as she spoke, causing Hugo to roll his eyes. So much for letting him take the lead!

Gale blinked. 'What about him?' she asked.

'Do you know him well? Do you like him?'

Gale shared a look between Hugo and Leona. 'What's this all about?' she asked on a note of suspicion.

'Look, Gale, I'm sorry, but I'm playing a hunch. You're friends with Dave's lady so I thought you might be able to shed some light.'

'I speak with Maggie when our paths cross. I feel a bit sorry for her, truth to tell. She's not the brightest of sparks but is totally dedicated to Dave. He plays away on a regular basis and doesn't try to hide the fact from her. Fancies himself as quite the ladies' man. He can do no wrong in her eyes but she's the only person who can't see that he has feet of clay. He and Steve go way back, of course.' Gale took a sip of her drink and then leaned towards Leona. 'So come on then, what's your interest?'

Leona glanced at Hugo, who gave an imperceptible nod. They might as well tell Gale what they really wanted to know – there had never really been an alternative open to them – but Hugo knew he'd be risking burning his bridges with Steve if word of their conversation got back to him. Gale didn't understand the meaning of discretion and would, at the very least, repeat to her husband what she was about to hear.

There was never any question of not going ahead, despite the risks, Hugo discovered, and he was surprised to find the experience cathartic rather than crippling.

Leona explained about her previous employment and her dispute with Steve. Gale touched Leona's hand when she ran out of words but didn't seem that surprised by what she'd just heard.

'You dumped him.' She chuckled. 'It's beyond time that someone did. It must have dented Steve's ego. We all know that Steve isn't the type to take a humiliation lying down.'

'He certainly didn't take my rejection well,' Leona replied with a wry smile. 'He's been vindictive and sly.'

Gale nodded. 'I'm sure he has. You know, Steve is my friend but I don't always like him very much and certainly don't approve of his methods.' She glanced at Hugo. 'I'm guessing you feel the same way, otherwise you wouldn't be here.'

'Steve crossed a line when he went to war with Leona,' Hugo replied, grinding his jaw. 'He's wrecked her chances of procuring the level of employment she deserves by implying that she's dishonest, and has conducted a harassment campaign against her ever since she walked out on him, scaring her witless. The police can't do anything because she has no actual proof that Steve's the responsible party. He's been clever that way.'

'Shit!' Gale muttered softly.

'I made matters worse by trying to take out a restraining order when he wouldn't stop harassing me,' Leona admitted. 'And it's now open war between us.' Leona paused to sip at her drink, smiling at a small dog that had broken free from someone and was charging round the bar like a lunatic. 'And from my perspective, it's time to fight back. I don't intend to live in the shadows, wondering when Steve will strike again.'

'Good for you!' Gale nodded emphatically.

Hugo explained about the latest incident of intimidation that had occurred during the dinner they had attended together. 'He's used me as his alibi. I had to tell the police that Steve hadn't left the restaurant because he didn't but I don't like being exploited.'

'You think Dave Marden did the dirty?' Gale asked.

'The possibility occurred to me,' Hugo replied.

'Did you know that Dave has a criminal record?'

'Nope, but it doesn't surprise me,' Hugo replied. 'What for?'

'Assault, GBH. Beat a guy half to death for looking at his then woman funny. It was about five years back. Steve paid his legal fees. Got him a top end brief which enabled Dave to get off with a suspended sentence.'

'It sounds as though he's hired muscle,' Leona said, tapping her fingers against the surface of the table upon which their half-consumed drinks rested.

'Well I can tell you with absolute certainty that Dave left that restaurant for over an hour on the night in question.'

Leona and Hugo shared an astonished look. Could it really be that easy?

'You sound very sure,' Hugo said.

'Oh, I am. I'd been in the ladies comforting Maggie. Dave had done one of his disappearing acts and she was getting worked up, wondering what was keeping him so long. I calmed her down and left her in the cloakroom repairing her makeup. I walked out just as Dave came in through the back door of the restaurant. He didn't see me but Steve was lurking in the shadows, clearly alerted to his return. Dave tossed some keys at Steve, winked and said, "Job done". I heard him quite distinctly.'

11

Steve had never seen Cleo look anything other than catwalk stunning so her haggard appearance when he met her in a local wine bar later that day took him by surprise. He hid his reaction, kissed her cheek and told her she looked good. Cleo waved the compliment aside, which worried Steve. She must really believe that she'd lost Farmer if she was *that* preoccupied. What did she know?

'Let me get you a drink.'

Steve ordered champagne without asking what she wanted, and a beer for himself. Once they'd ensconced themselves in a quiet corner table in the modern, trendy bar and their drinks had been placed in front of them, Steve saw no reason to prevaricate and cut to the chase.

'James and my wife...'

Cleo stuck out her lower lip. 'I don't know what to do about it, Steve. I've never seen him so infatuated before. I'm worried... worried that I'll lose him. I keep telling myself that Stella would never embarrass her father by leaving you but...'

Thanks very much, Steve thought but didn't say. It obviously hadn't occurred to Cleo that Stella would stay with him because deep down, beneath her craving for constant excitement, she actually cared about him.

'Well.' Cleo sat forward, leaning her forearms on the table, her eyes glistening. 'That directorship. You hadn't been warned that it was going to James, had you?'

Steve knew that he would only get her full cooperation if he laid his cards on the table. What did he have to lose? They were both down but not out, at least not yet, and if they combined forces, they would be formidable. Cleo, he sensed, would do whatever it took to hold on to what she considered to be hers by right and if that required her to snoop or play dirty then so be it.

'No. It was a shock, I won't deny it.'

Cleo reached out a hand and patted his arm. 'That wasn't fair.' She paused. 'You think Stella arranged it?'

Steve shrugged. 'I don't see how else it could have happened.'

'So she *is* serious about James.' Cleo's posture slumped. 'I knew it!'

'But I also think Bizham needs James.'

'Why?' Cleo looked becomingly blank, the ultimate dumb blonde, but Steve knew it was all an act. A sharp mind was hard at work inside that pretty head; a mama bear protecting her hunter-gatherer from all contenders. 'They are already in business together.'

'Ah, but what business? It has to be more than simply silk.' Steve asserted, playing a hunch. 'What is it that they're up to that enables James to manipulate such a strong man and for Bizham to turn a blind eye to his association with his daughter?'

'I don't know precisely.' Cleo screwed up her brow. 'But they've been a lot closer recently. I don't know what business meetings James has during the working day but he and I have been social-ising with Bizham a lot over the past few months *and* they've taken two trips to India together recently. I didn't think anything of it. I mean, they do have interests in common in that country, but after last night, I'm starting to wonder if it could be something more sinister.'

They did have interests, Steve knew, but those interests were well established and didn't require the personal intervention of either man; they had managers for a reason. And if there were problems, it didn't need them both to intervene. Steve's pulse quickened. His instincts were right. Bizham and Farmer were up to something. Something big. Steve had always known that there was a dark side to Bizham's character. The upstanding family man with political ambitions did not always play by the rules.

What are you up to?

'Did you get a gist of what the trip was for?'

Cleo shook her head. 'One or more of his sons and nephews were always in attendance, that much I do know.'

Bizham's inner circle. 'Any other outsiders, apart from James?'

'No.' She paused. 'They talked about shipping routes for a long time, I seem to recall.'

Steve's head jerked up. 'I thought James flew his silk back to the UK.'

Cleo blinked. 'He does, but I heard a lot of snippets about weight, now I come to think of it.'

Steve leaned back in his chair, rubbing his lips with the side of his index finger as he mulled that information over. Were they smuggling? he wondered. Avoiding the dreaded taxman. It was a common enough pastime but risky for someone in Bizham's position. Then again, Steve had been aware of belt-tightening recently in Bizham's empire. Perhaps his generous donations to his political affiliates, as well as his extravagant lifestyle, to say nothing of his lavish entertaining, had taken its toll on the bottom line. Bizham had always given the impression of being financially secure but appearances, Steve knew, could be deceptive. And the man had the temerity to lecture him on the necessity for financial prudence!

Steve felt better about life for the first time since the axe had fallen at that damned dinner. So, Bizham could be in financial straits too. Presumably Stella was aware, accounting for her own behaviour. What to do about it, though?

'Hugo wasn't very sympathetic so I—'

'Hugo?' Cleo's voice had taken on a whine but the mention of his nemesis's name recalled Steve's wandering attention. 'You discussed this with Hugo?'

'I didn't know who else to turn to. Hugo has always been there for me. I went to see him after the dinner, once James had told me he had to go back to work.' Cleo snorted. 'Working on your wife, more like.'

'What did Hugo suggest?' Steve asked, grinding his jaw.

He couldn't have said why Cleo turning first to Hugo should annoy him so much. He had made more of a success of himself financially: lived in a mini mansion, drove a top end car, flew first class. It was the only marker by which people were judged in this modern world. His temporary financial problems were just that: temporary. Losing the directorship had made matters worse, there was no denying it, but he would bounce back. He always did.

Hugo preferred to perfect his damned computer chip and live like a monk. And yet Steve always felt as though his old friend looked down on him. The episode with the woman at uni – Steve couldn't even recall her name – hadn't been his finest hour. He'd be the first to admit that but how was he supposed to have known that she was mentally unstable? Besides, they'd been kids at the time. These things happened. Hugo had never voiced his disapproval or castigated blame but he'd let it show in lots of small ways and their friendship had certainly cooled in the past few years.

News of Steve's disappointment over the directorship would

have reached Hugo's ears and Steve would have found a way to shrug it off in front of Hugo. For reasons he failed to understand though, Cleo running to him and spilling the beans made him feel distinctly uncomfortable.

'Hugo said I should turn a blind eye. That Stella would never leave you and that James would come back to me.' Cleo sniffed. 'It's humiliating. How do you cope with it?'

'Darling, in order for it to get to you, you first have to give a damn.'

Cleo shuddered. 'That's cold.'

'That's reality. Life's a game and you just have to make sure you understand the rules if you want to rise above the humdrum.'

'Very well then.' Cleo folded her arms on the table and leaned towards Steve, her expression combative. 'Since you understand this game of life so well, and since you have almost as much to lose as I do, you tell me what we're going to do to save our respective situations.'

Steve had already made a decision in that regard. The slight was too serious to be ignored and required almost immediate retribution. To bring it about would require careful planning, to say nothing of a strong nerve, but Steve was more than capable of stepping up to the plate. 'That rather depends upon how far you're prepared to go to protect your corner.'

'As far as it takes,' she shot back, a determined glint in her eye. 'Tell me what you have in mind and how I can help you achieve it.'

* * *

'At least we now know that I haven't lost the plot,' Leona remarked as Hugo drove her home from the meeting with Gale. 'But it doesn't really take us any further forward, does it? I mean, it's not as if we can prove what Gale just told us.' She threw up her hands. 'It is *so* frustrating. If crossed, Steve could invent any number of plausible reasons for Marden having taken his car. He is, after all, Steve's gofer.'

Hugo nodded. 'But it does prove that Steve thinks he's invincible, and that makes him vulnerable.'

'He believes his own hype.'

'Yep. But his priorities will have changed. We've already agreed that he'll be hurting both personally and financially after the humiliation of the directorship and looking for revenge.'

Leona opened her mouth to reply but before she could do so, her phone rang. 'It's Patsy,' she said, taking the call. 'Hey, what gives?'

'I have news on Bizham.'

'Blimey, that was quick.'

'Well, what can I say. I know people who know people. It's all third-hand rumour, of course, but your friend Hugo might know if there's any truth in it.'

'I'm with him now, as it happens.' She glanced at Hugo's profile as he concentrated on his driving, clearly listening to her side of the conversation. 'Where are you?'

'I can be at yours in ten.'

'Okay, see you soon.' Leona cut the connection, then turned to Hugo. 'She has news for us.'

Hugo flexed a brow. 'Already? I'm impressed.'

'She's coming to my place now. Let's see what she has to say for herself.'

Leona and Hugo hadn't been in the cottage for five minutes, which wasn't nearly enough time to satisfy Mulligan's demands for attention, before a breathless Patsy arrived. Leona gave her friend a hug and introduced Hugo, watching with amusement the widening of Patsy's eyes as she took in his rugged good looks and muscular physique.

They settled with drinks in hand, Mulligan stretched between them, and Patsy took centre stage.

'A few of the people I've arranged corporate hospitality for have had dealings with Bizham Nawaz,' she said. 'I found a reason to contact a couple of them who have expressed an interest in future events and used the surprise announcement of the directorship as an excuse to ask their opinions about it going to Farmer.'

'You got past their PAs?' Hugo asked, making no effort to hide the fact that he was impressed. 'I thought these highflyers hide behind layers of underlings.'

Patsy winked at him. 'They must have given me their mobile numbers.'

Leona laughed and shook her head. 'Of course they did!'

'Well anyway, the word is that Bizham's been quietly selling off a lot of his assets. Property, share portfolios, that sort of thing. Even his luxury yacht, which was his status symbol. It's been done behind shell corporations but word still leaks out.'

'He's hurting financially,' Hugo muttered.

'Seems that way,' Patsy replied cheerfully. 'Couldn't happen to a nicer guy. Personally, he gives me the creeps. I've met him a few times. He's a sanctimonious prig, gives the impression of being holier than thou but I've seen the way he looks at some of the girls who work in corporate hospitality. And as for his sons... well, don't get me started.'

Hugo nodded. 'That's always been my take on him. Bear in mind he supports a huge family network. Stella is the only one who's never properly toed the line. Her brothers have simply taken up positions in Daddy's empire, doing as they're told and raking in the rewards. Stella has not only carved her own path but also made a success of it.'

'I wonder what he thinks about Steve and Stella having no kids,' Leona mused.

'I can tell you that he raised the subject with Steve two years into their marriage,' Hugo replied. 'Steve anticipated it and so had a test to prove he wasn't firing blanks. He thought it was amusing.'

Leona chuckled. 'I can just imagine him doing that.'

'It implied that Stella was to blame and as far as I'm aware, the subject was never raised again.'

'He's got enough grandchildren: eight, I think at the last count,' Leona said. 'That makes for a lot of private school fees. Plus the expense of all the nephews and nieces he supports within his family and business worlds.'

'I do wonder why he finds himself in financial straits though,' Hugo said. 'He's a shrewd operator, a tough negotiator, and he diversifies so if one enterprise fails, it doesn't bring the whole house of cards down. Was there any flesh to that particular rumour of financial instability, Patsy?'

Patsy shook her head. 'Nothing substantial but I wouldn't bet against it being on the button.'

'Bad investments, perhaps?' Leona suggested. 'The stock market is volatile and Bizham is a gambler who likes to take risks.' She restlessly tapped her fingers of one hand against the arm of her chair. 'Him and Steve both hurting financially. What are the chances?'

'Joint bad investments, perhaps?' Patsy suggested.

Hugo waggled a hand from side to side. 'Possibly, but I'm thinking they've both overreached themselves. They've responded by spending lavishly to keep up appearances, thereby digging themselves into deeper holes.'

Leona nodded. 'Exactly. Image is everything to both men.'

'The question is, what has Farmer done to help Nawaz that resulted in his being awarded such a lucrative reward, a reward that had Steve's name on it?' Hugo leaned back in his chair and stretched his legs out in front of him, nudging a dozing Mulligan with the toe of his shoe. 'It must be something substantial. That directorship was a big prize, worth a lot both in terms of financial reward but, more importantly, kudos.'

'That I couldn't say,' Patsy replied with a sad little shake of her head.

'And why are Stella and Farmer in cahoots so openly?' Leona added.

'If Nawaz is losing his grip then it would explain why Stella's making a break for freedom, if that's what she's actually doing. And she's being clever about it,' Hugo mused. 'If Farmer is somehow bailing Nawaz out then he can't object to his daughter taking up with him, however much it goes against his family image, to say nothing of marring his political ambitions.'

Patsy waved that suggestion aside. 'The world has moved on since politicians' families were obliged to be squeaky clean. He'd be better advised to look to his financial activities. Those can and will be raked over by opponents and any discrepancies used against him. But I think I know someone who knows Farmer,' Patsy remarked.

Leona grinned. 'Of course you do.'

'Do you want me to sound him out? See what the man's been up to in his spare time, other than helping himself to Steve's wife, that is?'

'Or Hugo could go straight to Farmer's partner,' Leona said with a sweet smile.

Hugo laughed. 'Best not. Her first priority is to save her relationship and if she thought we were looking into Farmer's activities in order to discredit him then she'd more than likely give him the heads up.'

'Then we're no further forward.' Leona felt defeated. 'We know Steve sent his mate Marden to scare me but can't prove it and, don't forget, my only interest is in getting Steve to back off so I can get on with my life. I really don't care much about Nawaz's financial shenanigans.'

'But if we bring down Bizham, the chances are that Steve will fall with him,' Patsy said.

'Not necessarily,' Hugo replied.

'Well then, there's only one thing for it,' Leona replied, lifting her chin. 'I shall just have to go and offer my services to Steve in his hour of need.'

'No!' Patsy cried.

Hugo looked at her and shook his head. 'A seriously bad idea.'

'I said it was my intention but promised to wait until we knew what Patsy dug up. Well, we now know and forewarned is forearmed.' She shared a defiant look between them. 'I appreciate your concern for my welfare, both of you, but my mind is made up. I'm going to do it.'

12

Steve left his car directly in front of Bizham's front door as opposed to the large parking area to its left – a petty act of defiance that amused him. The actual front door was more an elaborate entrance portico, designed to impress. Steve thought it wouldn't have looked out of place in a high-end, nineteenth-century bordello. In the early days of their marriage, Stella and Steve had laughed about Bizham's pretentious attempts to turn on the style. Steve could have told his father-in-law that style and good taste came naturally but where would the fun have been in that?

He climbed out of his car and straightened his jacket. He hadn't heard from Bizham since the directorship fiasco and had deliberately delayed calling on him, simply because that would be what was expected of him and Steve hated being predictable. For all his wealth and influence, Bizham wasn't a lateral thinker and was wrong-footed whenever things didn't go according to his expectations.

And so Steve had waited to be summoned, thereby scoring the first points in this battle of wills.

'Keep 'em guessing,' he muttered, glancing up to the first-floor window that housed Bizham's ostentatious study, aware of the faces of two of Stella's brothers peering down at him. He'd always gotten along well enough with the three boys and had clocked their sympathetic expressions when the announcement had been made. Bizham liked to play them off against one another and they never knew which of them would earn parental disfavour for some nebulous reason. Steve had never expected to find himself in that position but unlike the boys, he wouldn't take it lying down.

The boys – grown men with families of their own – were Bizham's puppets without original thoughts or agendas of their own. Steve could run intellectual rings around the three of them with his hands tied behind his back but had never felt the need. He had no axe to grind with any of them but unfortunately, there was no room for sentimentality in business. Bizham would get his soon enough and the boys would take the fall right along with him. Steve fully intended to turn his humiliation into a triumphant form of revenge and had already put the first bricks of his plan in place.

He was admitted to the house by Bizham's turbaned butler and conducted to the study, where Bizham and all three of his sons formed a welcoming committee. The room was another example of gross over-exuberance: East meets West in a gaudy display of wealth. Pride of place went to Bizham's collection of katars, vicious weapons posing as Indian ceremonial daggers. Bizham was a renowned collector and added to it from all parts of the sub-continent. He had dealers on speed dial. Steve glanced casually at the illuminated display cases as he strode across the room, not so idly wondering how much damage such a weapon could wreak.

'Steve.' Bizham stood, hand outstretched. 'Good to see you. Thanks for making the time to call in. I know how busy you are.'

'Likewise,' Steve replied, shaking Bizham's hand and repeating the process with the three boys, before taking a chair and leaning back in it, his pose casual. 'To what do I owe the pleasure of this summons?' he asked, declining an offer of refreshment. 'I wasn't aware that we had a meeting scheduled.'

'I just wanted to clear the air, make sure there are no hard feelings about the directorship,' Bizham said, sharing a brief look with Chetan, his eldest son. 'It's business, nothing personal.'

'No hard feelings whatsoever.' Steve flexed a brow. 'The fact that all four of you are so concerned about my finer feelings is appreciated but totally unnecessary.'

Bizham looked taken aback, just as Steve had intended that he should.

'I know you must be disappointed but—'

'I am disappointed, there's no denying the fact, but probably not for the reasons you suppose.' He sat straighter and held Bizham's gaze. 'I'm disappointed because you pride yourself upon being a man of your word. I have never known you to renege on a promise before and certainly never so publicly, without at the very least affording me the courtesy of a warning, as any gentleman worthy of the name would have instinctively done.' Steve lifted one shoulder, amused to see Stella's brothers all looking on anxiously. No one, but no one questioned Bizham's integrity and got away with it. It felt damned good to buck that particular trend. 'Anyway, I dare say you had your reasons. What's done is done. Don't give it another thought.' Steve wished they were standing so that he could slap Bizham's shoulder in a patronising manner. 'Besides, word on the street is that you did me a favour.'

Bizham and Chetan again locked gazes, this time with an air of nervous uncertainty that did Steve's ego the power of good. *Never be predictable.* 'What on earth do you mean by that?' Chetan asked, an edge to his voice.

'The financial markets are a hot bed of gossip; you don't need me to tell you that.' Steve shrugged. 'Word gets around.'

'What have you heard?' Bizham asked curtly.

'That you are selling off assets by the shedload, which makes the directorship you failed to give to me look far less desirable now.' He privately thanked his investigator for coming up with that rumour, albeit belatedly. 'I have mentioned to you before now about overstretching yourself,' he added, choosing to ignore the fact that he himself had done precisely that. 'Of being tempted into taking risks, which is I assume what you've done. When something seems to be too good to be true, it almost certainly is.'

'A momentary glitch, nothing more.'

'Right.' Steve imbued the single word with a wealth of scepticism. 'But mud sticks in the financial world, which will affect your share price.' It already had; Steve had made sure of that by placing a few inventive rumours of his own based on what he knew of Bizham's spending spree. A word in the ear of a formidable broker, in the strictest confidence, when he'd wanted to know why the directorship hadn't gone to Steve was all that it had taken. An embellished account of Bizham's financial instability and a hint that Steve had actually declined the directorship for that reason helped to swell the rumours.

'I needed to liquidate some capital in order to complete a complex deal in Bangladesh. The particulars are confidential.'

Steve fixed his father-in-law with a firm look. 'I am family and have proved both my loyalty and discretion. I don't mind that you gave the directorship to someone else, particularly in view of the tumbling share price.' Steve suppressed a smile when he noticed Depan, Stella's second brother, reach for his phone, no doubt to check the markets. 'But I do mind being sandbagged in the way that I was at the presentation.' Steve kept his voice low and conversational, but it had developed a steely edge. 'It was unprofessional, disloyal, and as far as I'm aware, I did nothing to deserve not being given a heads-up at the very least. You are, of course, free to give the directorship to whomsoever you please but I do deserve to be treated with respect.'

'The fact of the matter is,' Bizham replied after a prolonged pause, 'that one of our suppliers has gone under with a full order book. If I don't fulfil those orders then I will lose valuable custom.'

It was complete tosh and Steve didn't believe a word of it. 'Competition is rife in that part of the world. Surely someone else can take up the slack. Besides, how does a supplier with a full order book go bust and why have you got so much invested with him that you need to have a January sale?'

'A very good question.' Bizham glowered at his oldest son, who looked away. Clearly, he'd been responsible for the cock-up, *if* it was genuine. 'There are other suppliers, of course, but none who produce goods to the same high standard, which is what sets our merchandise apart from all the rubbish invading these shores. We are making a fortune in the current economic climate, where everyone wants a bargain, but we can only continue to do so if we keep up the supply chain. It's vital. Our current suppliers over-reached themselves, got over-ambitious and their creditors called in their loans, someone took his eye off the ball and... well—'

'Farmer can fill the void?'

'He can, but his price was that directorship, about which discretion was vital.'

'I take exception to the fact that you think me incapable of keeping a secret,' Steve remarked mildly.

'You would not have behaved naturally the other night if you'd known what was coming,' Chetan had recovered some of his poise and spoke scathingly, displaying a disapproval of Steve that he had previously taken care to conceal. 'If a man cannot even control his own wi...'

At a look from Bizham, his words trailed off but what he had almost blurted out was interesting. So, Bizham knew that Stella played away; there could be no further doubt. Why hadn't he done anything to bring it to an end and, more to the point, why had he rewarded her current lover quite so lavishly? Perhaps she no longer needed his financial support for her company, especially if Farmer was bankrolling her, and had told him to take a hike. But then, why would Bizham publicly acknowledge Farmer if that was the case?

Steve knew that Stella had grown tired of being what her father and brothers expected her to be and wanted to spread her wings like the successful twenty-first century businesswoman that she had become. Steve would have encouraged her to do so if she had come to him, putting him ahead of Daddy dearest; all women needed his help sooner or later, even that little tramp Leona. Instead, she'd chosen to lean on Farmer. Big mistake! The silly mare had forgotten just what her husband was capable of when crossed. A timely reminder was clearly overdue.

'I will make it up to you, Steve.' Bizham's voice had turned conciliatory. 'This is just a bump in the road. Get past it and we will be untouchable.'

Keep telling yourself that. 'No need.' Steve shifted position and stretched his limbs. 'But whilst on the subject of agreements, you will recall that my investment in your silk enterprises is up for renewal.' It was an investment that Steve had insisted upon making when his own business had become successful. Bizham had bankrolled him and Steve wanted to prove a point by returning the favour. 'Since you have a new partner already working in that area, my input will be surplus to requirements.'

'Nonsense.' Bizham held up a hand. 'There is more than one string to my bow.'

'But it didn't occur to you to run the problem past me when you needed help replacing your defunct supplier.'

Bizham's eyes darted from side to side, clearly wrong-footed. He had either forgotten about Steve's support of *his* enterprise, or hadn't realised it was due for renewal. It seemed that he was haemorrhaging cash and given his company's sliding share price he couldn't afford to risk losing more investors, especially one of Steve's not insignificant stature. This time, the parental look of disapproval fell upon Depan, a qualified accountant who kept Bizham's books.

'I hope you will not be that petty,' Bizham said, an edge to his voice. The man looked strained, as though he wasn't sleeping well. Steve had never seen him anything other than suave and self-assured before. The current view was almost worth the disappointment of the directorship.

'Petty?' Steve ensured that his smile didn't trouble his eyes. 'Don't take this personally, Bizham. It's just business,' he said, throwing the older man's earlier words back at him.

'Ah, so that is how it will be.' Bizham rubbed his chin, breathing deeply as he clearly struggled to contain his anger. 'What do you intend to do about the silk investment?' he asked.

'Well, now is hardly the time or place.' Steve rose to his feet. 'The trust is gone, Bizham, so we need to have our lawyers present if we are to renegotiate. I will have my people contact yours and arrange a meeting. I have a lot on right now so it might have to wait a week or two.'

'But surely you can make time for...'

Steve offered Bizham his hand together with a reptilian smile. 'Later,' he said, nodding to the boys, who'd stood also, huddled together as though for protection. Well they might, Steve thought, suppressing a chuckle. Bizham was not a pleasant man to be around when he was unhappy and right now, antagonism wafted off him in waves. Steve had had the temerity to stand up to him and Bizham was spitting tacks as a result.

What else had he expected, Steve wondered, as he made for the door, surreptitiously lifted the front flap to the display cabinet closest to it and deftly palmed the katar that he'd selected at a glance before sitting down. The cabinet was concealed from the body of the room by an alcove but anyway, the occupants of said room were too distracted by Steve's behaviour to watch his departure.

No one noticed a thing.

The katar disappeared into Steve's sleeve as smoothly as the silk now under dispute. He whistled to himself as he left the house, thinking that some of the skills he'd learned from a criminal father whilst growing up on the mean streets of London had come in far more useful in later life than the obscure subjects disinterested teachers had failed to drum into the heads of the kids they were paid to inspire.

* * *

'Have you heard? It's all over the news.'

'Heard what?' Hugo held the phone away to distance his eardrum from Leona's breathless shout.

'Stella's been attacked.'

'What? When? Where? Is she badly hurt?'

'Turn the news on.'

Hugo did so and saw scant details of a woman's brutal mugging outside a hotel in central London flickering across the tape at the bottom on the screen. She was said to be in a critical condition. 'How do you know it's Stella?' he asked.

'She's been named. They showed Steve arriving at the hospital a while ago, followed a bit later by Bizham and all her brothers.'

'I really didn't think he'd go that far,' Hugo said softly, scrolling through his phone for more details.

'You think Steve's responsible?'

'A hundred quid says the hotel she was leaving is where Farmer has a suite.'

'Which means the police will make enquiries inside and her association with him will leak out.'

Hugo nodded, then recalled that Leona couldn't see the gesture. 'I wouldn't bet against it,' he said. 'Steve will have seen an opportunity to revenge himself on a disloyal wife, gets back at Farmer who, if he really is taken with Stella, will be heartbroken, *and* he gets one over on Nawaz. The man won't recover if Stella doesn't.'

'But murder?' Leona sounded shocked by the suggestion, which told Hugo just how much she still underestimated Steve's determination to come out on top, no matter what the cost. Hugo could understand that since he'd been underestimating his friend, then making excuses for him, for far too long. 'I don't have a high opinion of Steve but even I wouldn't have thought he'd go that far.'

'Look what he did to you, just because you rejected him.'

'True, but—'

'He and Stella had an agreement, as did he and Nawaz,' Hugo reminded her. 'Both reneged and that will have been a bitter blow. Oh yes, I think his revenge will have been swift and brutal.'

'Hmm. Perhaps. But how could he have put the arrangements in place so quickly?'

'Steve has all manner of dodgy characters on speed dial.'

'I'm aware of that, but would they commit murder and would Steve place himself at risk of being blackmailed by getting them to do it?' Leona asked, on a note of anxiety as she reminded herself that she'd almost entered into an affair with a dangerous and vindictive man.

'Murderers for hire are easier to get hold of than you might imagine.'

'I'll have to take your word for that.'

'Have you seen Nawaz's share price today?' Hugo asked.

'Can't say that I have.'

'It's taken a tumble. Someone's been starting rumours about his financial instability.'

'Steve?' Leona bit her lower lip anxiously. 'Now that I can imagine him doing.'

'Me too. We found out that Nawaz was selling off his assets so he will have too, and it would have been too much of a golden opportunity for him to pass up.'

'He certainly doesn't waste any time, and nor do I. Much as I hate to grasp Stella's assault as an opportunity, it gives me a plausible reason to call Steve, offering both my sympathy and my services. I'll pretend that I want to bury the hatchet, even if I don't add that I'd prefer to bury it in his head.'

'What will that achieve?' Hugo asked, an edge to his voice.

'Think about it. If Steve *did* arrange for his wife to be attacked then I'll be best placed to find the evidence if I'm on the inside. He won't have done it himself, of course, and will have made sure that he was somewhere in plain sight when the attack went down. His ego will make him think I'm using Stella's absence from the scene to get my feet back under the table.' Her sigh echoed down the line. 'It was only when I found out that his marriage was solid that I rejected his advances, remember.'

'Leona, take a breath and think this through. Knee-jerk reactions seldom end well.'

'Not that he'll open up to me,' she added, talking over Hugo's interruption, 'he's not that careless, but still, he'll be distracted and I'll have an opportunity to do a spot of snooping. I still know all his passwords.'

'Use the sense you were born with! There won't be anything incriminating in writing.'

'I need to prove to the world in general and Sergeant sodding Potter in particular that I'm not a hysterical female and that I was right about Steve all along.' Leona felt surprisingly calm, despite the possible danger that she would be exposing herself to. She was sorry about Stella, of course she was, but she wouldn't hesitate to use her misfortune for her own advantage. It was almost as though it was supposed to be and she would not squander the opportunity.

'He'll leave you alone now, Leona. Our job is done. Let it be.'

'Even if he's finished with me, I'm not through with him. If he's a would-be murderer then someone needs to bring him to justice and he will have covered his tracks too well for the police to stand a prayer. I'm better placed to stir the pot.'

'Let's meet tonight and talk about this.' Hugo's deep voice echoed down the line, firm and persuasive.

'Nothing to talk about. I'm not asking for permission but telling you what I intend to do as a courtesy.'

'Even so, let me buy you a drink.'

'I'll do better than that. I'll cook dinner for you as a thank you for putting your faith in me. Provided you don't use the opportunity to try and change my mind.'

They agreed a time and Hugo hung up, leaning back in his chair to mull over what he'd just heard. Could Steve really have turned murderer? Given that he'd been indirectly responsible for the death of the girl at uni and hadn't lost any sleep over the matter, Hugo found it surprisingly easy to imagine him doing so. He'd been backed against the wall by Nawaz's actions and blindsided by his wife's association with Farmer. A narcissist and misogynist, that double blow would have caused a red mist of anger to blur his vision and create an unquenchable thirst for revenge.

Yes, Hugo decided, grinding his jaw, he could easily imagine his old friend committing murder and Leona, hot-headed and annoyingly determined, had decided to ignore all the warning signs and throw herself headfirst into the fray.

How, he wondered, as he returned to his research, was he supposed to talk some sense into her?

Steve stood outside the window of Stella's intensive care room, watching her chest moving up and down. She was attached to a bewildering array of machines that were keeping her alive, but for how much longer, that was the question. Her doctors had shaken their heads and told him to prepare for the worst. They had done all they could do to save her life. It was now up to her.

Bizham and his sons had arrived half an hour after Steve. Distraught, Bizham had demanded to know why he had not been called first. He was her next of kin. A harried but experienced staff nurse had no time for his rank-pulling and calmly told him that her husband was her nearest and dearest. It had been up to him to call Bizham, which he had done.

Eventually.

To add insult to injury, Bizham had been told that he couldn't stand where Steve was and he and his sons had been relegated to a nearby waiting room, where Bizham's irritating voice could be heard demanding progress reports from every member of staff who passed the door. Steve wondered how long it would be before he was thrown out and when anyone had last dared to throw Bizham out of anywhere for that matter. Perhaps now he understood what happened to people who crossed Steve, although unfortunately Steve couldn't claim the credit he deserved for the attack on Stella that had so devastated Bizham.

Even so, there were subtle ways to make Bizham understand that he only had himself to blame. Whoever said that women were more dangerous when it came to exacting revenge had a lot to learn. Steve had decided that Bizham deserved the deluxe treatment: a two-pronged attack on his financial base whilst hitting at the heart of his personal life.

'Sleep well, my darling,' Steve breathed, blowing his comatose wife a kiss. 'You've brought this on yourself.'

Steve almost jumped out of his skin when a hand landed gently on his shoulder. God forbid that he'd spoken louder than he realised and that he'd been overheard. His blood ran cold. Not normally careless, this was a timely reminder to stay on his guard at all times, especially now.

'Mr Jessop?'

Steve's head swivelled round. 'Who are you?'

'Detective Sergeant Potter, sir. How is your wife?'

'As you can see, it's touch and go.' Steve let out a long sigh. 'They can't do anything more for her.'

'Let's hope she's a fighter, sir.'

'Oh, there's no question about that.' Steve paused. 'I hope you find out who did this, Sergeant. In broad daylight in a crowded city. How is it even possible?'

'We will do our very best. There are cameras everywhere nowadays, which is helpful.'

Steve nodded. He hoped to Christ that his man had avoided them. Not that Steve really cared if he was caught. The attacker didn't know who had commissioned the hit. Even so, it would be less hassle if it went down as a random mugging. He glanced again at Stella, idly wondering if she would beat the odds and pull through. If she did, she would be a different person. Steve would finally have her firmly beneath his control and she wouldn't dare to break their agreement.

Not again.

Besides, if she did survive then Steve would rewrite the terms of the agreement in question.

'All for the contents of her bag,' he mused, shaking his head.

'She had come from the Randolph Hotel,' Potter said. 'Do you have any idea what she was doing there?'

'None whatsoever, but my wife is a successful businesswoman. She had meetings all over the place with clients and investors. Presumably the hotel will be able to tell you who she was there to meet with.' *They'd damned well better!*

Potter paused, eyeing Steve in a manner that made him feel uncomfortable. 'You are aware that your wife was stabbed.'

'Yes, they told me.' He shook his head. 'Why was that necessary? She would have given up her bag without a struggle if she feared for her safety; I'm absolutely sure of it.'

'Not necessarily. We think she might have resisted when her assailant attempted to grab her bag. That's the only explanation that makes any sense.'

Steve tutted. 'That would be typical, I suppose, and very stupid of her. But she's always been a fighter and on the spur of the moment, perhaps...'

'We have people scouring the area, hoping to find the weapon, as well as teams looking at CCTV. There's a lot of homelessness in London and high-end hotels are easy pickings. You will be astonished how careless people can be with their possessions simply because they feel that they're in a safe part of town.'

'Isn't it a leap to blame this on a homeless person?'

'I'm speaking from experience, sir.'

'Yes, sorry. I didn't mean to tell you how to do your job.' Steve let out a slow breath. 'Just catch who did this, Sergeant. I don't want anyone else to have to suffer in the way that my wife is.' *Unless they do anything to deserve it.*

'We will do our very best, sir, but I can't make any promises. Did your wife have any enemies?'

'Good heavens!' Steve gave a convincing display of shock. 'You don't think this was anything other than a random attack, do you?'

'Just covering all the bases.' Potter's bland expression gave nothing away about the nature of his thoughts. 'A routine question, sir. Where were you at eleven this morning?'

Steve gave the policeman a disbelieving look, despite the fact that he'd been expecting the question. 'In a meeting at my offices with potential clients. There were six of us there from ten-thirty. We had lunch in the directors' dining room. My PA can give you the names of the attendees.'

'Thank you, sir.' He had been making notes on his phone but closed it down now and pocketed it. 'Well, I'll leave you to it and speak with your father-in-law. I really hope that she makes it.'

'Me too, Sergeant, me too.'

Steve watched in the window as the detective walked away, feeling totally satisfied with the way the meeting had gone. Now it was a waiting game. He would see how hard Stella fought for her life before he decided on his next move. He would wait for it to be discovered that Stella had been meeting with Farmer for reasons that had nothing to do with investments. He would wait for the katar to be found, which it would be, he'd been most specific in that respect, and linked to Bizham. Then the shit would well and truly hit the fan and Steve would ensure that he had an unimpeded view of Bizham's downfall. Even if the crime couldn't be pinned on him, Steve would ensure that his being questioned hit the headlines.

'See what that does to your share price, arsehole,' he muttered.

* * *

Leona wondered why she'd offered to cook for Hugo. They would have been better off having a drink in an anonymous pub and eating bland scampi and chips, surrounded by other people. That way, it would have been harder for him to work his persuasive charm on her and talk her out of offering her services to Steve. She hadn't needed to accept the offer of his company at all, come to that. She smiled at Mulligan, who tilted his head in expectation as he watched her rolling out pastry for her beef wellington. His tongue lolled from the side of his mouth as he sent her a *seriously?* look. Her dog seemed to know better than her that she'd be hard pressed to reject any invitation issued by the charismatic research engineer.

'So much for my swearing off all men except you, Mulligan,' she said, wrapping her pastry carefully around the prepared meat, placing the results on a baking tray and popping it in the oven.

Table set and everything prepared, Leona nipped out with Mulligan for a brief ramble, thinking about Stella's attack. There was no further news, so presumably she was still alive. Leona hadn't liked the woman much but then she could be accused of bias, given that she'd only met her when she herself was being bombarded with a charm offensive by her husband and not fighting too hard against it. Even so, no one deserved to be bashed brutally over the head, stabbed and left for dead which, according to the sketchy details that had emerged, is what had happened to Stella.

Leona picked wild flowers as a centre piece for her dining table as she thought the matter through. People like Steve and Bizham deserved one another but couldn't be allowed to get away with breaking the law, even if it was only one another that they hurt. No one was above the law but those who amassed a fortune usually ended up believing their own hype and reckoned that the rules didn't apply to the likes of them. Bizham was as bad as Steve in that regard, certainly when it came to cutting corners in the business world, shafting the opposition by unscrupulous means, courting the movers and shakers and cheating the taxman. Steve had often spoken about his methods to Leona and she had sensed a combination of admiration and resentment in his attitude. They were, Leona thought, kindred spirits and therefore rivals. Men with their massive egos didn't countenance opposition.

Hugo was right to say that Steve wouldn't be thinking about antagonising her any more but that didn't change the fact that he'd screwed up her career, implied that she had criminal tendencies and made her scared to live like a normal person. She simply couldn't let that go, even if it meant putting herself in danger. But if she did that, this time it would be on her terms and Steve's charm offensive, if it was renewed, would be played to her own advantage.

'See how you like a taste of your own medicine,' she muttered, thinking that she really ought to have a clearer campaign strategy before putting herself in the line of fire.

She returned to the cottage, checked the oven, turned it down and then arranged the flowers she'd picked, placing them in the centre of the table. With nothing else left to do, she hit the shower and stood under the hot jets of water for a long time, hating the fact that she'd locked all the doors and made sure the windows were closed before retreating to the bathroom, despite the fact that Steve definitely wouldn't bother her today.

'I cannot live like this,' she said aloud, the sound of her own voice reinforcing her determination to regain control of her life.

With hair washed, brushed out and left to its own devices, she opted for casual clothing. It was a warm evening. They could have drinks on the terrace and watch the sun go down, she thought, applying make-up with a light hand. If Hugo didn't get involved with his research, of course, and lose track of time.

But Hugo arrived dead on time with flowers and a decent bottle of wine.

'Thanks,' she said, proffering her cheek for a kiss.

'Something smells good,' he said, bending to make a fuss of an ecstatic Mulligan, whose tail whipped across Hugo's shins as he soaked up the attention.

'Let's sit outside,' she said, after she'd poured drinks for them both.

Hugo lowered himself onto a patio chair, stretched his long legs out in front of him, leaned his head back and closed his eyes. 'This is nice,' he said. 'I can't remember the last time I got home before sunset.'

'You know what they say about all work...'

'True, but there's not much point to this if you don't have anyone to share it with.' He opened one eye and regarded her closely as he spoke.

'Like you'd struggle to find someone, if you really wanted to. I think you use your research as an excuse *not* to get involved.'

'Hey, you already know me too well,' he said, winking at her.

'Cheers.' She raised her glass to his, thinking their conversation had gotten too intimate far too quickly.

'Cheers.'

She took an opportunity to look at him, enjoying the view a little too much. If being broad shouldered and handsome wasn't enough, there was also an integrity about him that she found compelling, which was annoying since she had no desire to be compelled, not by him or any man. Once bitten and all that. She wondered if it was even possible to sense integrity. What she knew for a certainty was that she couldn't trust her judgement when it came to men. Besides, Hugo hadn't given any indication that he was in the market for a significant other, casual or otherwise.

He did seem stoutly determined to protect her from Steve, though, and that did make her wonder about his motives. Was it their rivalry that drove him or did he hope to prevent history from repeating itself? There was something about his past dealings with Steve that he still hadn't shared, she sensed. Something sensitive, more likely, and she wondered if he would ever trust her enough to confide in her.

Could Hugo be using her to get back at Steve for that as yet unidentified reason? She quickly dismissed the possibility. If that was the case then he wouldn't have tried nearly as hard as he had to talk her out of returning to Steve's employ.

'How's Patsy?' he asked.

Leona smiled. 'She's been on the phone, speculating wildly about Stella's attack. She doesn't have any difficulty in thinking that Steve might be responsible.'

'All the more reason to...' He broke off and smiled at her. 'Sorry,' he said contritely. 'I promised myself that I wouldn't raise the subject.'

'A bit ambitious, that. It's the elephant in the room.'

He grinned and nodded. 'True.'

'If Steve's responsible then he wouldn't have done the deed himself. He's not daft, Hugo, and I don't think he'd try to harm me. He knows I put the police onto him and if anything happens to me, whose door is the first one they'll knock on?'

'That won't be much of a comfort if you're dead.'

Mulligan barked, jumped up from his place at their feet and tore off down the garden in pursuit of a squirrel. They both laughed as they watched his ungainly gait and inept attempt to keep the garden a squirrel-free zone.

'More enthusiasm than skill,' Hugo remarked, as Mulligan

planted himself at the base of the tree in which the squirrel had taken refuge, barking up a storm.

'Come on,' she said, 'if you've finished your drink, the sun's gone and dinner ought to be ready.'

'Good. I'm starved.'

Hugo elevated himself elegantly to his feet and collected up both of their glasses. Mulligan gave up on the elusive squirrel and gambolled up to them, paws flying in impossible directions.

'What can I do to help?' he asked, following her into her small kitchen.

'You can open the wine and let it breathe. I should have done it earlier.'

'Not a problem.'

He wielded the corkscrew with the same precision that he seemed to apply to everything he did. Leona watched him in the periphery of her vision, a little daunted by his dexterity. *It's only a damned corkscrew. Get a grip, girl!*

They settled across from one another at the intimate round table and Leona was pleased to see Hugo do justice to her food. She was a proficient cook but often didn't bother for herself, so it was good to cater for someone who appreciated her efforts.

'This is excellent,' he said. 'Restaurant standard.'

'Only that good?' she quipped. 'But thank you. I find cooking cathartic. I did a cordon bleu course when I was younger but don't often get to entertain. Certainly not since I've become a virtual prisoner in my own home.'

'Did you cook for Steve?'

Leona momentarily froze, wishing he hadn't ruined the intimacy of their flirtation by mentioning Steve's name. 'Frequently. He preferred to eat at home and *have me to himself*.' Leona snorted. 'And I fell for that old line. Of course, I realise now that he preferred not to be seen dining out with me too often. There are only so many instances that can be passed off as business dinners before someone notices and speculates. In retrospect, I get the impression that there was more than one person who'd have been happy to drop him in it.'

'He hurt you very badly, didn't he?' Hugo said, watching her intently across the narrow space that separated them as he picked up the wine bottle and topped up their glasses.

'Hurt?' Leona took a moment to consider. 'At first, yes. But I was the one to end it when I realised that he was never going to leave Stella, so I'm not sure if I was actually in love, although I thought I was at the time. And if it was love, is my burning desire to get back at him an act of revenge, a woman deceived, or do I genuinely want to get my life back?' She took a sip of wine and shrugged. 'Sometimes, I don't even know myself.'

'You need to have a clear head and clearer objectives if you really intend to return to the lion's den,' Hugo remarked casually, pushing his empty plate aside with a sigh of contentment and smiling at her. 'Otherwise, he'll sway you with that persuasive charm of his. I've seen him operate more times than enough.'

'Forewarned and all that. When someone goes to that much trouble to make a point by posting dog shit through your door, it kinda focuses the mind.'

'Even so. I can help you to get your career back on track. I do have some influence in the employment sphere.'

'Thanks, Hugo, but I don't need your help. Besides, unless I can disprove the implication that I stole from Steve then it will always be a cloud hanging over me and I won't be able to move on.'

He smiled across at her once again. 'Everyone needs help from time to time. They just need to have the sense to realise it.'

'Perhaps.' She sighed as she leaned forward to collect up the plates.

'Here, let me help.'

He was on his feet in seconds, taking over, and somehow she didn't mind. She left him to do the clearing and attended to dessert.

'Apple crumble and cream,' she said apologetically.

'Reminds me of my childhood,' he said.

'Not very inventive but I didn't have much time.'

'Don't apologise,' Hugo replied, picking up his spoon and tucking in. 'This is delicious. I can't remember the last time someone cooked for me like this.' He glanced up at her, his eyes dark and gleaming with an emotion she found it hard to put a name to. 'Thank you.'

'No thanks necessary. It's my pleasure,' she replied, wondering why they were suddenly being so formal. Wondering why her stomach lurched with a pleasurable sensation when he continued to look at her with such focused intensity.

Leona toyed with her own dessert and pushed the half-finished plate aside.

'Coffee?' she asked.

'Please.'

He poured the remainder of the wine into their glasses and again took over on the clearing-up front, whilst Leona fiddled with her coffee machine.

They took their coffee into the sitting room, which is when Leona suspected that Hugo would recommence his efforts to talk her out of returning to Steve's employ. She put some music low on the system, sat across from him in an oversized armchair and tucked her feet beneath her backside.

'I'd forgotten how real people live,' Hugo said into the ensuring silence. 'This is nice. I could get used to it.'

'This isn't how real people live,' Leona replied with a significant glance towards the multiple locks on the front door, visible through the sitting room's open door.

Hugo acknowledged the point with a tilt of his head. 'Even so...'

'Real people have the telly blaring away virtually non-stop. I seldom switch mine on. There always seems to be something more pressing or interesting that needs my attention. Besides, I hate all those reality shows that seem so popular.'

'I work too much. Can't remember the last time I watched the box.'

Leona smiled. 'I don't think we're missing much.'

She knew they were making banal small talk in preparation for the main event. She was proven right when she allowed a significant pause and Hugo filled it with the question she'd been anticipating.

'What can I do or say to persuade you not to go back to Steve?' he asked.

'Why are you so determined that I shouldn't?' She leaned forward, absently scratching Mulligan's ears when he stirred and rested his chin on the edge of her chair. 'What is it that you're not telling me about your history with Steve? Surely there can't be anything worse than the girl who killed herself over him.'

Hugo crossed one foot over his opposite thigh and leaned back in his chair, pinching the bridge of his nose, as though warding off a bad memory. Clearly, he was trying to decide what, if anything, to tell her. She left him to his cogitations. No way would she attempt to coerce the information out of him. He either trusted her or he didn't. She was interested to see which way he'd jump.

'Steve impregnated my sister,' he said softly.

Leona's mouth fell open. 'Seriously?'

'Hardly the sort of thing you'd joke about,' he replied, his jaw rigid. 'I have a fabulous ten-year-old nephew and a now happily married sister with two other kids with her husband, but things could have turned out very differently.'

A thousand questions jostled for dominance inside Leona's head. 'What? When did this happen?'

'Jess was fifteen.'

She tugged absently at the ends of her hair. 'Christ!'

'He entered into an affair with Jess before we went up to uni. Steve was my best mate. I didn't know his true colours then and I was glad to see him and Jess having fun. I didn't think it was serious. Anyway, long story short, despite being smitten, Jess had her head screwed on, even as a teenager. When she caught Steve cheating on her, it was her pride rather than her heart that was damaged and she dumped him.' He smiled across at Leona. 'You remind me a lot of her. She wouldn't take any bullshit either, even as a youngster.'

'Does Steve support his son?'

'He doesn't know to this day that he has a son. Like I say, Jess knew her own mind, refused to have an abortion and also refused to tell Steve that he was going to be a father. She didn't want anything more to do with him and certainly didn't want him influencing her son.'

'You still remained friends with him?' Leona's disbelief probably showed in her expression.

'I wanted to keep him close; make sure he didn't try to get back in with Jess. Not that it was likely, given that we were at uni and the world was his oyster, so to speak. Even so, I could tell that he hadn't enjoyed being dumped, thought he might try to get his revenge, a bit like he has with you, and wanted to be on the scene to manage damage control. That was when I stopped making excuses for him and no longer looked upon him as a friend, but to this day he doesn't know it.'

'How did your sister cope?'

'The family rallied round, helped with the baby whilst Jess finished her education. She's a social worker now, helping kids who find themselves in a similar situation to the one that she landed herself in. She says it helps her to empathise because she's been there. She's popular, good at her job and has risen through the ranks. She married a police officer and is happy now. Contented.'

'How did your parents respond?'

'My father wanted to go after Steve with a blunt carving knife but my mother and I talked him out of it. Steve was better left in the dark, we all agreed. Anyway, they were very supportive of Jess.'

'They sound very sensitive.'

'They were. My father died five years ago. A heart attack. My mother was wonderful but she went downhill herself when she lost him. Jess and I were recently forced to put her into care. She has Alzheimer's and can't live alone.'

'That's so very sad.'

'Yeah, it is.'

'You've waited for your revenge on Steve all this time,' Leona said softly. 'You must really hate him.'

'Not necessarily hate.' Hugo waggled a hand from side to side in a considering fashion. 'I would like to see Steve brought down a peg or two. After the suffering my sister went through, I'd be less than human if I didn't, but not at any price. It's so damned frustrating, having to depend on him for my bread-and-butter trade, knowing what I do about his methods. I have Jess on my conscience and have seen how Steve treated Jane, and now you.' His expression turned to granite. 'The time's come to stop him once and for all.'

'So why fight my decision to go back and work for him? We both know it's the best way to get to him.'

'Doesn't mean I have to like it.'

'You could have reported Steve for having sex with your sister, who was a minor at the time.'

'I could but that would have dragged Jess through the mire and she already had enough to contend with.'

'Have you ever spoken to anyone else about this?'

Hugo shook his head. 'It's not the sort of thing that comes up in every day conversation.'

'Then thank you for telling me, but if it was intended to change my mind, it's had the reverse effect.' Leona set her features in a stubborn line. 'I'm now more determined than ever on getting back at Steve; not just for my own sake but for that of your sister, the poor girl at uni and for Jane.'

'What about your own childhood? Was it a happy one?'

'It was until my father ran off with another woman when I was ten.'

'Ouch!'

'I'm an only child and my mother, left to raise me alone, was full of resentment. There wasn't a great deal of maternal interest and I was more or less left to bring myself up.'

'Is your mother still alive?'

'Living in Bournemouth in a retirement home. We don't have much contact.'

'You have no relatives to take an interest in your welfare, which is a situation Steve would have seen as ripe for exploitation.' He sighed. 'I don't suppose there's anything I can do to talk you out of contacting him. You seem determined to do it.'

It was a rhetorical question and Leona simply shook her head. 'Nope,' she replied, 'but you can have my back if you like.'

14

At the request of the harried ICU staff, Steve had vacated the corridor outside Stella's room and joined the rest of her family in the waiting area. Slouched on uncomfortable plastic chairs, the brothers looked terrified. Bizham, still with tie expertly knotted, his Savile Row suit failing to completely disguise the slope to his narrow shoulders, not a hair out of place, showed no emotion whatsoever. Appearances were everything to the man; emotional turmoil a weakness that could be exploited by his competitors. Steve had never known him to lower his standards, not even in front of his family. It seemed he had no intention of doing so now, not even when his favourite child was fighting for her life.

They looked up expectantly when Steve joined them but no one spoke a word. Everyone except Steve was existing in a personal form of hell. Steve, conversely, was thoroughly enjoying the view.

All heads jerked up when a tired-looking doctor joined them.

'She's stable,' he said, answering Bizham's curt demand for information. 'We're keeping her sedated, giving her body time to recover.'

'What are her chances?' Steve asked.

The doctor waggled his hand from side to side. 'Too soon to tell. She's a fighter but there is severe internal trauma and a nasty head wound that's giving us concern. We did what we could for her on the operating table. The rest is up to her.'

'Can I see her?' Bizham asked.

'No point. She's unconscious It's a sterile area. Best to keep it that way. The next twenty-four hours are crucial. You would all be better off going home and getting some rest. We'll call you if anything changes. If she does wake up, that's when she will want to see you and that won't happen tonight.'

'You all go,' Bizham said once the doctor had left them again. 'No point in us all staying but I want to be here.'

'That's not your call,' Steve replied, pleased when he managed to insert a catch into his voice.

'It's you she will want to see when... if she wakes up,' Bizham replied, swallowing. 'You heard the doctor. That won't be tonight.'

'Yes, but—'

All heads turned and there was a collective intake of breath when the door opened again. But it was Sergeant Potter rather than the doctor who put his head round it.

'Ah,' he said. 'There you all are. How is she?'

'No change,' Steve replied. 'Do you have news for us?'

'Not yet but I do have questions,' he replied. Another plain-clothed detective entered the room. Potter introduced him as DC Smythe. Steve recognised him. He'd fired perfunctory questions at Steve when Leona had started making allegations against him in her futile attempt to take out a restraining order. The two men nodded at one another and Steve sensed in the young DC an ambition that balked at the prospect of ploughing through life on a policeman's salary.

He wants to be like me, God help him.

Even so, it might come in handy to have someone on the inside of the investigation willing to keep him informed of progress, Steve reasoned.

'Fire away,' Bizham said impatiently. 'Anything to help catch the bastard who did this to my baby girl.'

'Do any of you recognise this?' he asked, producing an evidence bag with the offending katar, its blade covered in blood, ensconced behind the plastic.

'It's ours,' Depan blurted out. 'Where did you get it?'

'Is that the weapon that was used?' Bizham asked at the same time.

'We believe so. It was discarded in a drain close to where the attack took place.' Potter turned to face Depan. 'You say it's yours. Were you aware that it had gone missing?'

'I have a large collection of them, Sergeant.' Unsurprisingly, having recovered from his initial shock, Bizham took control of the situation. 'I am a renowned collector, in fact,' he added. 'My interest is common knowledge. My son cannot possibly know that that particular katar is ours. We do have several like it but that is a very common example.'

'Is any of your collection missing?'

Bizham looked visibly shaken. His sons appeared bemused. Steve, enjoying himself enormously, congratulated himself upon the ease with which he had brought such an influential family to a state of defencelessness. It had taken him less than twenty-four hours. *And I have barely started.* 'I will have to check, but not so far as I am aware.'

'It implies that the assault was personal rather than random,' Steve said pensively. 'It's too much of a stretch to accept that my wife was attacked with a weapon similar to those collected by her father. It's a message. It has to be.' He turned to face the father in question. 'Perhaps the attack was orchestrated by someone who bears you a grudge, Bizham,' he suggested, his expression suitably sombre. 'Damned cowardly way of resolving differences, but there you have it.'

'Impossible!' Bizham snapped, but he sounded as though he was attempting to convince himself.

'You are a man of substance, sir,' Potter said in an urbane tone. 'Your name is often in the news. I dare say you have made your share of enemies during the course of your business life.'

'Business rivals, perhaps. I would not go so far as to say enemies. But none of the people I have had professional differences with would dream of striking at my family in order to get at me.'

'Well, sir, unless the choice of weapon and the victim are the coincidence of the century then someone is clearly intent upon making a point; you must be able to see that.'

Bizham reluctantly inclined his head.

'Whoever it is must be exceedingly aggrieved to have gone to such violent and extreme lengths.'

'We are agreed about the extreme lengths, Sergeant, but I still cannot persuade myself that anyone I have had dealings with would go that far.' He left unsaid that they wouldn't dare because clearly, they would.

Potter sniffed but it was impossible for Steve to decide if he bought Bizham's firm assertion. Steve thought he was probably sceptical. Policemen were paid to be suspicious and never took anything at face value. 'Are you and your daughter close?'

'Extremely but that's no secret.' Bizham's face turned beet red. 'Look, Sergeant. I really think your senior officer should be talking to me. You are too junior to handle such a sensitive matter.'

Steve, watching Potter closely, could see that Bizham had miscalculated. The man might only be a detective sergeant but he was clearly experienced and not about to be intimidated by Bizham's bluster. 'Be thankful you do only have a lowly sergeant, sir,' he said calmly. 'The big guns will come into play if this turns into a murder investigation,' he added in response to Bizham's visible wince. 'Let's hope that your daughter recovers and it doesn't come to that.'

Bizham's expression closed down when he realised that he'd met his match. And perhaps because the choice of weapon supported Potter's assumption that someone had attempted to get at him through Stella. He grew even more sombre, presumably because it had occurred to him that by insisting his business rivals wouldn't behave in such an underhand way, he'd put the suspicion squarely back onto his own family.

'Are there any tensions between you gentlemen and Mrs Jessop?' Potter asked, embracing all four Nawaz men with a sweep of his eyes.

'None whatsoever,' Bizham replied for them all.

Steve cleared his throat and said nothing but the gesture was sufficient to draw the attention of everyone in the room to him.

'Do you wish to add anything, sir?' Potter asked.

'Only that Stella had changed recently.'

'Changed in what regard?'

'She complained that her creativity was being stifled.' Steve gave an apologetic shrug. 'She'd reached out to some new PR people to help build her public image as a fashion designer.'

'She used my people,' Bizham snapped, defensive again and still clearly struggling not to blow his top. Steve knew exactly which buttons to push and at that precise moment, Bizham could not have looked guiltier. He *was* guilty. He'd brought all this on himself by shafting Steve. Steve wanted to rub his hands with glee but couldn't even risk smiling. For now, his satisfaction would have to remain internalised. 'She never expressed dissatisfaction with their services. She would have told me if that was the case.'

'She knew you would insist upon keeping your people on the

payroll and wanted to avoid a dispute with you. That's why she was talking to others in secret.'

Bizham's shoulders were set in a rigid slope. 'I fail to see what this has to do with her attack,' he said, his tone sour.

'I think it's important that the detective knows everything,' Steve replied, spreading his hands in an apologetic gesture. 'Who are we to say what might be significant?'

Bizham fixed Steve with a look of deep betrayal before returning his attention to the detective. 'My daughter and I disagreed about the direction in which she was taking her company; that much is true.'

'A fashion label?'

Bizham nodded. 'I thought she was expanding too fast. I am the largest investor in her empire and a board member, so I have a big say in the way she runs things. We had a professional disagreement.' He fixed Steve with a penetrating look that bounced harmlessly off Steve's thick hide. *I'm not one of your lackeys. You'll have to try harder than that if you want to intimidate me.* 'I did not realise she had taken her grievances home and discussed them with her husband.'

His tone turned accusatory. Bizham, accustomed to speaking his mind and riding roughshod over the feelings and opinions of his underlings, didn't seem to realise that it showed him in a poor light, further rousing the detective's suspicions about his involvement in the assault. Not that Potter would seriously consider Bizham capable of orchestrating the attack on Stella simply because they'd had a business spat. And even if he did, a few questions would suffice to satisfy him that Stella and he really were joined at the hip. It was simply another thread of evidence against Bizham that Steve was constructing, one brick at a time, before destroying both his business empire and personal reputation.

'We have no secrets,' Steve said evenly.

'Well, sir. If you wouldn't mind returning to your home and checking your collection of... katars, I believe you said they were called.'

'I can't leave my daughter,' Bizham replied impatiently. 'Can't this wait?'

'Unfortunately not. I should have thought that you would be keen for the answers you require my superior officers to unearth.'

'Count on it,' Bizham said through clenched teeth, by which Steve knew he intended to launch his own investigation. *Bring it on!*

'Perhaps one of your sons could check the collection.'

'They can and they will let you know if anything's missing.'

'If they could do it now, sir, DC Smythe here will accompany them.'

'Is that necessary?' Bizham looked rattled and highly affronted. 'Will my word not suffice?'

'Unfortunately, the law doesn't work on trust, sir. I am sure you can understand why.'

Bizham huffed. 'You are being very insensitive...'

'Besides, if a weapon *is* missing then its cabinet will need to be sealed off, fingerprints taken and so on. I dare say you can see how important that would be.'

Steve nodded, glad that he'd had the foresight to wipe the catch that opened the cabinet, the only part of it that he'd touched, with the tail of his shirt.

'Of course,' Bizham said gruffly, 'but it won't prove to be necessary. The katar you showed me is readily available from dealers. I have one like it in my collection but it is far from unique.'

Steve thought that Bizham sounded over-defensive. Glancing at Potter, he could see that the detective had reached the same conclusion. Excellent!

'If one of your katars is missing, who would have access to it?'

'Anyone who has been in my study. I entertain clients and

friends in the room on a regular basis and often show the katars off.'

'Are they kept under lock and key?'

'They are in cabinets. The more valuable items are locked but not the others.'

'Could a guest help him or herself to one without the loss being noticed?'

The four Nawaz men shared a look and simultaneously shook their heads.

'I suppose it would be possible if the room was crowded,' Bizham conceded, 'but the gap would be quickly spotted, if not by me then by my servants who regularly dust the room.'

'Well then, I'm sure this will be a wasted journey but it needs to be undertaken, so if whoever is going with Smythe is ready...'

'I will go. We all will,' Bizham said magnanimously, encompassing his sons with his gaze. 'Then I will return and relieve you, Steve.'

'The doctor said that no one need be here overnight. Nothing will change,' Steve reminded his father-in-law, imbuing his tone with pathos.

'Even so...'

'But of course, I will stay. Take all the time you need. Obviously, I will call you if there's any news.'

Steve watched the party leave, wishing he could be a fly on the wall when they discovered that a katar was not only missing but was the actual one that had been used to attack Stella, or so similar that it couldn't possibly be a coincidence. Bizham kept up-to-date photographic records of his collection for insurance purposes, so identification would be a doddle, as would self-incrimination.

Aware that Potter had lingered, Steve made sure that he schooled his features into an expression that combined anxiety with confusion. 'What a mess,' he muttered, scrubbing a hand down his face.

'Do you have any opinions, sir, as to who could have done this, or why?' Potter asked. 'Do you think your wife was deliberately targeted? Excuse me, but I happen to know that a lady bears you a grudge.'

'Leona?' Steve's head snapped round, his shock totally genuine. 'You think she tried to bump my wife off so that she and I could be...' He shook his head and smiled. 'Impossible. She would never go that far.'

'Ah, so you were involved with the lady.'

Fuck! Steve had given himself away. 'Barely. We worked together, long hours that often required us to stay away from home overnight. We became friendly, nothing more. Leona read more into it than was actually there, became a little obsessed,' he added with a self-deprecating shrug. 'Her position became untenable as a result and I had to let her go.'

'I see.'

'I do think that Stella was deliberately targeted, to answer your original question.' Steve was anxious to steer the conversation away from Leona. He didn't want Potter going off on a tangent. The only person he wanted him to harass was Bizham. 'The katar doesn't leave much room for doubt in that regard.' Steve inhaled deeply as he stood, hands in pockets, jingling his change. 'But as to why...' He removed his hands and spread them wide. 'There you have me.'

Potter nodded. 'Do you have any idea what she was doing in that hotel?'

'Meeting James Farmer, I assume,' Steve replied with a casual shrug.

'Farmer?' Potter looked vague but Steve wasn't convinced by his nonchalance. He was sharper than his scruffy appearance suggested. Steve, who had already been caught out by him once, would do well to remember that and not underestimate the man. A brief Google of Bizham's name would have thrown up particulars of the directorship fiasco, Farmer's name and colourful accounts of Steve's disappointment.

'Stella and Farmer were having a fling.'

Potter blinked. 'You knew and didn't mind?'

Steve smiled. 'Stella and I have an open marriage. You've met her father. He demands total familial loyalty from all his children, even though they are adults no longer beneath his control, and that can be stifling. Stella is the only one who broke away from the family firm and struck out on her own, but she could only do that with Bizham's financial support, which is how he keeps control of her and why she gets so frustrated by his restrictions sometimes. Stella wants a more modern, westernised look for her range. She herself is very westernised but Bizham insists upon his old country's values.'

'Does he know that his daughter and presumably you, sir, have what you describe as an open marriage?'

'If he does then he knows better than to mention the matter to me. I am not his lapdog and would tell him to mind his own damned business, only not quite so politely. I'm pretty sure he hasn't mentioned it to Stella, either. She would have told me if he'd tried to interfere.'

'Mr Nawaz gave a directorship in his company to a man by the name of Farmer, I seem to recall reading.'

'You keep up with the financial news, Sergeant?' Steve realised that he'd sounded patronising and attempted to repair the damage. 'I'm surprised you find the time.'

'My interests are wide and various, sir.'

'Well yes, Bizham did give the directorship to my wife's lover,' Steve replied calmly.

'That must have been humiliating. I understand you were broadly expected to be given the position.'

'It was a possibility but I'm glad it didn't happen.'

Potter looked surprised. 'I thought these positions were highly sought after and offered a lucrative return for very little effort.'

'Ordinarily, but Bizham's star is no longer in the ascendency. If you keep up with the financial news, you will be aware that his share price is falling amidst rumours of financial difficulties.'

'He's overreached himself?'

'It happens, often temporarily, and in such cases, secrecy is vital. The stock market is a hot bed of gossip. Once rumours gain legs, even if unfounded, it can have a devastating effect on share prices. Investors are famous for panicking.'

'Even so, I should have thought that a man of his stature would recover and that you would have benefited from the directorship in the long term.'

'Possibly, but I am not the vindictive type. I have got where I am today through my own efforts and most certainly didn't attack my wife in some sort of manic desire to get revenge for a perceived slight. If I had issues in that regard, I would have taken them up with Bizham directly. Don't assume because we lead separate personal lives that we aren't a happily married couple, because we are.'

Or had been, Steve privately amended, before Stella broke the rules; a transgression for which Steve would find no forgiveness. Now she was surplus to requirements and if she recovered from the attack then Steve would ditch her. Stella, he knew, would be devastated because unlike him and despite her behaviour, her feelings were invested in the marriage.

'Stella and I are very fond of one another. We are both ambitious and make a good team. I have absolutely no reason to rock that particular boat and have only been so candid because I want you to catch whoever did this.' Steve tapped the fingers of one hand on his opposite forearm. 'I keep coming back to that katar. It has to mean something. I don't for one moment suppose that Bizham or Stella's brothers had anything to do with the attack; they all adore her.' *But I want you to think precisely that.* 'However, someone has gone to a lot of trouble to make it seem that way.'

'My thoughts exactly, sir.'

'Who, though? Bizham is not an easy man and tends to ride roughshod over the feelings of others. I have absolutely no idea who he could have upset to such a degree, though.'

Potter rubbed his stubbly chin. 'You say that you have no reason to rock your marital boat. But surely your wife's open support of Farmer must have hurt your feelings?' Potter said mildly.

Steve smiled and shook his head. 'I don't think Stella was responsible for Farmer getting the directorship. Bizham tells me that he and Farmer have some sort of new partnership. Something to do with imports from Bangladesh, although you didn't hear it from me. I'm not ordinarily indiscreet and am only telling you this so that you can get the full picture.'

'And very complicated it appears to be.' Potter nodded and closed his notebook. 'Well, I think that's all for now. I will leave you here and hope your wife's situation improves.'

'Thank you, Sergeant. And please keep me informed of progress.'

'I will tell you as much as I can, sir. Good evening to you.'

Steve let out a long breath and released the slow, satisfied smile that had been struggling to escape for too long as the door closed behind the detective. Things could not have gone better, leaving aside his slipup over Leona. Not that it really mattered. Nothing could be pinned on him with regard to her harassment claims. Now he'd sit back and watch the shit hit the fan. If Stella didn't pull through, it would be an added bonus because she would never be the same again and would be firmly under his control. As would her financial affairs be. Perhaps his own financial problems had come at just the right time. When he divorced Stella, *if* he decided to, *she* would be required to pay *him* a substantial settlement. If she died then he would inherit her entire estate.

Steve grinned and rubbed his hands together gleefully. His future suddenly looked a whole lot brighter.

When would women learn that they were the weaker sex for a reason? he wondered as he made himself as comfortable as possible in one of the uncomfortable plastic chairs. He closed his eyes, feeling tired yet elated, but knew that he wouldn't sleep. He wondered how long it would be before Bizham returned. A great deal of time presumably since he'd be required to answer questions about the missing katar and the heat would be turned up. He'd lawyer up, of course, but somehow Steve couldn't see someone with Potter's experience being intimidated by Bizham's expensive mouthpiece.

He threw his head back and closed his eyes. As always, when coming out on the winning side of a complex deal, Steve felt an overwhelming urge for sex. His thoughts automatically turned towards sweet little Leona – the one who got away. The one whom he hadn't finished with yet and who was never far from his thoughts. If he could bring Bizham's mighty empire crashing down in a single day then Leona's defences wouldn't take a lot of bridging. But still, he couldn't go near her yet. Shame, but she would keep.

Dare he call up someone else and have some fun once he got out of here? It was tempting but he knew better than to take the risk. Potter didn't seem to suspect him. His sights were centred firmly upon Bizham. The man might not be a complete idiot but he'd still followed the trail that Steve had lain that led to Bizham's door. He didn't give much about his inner thoughts away though and Steve didn't want to do anything to give the detective reason to transfer his attention to him.

The husband was always the first to be suspected, Steve knew, but this particular husband had covered his trail with precision. Even the extortionate amount it had cost him to hire the hitman had come from an offshore account that no one knew anything about. The man himself had no idea who'd hired him; it had all been done through an anonymous intermediary. There was absolutely nothing that could lead the police to his door.

Satisfied on that score, Steve again closed his eyes but his phone, on vibrate, buzzed in his pocket, bringing him instantly back to alertness. He glanced at the display, ready to decline the call, just as he'd declined all that had come in since news of Stella's attack broke, and did a double take. He rubbed his eyes, thinking at first that they were deceiving him, but when he looked again, it was still Leona's name filling the display.

Curious, he took the call without hesitation.

'Leona?'

'Steve. I heard about Stella and wanted to know if she's okay. If you're okay. I know we've had our differences but at times like these, they don't seem important.'

Steve allowed himself a slow, satisfied smile. Just when he'd thought the day couldn't get any better. His cock thickened as thoughts of Leona's curvaceous body filled his imagination.

'That is incredibly generous of you,' he said, his voice low and sombre. 'I'm at the hospital now. She's out of the operating theatre and being kept under sedation. It's serious, Leona,' he added, forcing a catch into his voice, 'and the prognosis isn't good. They've said it's now up to her and all we can do is wait and hope.' He paused. 'And as for how I'm doing... well, thank you for asking. You're the first person who has. I am, as you can imagine, pretty damn shellshocked but hanging in there. But this isn't about me.'

'Do the police have any idea what happened? Who did it?'

'Not as things stand. Investigations are underway, as they say.'

He heard Leona swallow at the other end of the line and imagined her eyes filling with tears, soft-hearted little soul that she was. Steve had said all he intended to. She'd called him and his trusty sixth sense told him that she'd done so for reasons other than enquiring after Stella.

'It occurs to me that you're going to be distracted for the foreseeable.' Her husky voice only served to harden Steve's erection. He briefly touched it and it jerked beneath his palm. God, but he wanted the damned woman! More so than he could recall wanting anyone for a very long time. Perhaps that was because she was proving to be so fucking elusive and he enjoyed the challenge. 'You need someone at the office who knows the ropes and whom you can trust. Like I say, we've had our differences but I'd be happy to fill the void on a temporary basis if you'd like me to.'

Steve's lingering smile transmuted to a full-blown grin. 'Darling, are you absolutely sure?'

'I'm not your darling, Steve. I need to make that clear. This is purely business.'

'Of course. It's merely a turn of phrase. You can't possibly imagine that I'm thinking along those lines at a time like this.' *Even though I am.* 'Besides, you've made your position plain and I respect that.' The sound of a dog barking in the background and a man's voice calling to the bloody hound echoed down the line. He knew she had a dog, of course, but the pretence had to go on. What he hadn't known was that she'd got a man in her life and that knowledge now filled him with a jealous rage. When had Steve last felt jealous of anyone or anything? He couldn't recall. What was it about Leona that could so easily stir him from bouts of burning lust to outright jealousy in the blink of an eye? He really would have to have her, by force if necessary, then he would finally get her out of his system. He hated anything controlling his emotions, such as they were. It always had to be the other way around. Steve was the master of control. 'Is that a dog I can hear?' he asked.

The background noise abruptly abated. Presumably she'd had him on speaker prior to that. 'Would you like to accept my offer?' she asked. 'Or have you already made arrangements?'

'You are the answer to my prayers, Leona.'

'Right. Well then, let Molly know that I'll be there in the morning. She can update me with what needs doing and you can concentrate upon Stella.'

'I might have to show my face briefly but you've set my mind at rest. I know I can depend upon you.' It was true. Leona had integrity oozing from her pores. Despite the fact that they had parted on such bad terms and that she'd tried to take out a fucking restraining order against him – for which she would have to be severely punished until she acknowledged the error of her ways – she would never try to get back at him by sabotaging his business affairs. Steve would have staked his life upon it. Besides, he would keep her well away from the sensitive stuff. There was such a thing as being too trusting.

'Thank you, Leona. I will make sure you are financially rewarded for your kindness.'

She cut the connection and Steve found himself listening to thin air. Smiling, he pulled up his list of contacts and called someone whom he knew he could depend upon to plant certain information in the financial press about Bizham's precarious situation. It was a gamble, but a calculated one. His contact wasn't averse to the odd spot of insider trading and Steve had the proof. In other words, they needed one another and no one would ever know that Steve had been starting rumours about his father-in-law's business affairs whilst his wife was fighting for her life.

15

Leona cut the call. Her throat felt dry, her palms were sweating and her heart was galloping at twice its normal pace. She slumped back in her chair, feeling a raft of conflicting emotions. She'd done it! The emotional side of her wondered what she realistically expected to achieve by taking on such a dangerous and amoral man – a man whom she would be happy never to set eyes on again.

'That was easy,' she said, letting out a long breath.

'A little too easy.'

Leona waved Hugo's remark carelessly aside. 'He's too up himself to read anything into it. He'll just assume that I've come to my senses and can't live without him.' She snorted. 'The bastard!'

'Think about what you plan to do, Leona. Just talking to him has reduced you to a quivering wreck so how will it be when you have to actually face him?'

'Well, thanks a bunch! Just what a girl needs to hear.'

Hugo smiled that lazy smile of his, sat beside her and took her shaking hand in his. 'My point is, you will have to face him. He will make excuses to come to the office when he knows you'll be there, regardless of the fact that his wife is in intensive care. You can count on it.'

'I'll be okay,' Leona replied, with more conviction than she actually felt. 'I won't deny that I found that conversation harder than I'd expected to. The sound of his voice gave me the creeps. But the initial contact is over now and I'll be fine. I'm tougher than I look and besides, I have a vested interest in bringing the scumbag down.'

'Right well, if you're sure.'

'I am. Steve will think I'm using Stella's accident as an excuse to offer an olive branch.' She blew air through her lips indignantly. 'He's too arrogant to look at it any other way and probably thinks I've had time to regret rejecting him.'

'Very likely, which makes him dangerous and unpredictable. You *did* reject him and he will take that as a personal slight. Stella being in ICU won't prevent him from hitting on you again. You know that, don't you, and once he thinks he's got you, he won't play nice?'

Leona nodded, unsure of herself suddenly and yet also fiercely determined. She *had* to do this, otherwise her life would remain stalled indefinitely and she would hate herself for being such a coward. 'The possibility had occurred to me.'

Hugo glanced at his watch. He was obviously thinking about leaving and Leona was filled with a ridiculous urge to beg him to stay. She didn't want to be alone, even though she knew where Steve was for once. She'd offered to work for him again, so she would be safe from his retribution for the foreseeable.

Even so, the thought of having Hugo sharing her space filled her with an inner peace that she hadn't known for weeks, which annoyed her. She was a strong, independent woman and didn't need any man other than Mulligan to make her feel safe.

'It's getting late,' he said.

She nodded. 'You should go.'

'I'll let Mulligan out for you first.'

She wasn't sure how she felt about Hugo so effortlessly taking over her domestic duties but didn't dwell on the point. She watched as he whistled to the dog, who was at his side in seconds, staring up at Hugo through adoring eyes as he wagged his entire rear end. The dog appeared to be even more devoted to Hugo than he was to Leona: a further cause for irritation. She watched man and dog wander down the length of her garden. The former with hands clasped behind his broad back as the latter sniffed at the undergrowth, pausing to lift his leg every few yards.

'He's empty,' Hugo said, returning to the cottage and double bolting the French doors behind Mulligan.

'Thanks.'

Leona hadn't moved and Mulligan came up to her, placing his cold nose beneath her hands. She scratched his ears as she extricated her curled legs from beneath her backside and stood up, ready to show Hugo out.

'Thanks for dinner,' he said. 'It was superb.'

'My pleasure.'

'I suppose you intend to report to Steve's offices first thing.'

'Yep, before I lose my nerve.'

'Promise to keep me in the loop.' He placed his hands lightly on her shoulders, dropped his head and placed a soft kiss briefly on her lips. Taken aback by the gesture, Leona instinctively responded to it but Hugo broke the kiss before it could get interesting. 'I wish I could talk you out of it but I know I'll be wasting my breath.'

She smiled up at him. 'I have to do this. It's the only way to get my life back; I thought you could see that. Besides, if he has done something to Stella then perhaps I can find the evidence to prove it.'

His grip on her shoulders tightened and he gave her a gentle shake. 'Leave it to the police. I do not want you to be his next victim. I'm just getting to know you and I kinda like what I see.'

She shuddered, even as a waft of warmth heated her body. Hugo liked her. He wasn't a man to throw out compliments and so she felt the full force of that particular one. 'It won't come to that. I'll be careful and won't do any snooping unless the coast is absolutely clear. I know a few things about his personal affairs that he's not aware of. Where all the bodies are buried, financially speaking. I can do a bit of sleuthing online once I'm back on the premises.' She grinned up at Hugo, who shook his head, clearly accepting that he wasn't going to win this particular battle.

'Just keep your phone on at all times. If I can't get hold of you, I'll come looking.'

She nodded her agreement. Her forehead rubbed against his shoulder and she moved out of his grasp, forcing him to drop his hands from her shoulders before she gave in to temptation and leaned on him a little harder. She opened the front door, smiling as he ruffled Mulligan's ears.

'Take care of your mistress and try and talk some sense into her,' he said to the dog. 'Not that I hold out much hope of you succeeding.'

She stood where she was, watching him as he climbed into his car, turned on the engine, flashed his lights at her and reversed out of her driveway.

Once his rear lights had disappeared from view, Leona returned to the cottage and locked the door securely behind herself. She cleared away their glasses and coffee cups, stashed them in the dishwasher, turned out the lights and headed for the stairs with Mulligan at her heels.

'Returned your attention to me, have you, now that your new bestie has left us?' she asked the dog.

Mulligan woofed, jumped onto the bed, curled into a tight ball and was snoring by the time Leona had attended to her ablutions and climbed between the sheets herself. She envied her dog his simple existence. Unlike her, his sleep would not be interrupted by nervous anticipation, or thoughts of Hugo's dark eyes and intense expression begging her to rethink her options. Or the feeling of his lips touching hers either, for that matter, which only served to complicate the entire picture.

'Get a grip!'

She angrily punched her pillows as though she bore them a grudge and waited for sleep to find her. It was a long time coming.

She woke early with a slight headache but fresh resolve. She could do this. She *had* to do this. In the cool light of dawn, it felt good to have made the first move to reclaim her life and hopefully to expose Steve for the scumbag misogynist that he was. Someone had to take him on. Besides, she was pretty sure that he'd been responsible for Stella's attack and if by some miracle she could uncover evidence to support that belief then she would feel vindicated.

She whistled to Mulligan, still sound asleep. He stirred himself, blinked at her as though asking what the hell time she thought it was and then jumped from the bed, happy to get a head start on the day. She took him for a long run. He would be left to his own devices for a big chunk of the day so she felt that she owed him. Returning to the cottage an hour later, she made herself some breakfast that she forced past the lump in her throat and drank two cups of coffee. Dressed casually in tailored trousers and a favourite top, she piled her hair on top of her head and applied light make-up.

'Okay, Mulligan,' she told her dog. 'I'm ready to go into battle. You're on guard duty. No sleeping on the job,' she added, grinning. 'Wish me luck.'

She was about to leave when her phone rang. It was Patsy asking for an update and Leona told her what she was about to do.

'Hmm. Your hunky Hugo doesn't approve, I'm betting. Can't say that I do either, although in your situation, I'd probably do exactly the same. I don't like being a victim either.'

'Hugo isn't mine and doesn't get to tell me what to do.'

'He can give me orders any time he likes!'

Leona laughed. 'You're incorrigible.'

'And you should take note of the way that man looks at you. If I was the recipient of that look, I'd have jumped his bones long since. I know you've had your fingers burned, darling, but for what it's worth, not all men are bastards.' Patsy paused. 'Just the majority of them. But Hugo, I'm thinking, is likely the exception that proves the rule.'

'I'll have to take your word for it. Right now, I'm off to put my head in the lion's den. Steve won't be there but even so...'

'Stella must have been leaving a liaison with Farmer, given where the attack took place. It's on the news that she'd been at the Randolph for *a meeting*.' Patsy's laugh echoed down the line. 'That seems to be the euphemism for it this week.'

'Yeah, that's what we're thinking. Steve will know it and I'm betting that he's told the police, just to drop Farmer in it. He will think that Stella and James Farmer are jointly responsible for him not getting that directorship – a public display of disloyalty on Stella's part that can't go unpunished.'

'You really think he arranged for Stella's attack? You've come round to my way of thinking?'

'Yep, I really do now that I've had time to dwell on it. Farmer will suffer from the fallout when news of the affair breaks in the press, and you can bet your life Steve will ensure that it does. I dare say it's just the start of Steve's campaign against him.'

'Well, I'm ringing to tell you that Bizham's company's share price has taken a slide since news of the attack on Stella broke. Stella's company's shares are holding up but word is that situation is unlikely to endure with the driving force behind the fashion line clinging to life by a thread. The markets like certainty.'

'How can Stella's attack affect Bizham's position?'

'It's assumed he'll take his eye off the ball, I'm guessing. But people in the know tell me that the rumours about his financial problems have grown legs overnight. That could have something to do with it.'

'Okay, that's interesting. I wonder if Steve's been stirring the pot.'

Patsy snorted. 'Nothing would surprise me.'

'Me neither. But look, I'd best get going.'

'Keep your phone on and call me if you need me. Laters, darling.'

Leona found herself smiling as she cut the connection. A chat with Patsy was just what she'd needed to bolster her flailing courage. There was a spring in her step as she said goodbye to Mulligan and let herself out of her cottage.

The drive to Steve's offices was a familiar one and Leona undertook it on autopilot, the car's radio tuned to an oldies station to distract her. She absolutely didn't want to overthink the situation but instead needed to be reactive. She pulled into the office's car park, cut the engine and checked her appearance in the rear-view mirror. She thought she looked gaunt. Hardly surprising, given what little sleep she'd managed to achieve. She checked her phone for missed calls, hoping that Hugo might have been in touch to wish her luck.

He hadn't.

Fair enough. She didn't need him, or anyone. She climbed from the car, locked it and headed for the entrance.

The security man greeted her warmly.

'Welcome back,' he said. 'I was told to expect you.' He handed her a pass. 'Terrible what happened to the boss's wife. No one's safe in the streets any more. Terrible, so it is. Anyway, it's good of you to step into the breach.'

'Least I can do.' She wondered if the man knew she'd left under a cloud. 'We all have to pull together under such circumstances.'

'Well, anyway, Molly's expecting you. You know the way.'

Leona smiled at the man whose name she couldn't recall and headed in the appropriate direction.

Molly was on the phone but grinned when she looked up at Leona and indicated the chair in front of her desk.

'Are you a sight for sore eyes,' she said, ending her call and walking round her desk to give Leona a hug. The gesture took Leona by surprise. They hadn't been *that* close before. Even so, she was glad that the older lady had instigated the bonding gesture. 'It's terrible what's happened to Stella.'

'Indeed. Do the police have any leads, do you know?'

Molly shook her head. 'Steve called a bit earlier. I think he was at the hospital all night. But if he knows anything, he didn't say and I didn't like to ask.' She resumed her chair, glanced at her phone when it rang again and diverted the call to the main office. 'Press.' She rolled her eyes. 'Again. The phones have been ringing off the hook but there's nothing we can tell them because we don't know anything. Anyway, I'm very glad to see you here. Glad but surprised,' she added, her gaze sapient.

'At times like this, people need to pull together. I figured Steve would need help so I offered my services on a temporary basis.'

'He does need help, and did even before this awful thing happened. Your old position hasn't been filled so you can have your office back. Anyway, get yourself settled in and I'll bring you the most urgent cases that need chasing up.'

Leona stood and smiled. 'Thanks, Molly. Have the systems' passwords changed?'

Molly shook her head, obliging Leona to suppress a smile. She had constantly berated Steve for his lax attitude to cyber security. That laxity could now work to her advantage.

* * *

Steve was dozing in his uncomfortable chair when the door opening jolted him abruptly back to the here and now. Shame that. He'd been in the middle of a rather pleasant dream in which he had a willing Leona at his complete mercy. He sat up straight, rubbed the sleep from his eyes and glanced at the loudly ticking clock on one wall. Two in the morning and Bizham had only just returned, looking uncharacteristically shaken.

Excellent!

'Any change?' he asked.

'None. You've been a while. What happened?'

'The katar used to attack my daughter was part of my collection,' he said through gritted teeth.

'No!' Steve's jaw dropped open in what he hoped would come across as genuine-seeming shock. 'How the hell...'

'Precisely what that annoying detective wants to know, but not nearly as much as I want to know myself. I've been at the police station for hours, giving a statement, answering banal questions. How many ways is it possible to say that I don't know when the katar disappeared, or who took it? It was accounted for three days ago but dozens of people have been in and out of that library in the meantime.'

'I assume the police have no leads.'

Bizham threw up his hands. 'They're clueless. Seem to think it was one of us because that's the easy option and lateral thinking isn't their forte.'

'That's ridiculous!'

Bizham snorted. 'Try telling them that.'

'It must be someone with a serious grudge against you, Bizham. Someone who's pretty desperate and has nothing left to lose. Try to think who that could be.'

'What the hell do you think I've been doing! Sorry,' he added in a more conciliatory tone, 'but I won't have them pinning this on me or any of my boys because they can't be bothered to conduct a proper investigation.'

'There's no evidence other than the katar belonging to you. I'm not sure precisely what time Stella was attacked but I dare say you can account for your time.' Steve waved a hand. 'They're bound to ask. I think they have to.'

'They have and unfortunately, I wasn't at home, so no one can vouch for me.' He looked away from Steve. 'Inconvenient but since there's nothing to suggest that I had any desire to harm my beloved daughter, I'm not unduly worried.'

'Why not simply tell them where you were?' Steve suspected that he'd been with a woman, probably a married woman, which would give the lady's husband a justifiable reason to strike back at Bizham where it hurt the most, assuming he'd gotten wind of the affair. 'It could be significant.'

Bizham shook his head decisively. 'It isn't.'

Widowed for years, Bizham had never remarried, despite being targeted by a plethora of glamorous and determined gold-diggers. Instead, he enjoyed a series of dalliances that he thought no one knew about, preferring to retain his family man image in public and enforcing rigid standards of conduct within his immediate family circle. Stella and Steve used to laugh about his double standards.

'No one could seriously suspect me of ordering such a vicious attack on my daughter.' His voice caught in his throat. 'And even if, for some bizarre reason I did so, why the devil would I have had the assailant use one of my own katars?'

'I agree, the idea is preposterous,' Steve replied smoothly. 'But I'm betting that weirder things have happened in the heat of the moment and... well, I'm sorry, but you and the boys will be the primary focus of the police investigation now, unless you tell them where you were. I assume a lady is involved.'

Bizham gave Steve a sharp look and slow, reluctant nod.

'Well then, that puts her husband squarely in the frame.'

'He is not in the country at present and anyway, he knows nothing about the liaison. I am the last word in discretion.'

'Someone always knows,' Steve replied with conviction. 'And the husband need not be in the country in order to make it happen. In fact, it would be better for him if he was not.'

Bizham, tight-lipped, nodded for a second time. 'It's possible, I suppose. But the man has not been in my library since long before the katar went missing.'

'But someone acting on his behalf might well have been. You need to think about who that could have been.'

'What the hell do you suppose I've been thinking about these past hours? As well as worrying incessantly about Stella, of course.'

Steve dipped his head. 'Of course.'

'It's a damnable mess. Tariq is rattling a few cages. He has people checking on the few businessmen I have crossed recently, calling in favours. Someone somewhere will know something and he'll root it out.'

'Good thinking.'

But it also concerned Steve. Tariq was Bizham's youngest son and easily the cleverest. He was Bizham's right-hand in many respects, his fixer, especially in political circles. He and Steve enjoyed a cordial relationship but Steve had always felt uneasy in the man's company. It was almost as if he could see through Steve and understood what really drove him.

'You aren't going to give me the lady's name?' Steve asked, returning to the question of Bizham's latest squeeze. 'I'd like to try and help. I have a vested interest in resolving this business too, in case you'd forgotten.'

Bizham waved the offer aside. 'I will deal with it.'

'What about Farmer's connections?' Steve asked. 'You realise, of course, that's where Stella had been. Farmer has a suite at the Randolph. You must be aware that they're having an affair.'

Bizham scowled. 'Why do you allow it?'

Steve responded with a tight smile. 'Stella enjoys her little dalliances and I see no harm in them.'

Bizham shook his head. 'A man should control his wife.'

'She isn't a chattel. Even you were unable to clip Stella's wings. I know you've had a lot of disagreements recently about the direction her business is moving in.' Steve withstood Bizham's blistering glower without backing down. It felt good to stand up to the man. 'Anyway, if you disapprove of Stella's behaviour so much, why did you give Farmer that directorship?'

'I never permit personal considerations to get in the way of business.'

'Back to my original question. Could someone connected to Farmer have sought revenge?'

Bizham waved the suggestion aside. 'He only has that silly female whom he's never married to care about his personal entanglements, as far as I'm aware. She wouldn't have the brains to come up with such a vicious form of revenge, much less carry it out. Besides, she has never been in my library as far as I'm aware. Certainly not recently.'

'I've been thinking all night, trying to come up with ideas, explanations, but you seem less than impressed by my suggestions.'

'Sorry, Steve, but you haven't said anything that hasn't already occurred to me. Not to worry. I will conduct my own investigation too. I don't trust the police to do a thorough job, especially with a lowly sergeant in charge, and the crime will likely never be solved if I leave it to them. They are overstretched.'

'What do you mean?'

'I mean to offer a substantial reward for information leading to a conviction. Not even a conviction. I just need a name and some evidence.' He firmed his jaw. 'I will take matters from there personally.'

Steve's heart stalled. He hadn't considered that possibility but probably should have. He did a quick re-evaluation, just to reassure himself that he'd not left himself open to exposure, and breathed a little more easily when he couldn't think of anything he'd overlooked.

'Good idea,' he said. 'How large a reward are you thinking of?'

'A million pounds ought to jog a few memories,' he replied calmly, fixing Steve with a look that made his skin crawl. *He suspects me.*

'It certainly should. You'll be inundated with time wasters, though.'

'I will have my people sort through the calls that come in and deal with the most promising ones myself. Once Stella is back on her feet, there's always the possibility that she might remember something.'

'The police seem to think that she was struck from behind whilst on her phone, so don't hold out too much hope.'

'Hmm. The police have seized all the CCTV in the area and are going through it but, of course, there are camera blind spots. Besides, I don't suppose Stella's assailant obligingly looked at a camera with his face uncovered. In fact, I know he did not. That annoying sergeant mentioned that the perpetrator had briefly been caught fleeing the scene wearing one of those hoody monstrosities. They have only so far found a camera image of his back view. They have a rough idea of his build but don't even know the colour of his skin.' Bizham threw up his hands. 'It's hopeless.'

'There's always hope,' Steve replied quietly, reminding himself that every cloud had a silver lining. Leona would be ensconced in his offices in a few hours' time, chewing her lower lip in that engaging manner of hers when she concentrated. He ached to see her, to be there to welcome her back in person, but knew that he must bide his time. He'd give her a while to get comfortable first and immerse herself in a job she enjoyed, was good at and probably missed.

Besides, he really did need her input into some of the new client accounts he'd been chasing, and others that she'd been negotiating but which had stalled without her at the helm. *That* had contributed to his financial problems. Even since she'd left him, the new business accounts had been neglected. He'd lost a few promising leads because of Leona's stand-in's inability to follow up properly: another situation for which she would have to be punished in due course. Steve briefly fantasised about the form that the punishment in question would take.

'Well, why don't you get home.' Bizham, still impeccably suited and booted, perched his buttocks on the edge of one of the chairs. 'I will stay here, just in case.'

Steve yawned. 'I think sleep will be impossible. But I would appreciate a shower and a few hours respite. I'll be back at first light. Call me if there's any change. Any change at all.'

Bizham nodded and made shooing motions with his hands.

Steve left the room, closing the door quietly behind him, feeling relief as he quit the cloying atmosphere of ICU. He nodded to the nurses, who smiled sympathetically, but held his own smile in until he was in the car park, well clear of interfering cameras. He breathed deeply of the clean night air as he climbed into his car and fired up the engine. He worried about Bizham's determination to offer a reward and decided it might be useful to increase the pressure on Bizham's share price by starting more rumours about financial instability. That would give the man something else to occupy his mind.

All Steve needed now, he thought as he drove out of the car park, was for Stella to die and then everything in his garden would be rosy. Her company was solid and Steve reminded himself that he was her sole heir. Steve had insisted upon their making wills soon after they married, naming one another as their beneficiaries. He also knew because he'd checked that she had not amended her will since then.

16

Everyone in Steve's company seemed pleased to see Leona back and made a point of stopping by her office to welcome her. The welcome in question was tempered by their shocked reaction to Stella's attack, their sympathy for the boss universal. That was the thing about Steve and the reason why Leona had almost fallen for his toxic charm offensive. It hadn't seemed toxic at the time but rather totally genuine and plausible, which was what made him so dangerous. She'd watched him with junior members of his staff, focusing his full attention on whatever they had to say to him; congratulating them upon their foresight when they responded to his request and made suggestions to improve efficiency.

They all went that extra mile for him because he made them feel valued. And because he recognised quality and paid above the going rate. For that reason, she did wonder why he'd dragged his feet when it came to finding a suitable replacement for her. Was he so arrogant that he assumed she'd come running back at the first opportunity, despite the fact that his interference had prevented her from getting a decent position elsewhere? Or perhaps because of it.

'Bastard!' she muttered beneath her breath.

Despite her reasons for being back, Leona found herself being drawn into her old client accounts, shaking her head at the slap-dash manner in which they'd been handled since her departure. She updated records, made calls and re-established herself with old clients, all of whom seemed delighted to learn of her return and equally concerned about Stella. She was plied with questions about the situation but was unable to tell them much, simply because she didn't have the answers.

The time flew by and when Molly put her head round her office door, she was shocked to discover that it was gone one o'clock.

'Come on,' Molly said, tapping the face of her watch. 'No excuses. This lot has been neglected for long enough. It can wait for a bit longer. You and I are going to have lunch.'

Since getting Molly alone and chatting was her precise intention, Leona didn't put up any objections. Even so, it did occur to her that although friendly, Molly had never sought Leona's company at lunchtime before, a fact that reminded her to be wary. Molly could conceivably have been tasked by Steve to find out if there were any hidden reasons for Leona's return.

'Good thinking.' Leona smiled at the older woman and closed down her computer. 'Lead on.'

They went to the local, where they ordered soft drinks and sandwiches.

'So, tell me what you've been up to since leaving us,' Molly said, as they settled at a small table and sipped at their drinks. 'Presumably you've not got work elsewhere, otherwise you wouldn't have been free to help us out.'

Leona sent Molly a speculative look, her doubts about her reasons for asking the innocent question intensifying.

'I've been freelancing from home while I consider my options.'

Leona took a bite of her sandwich. 'It's liberating, being one's own boss.'

Molly nodded. 'I can imagine. You make your own hours and your own rules. Must be a bit lonely though.'

'I have a dog.'

Molly laughed. 'Ah well, that would fill a void.' She paused with her own sandwich raised to her lips. 'Hardly the same though, is it?' she added with a significant look.

She knows and wants me to talk. And Leona would be happy to, if she could convince herself absolutely that Molly wasn't spying for Steve. But, she reminded herself, there were no guarantees in this life and sometimes one had to go with one's instincts. 'It's less complicated. Dogs don't have agendas, are unswervingly loyal and love unconditionally.'

'Well, there is that.' Molly paused. 'You left very abruptly.'

'I'm not the first to do so.' Leona allowed a significant pause. 'I'm thinking about Annie Blakely.'

'Ah yes, Annie saw the value of working from home too.'

'I'd like to talk to her,' Leona said, conscious of her heart rate quickening as she cut to the chase. What was the worst that could happen? she reasoned. If Molly was digging on Steve's behalf then she hadn't revealed anything that Steve didn't already know, at least insofar as his serial predator tendencies were concerned. Leona swallowed, decided to take a chance and met Molly's gaze head on. 'I think you know why.'

Molly shook her head and Leona was relieved when she didn't pretend ignorance. 'She won't want to talk about it. She's married.'

'You know what he is?' Leona fiddled with the stem of her glass, twirling it through her fingers, hoping she hadn't burned her bridges. 'What he does?'

Molly nodded. There was no prevarication and Leona felt a huge surge of relief, aware that she'd read Molly right. 'I tried to warn you in subtle little ways,' she said. 'I did the same with Annie but she didn't want to know. I have to be careful. Steve pays me generously and I need this job. My husband had an accident a few years back. He's now disabled and can't work. My salary is all that gives us any sort of life. And Steve... well, Steve demands total loyalty for his pound of flesh. I'd be out on my ear if he even suspected we were having this conversation.'

'Then why risk it?'

'Because he ruins lives. It's what he does. I've watched him for years, saying nothing, pretending not to know, but it goes against my principles.' She fiddled with the crucifix hanging on a chain around her neck. 'Against everything I believe in. You're the first of his victims who's been willing to fight back. I know a little about what you tried to do.'

'The restraining order?' Leona raised a brow.

'Yes. Steve is so assured of my loyalty that he sometimes forgets I'm there and of course, I hear stuff.'

Leona reached across to touch Molly's hand. 'I'm sorry about your husband. I didn't know. It must be difficult.'

'We get by.'

'You're conflicted. I can quite see that. Loyalty to Steve warring with disapproval of his operating methods.'

'Something like that.' Molly shifted her chair so that someone could walk behind it. She waited for that person to be out of earshot before speaking again. 'Like I just said, I see everything, hear a lot of stuff and am perfectly capable of joining the dots.'

'I almost fell for his line.' Leona rolled her eyes. 'I thought I was street wise. He's very plausible, but even so...'

'Why did you really come back?' Molly asked into the ensuing silence.

'Honest truth?'

'You have my word that whatever's said between us stays

between us. I wouldn't have lasted five minutes working for Steve if I didn't know how to keep my mouth shut.'

'Okay, I saw through him at the eleventh hour and wouldn't do the dirty with him. My position became untenable after that.' Her chuckle owed little to humour. 'I don't think he's been rejected before and his pride took a denting, which is why he implied that I'd been embezzling funds.'

Molly flapped a hand. 'I never believed that for a moment. But as to his pride, there's no question that it took a beating. He was like a bear with a sore head for days after you left. He hid it from most people but I work too closely with him for him to be able to disguise his moods from me.'

'He's put the word out about me, making it impossible for me to get a decent position elsewhere, *and* he's conducting a stalking campaign, hence the dog and my failed attempt to take out a restraining order against him.'

Molly chuckled. 'That infuriated him. I've never seen him so angry before.'

'Yes well, it came to nothing. He spun the police a line about me being a crazed ex-employee, hung up on him, and they fell for it.' Leona huffed indignantly. 'I no longer feel safe in my own home.'

Molly tutted when Leona went on to explain some of the tricks he'd pulled.

'I can't pin any of it on him, of course. He's far too clever for that, which is why the police won't take my complaints seriously.'

'He didn't find it suspicious that you offered to step into the breach here after falling out with him so seriously?'

Leona shook her head. 'I haven't seen him, only spoken to him on the phone. I was counting on him assuming that I'm using Stella's situation as an opportunity to rebuild bridges. He's too up himself to think that I don't regret walking away.'

Molly fiddled with a drip mat and nodded. 'That sounds about right.'

Leona grinned and clinked her glass against Molly's.

'What do you make of the Stella situation?' Molly asked after a reflective pause.

'Do I think that Steve might be responsible is, I think, what you're asking me.'

Molly nodded. 'I know he was depending upon that directorship. To have it so publicly awarded elsewhere...' She shrugged. 'If he couldn't bear the thought of you dumping him, how much more would he resent his father-in-law shafting him so publicly? He'd blame Stella as much as him, I'm thinking.'

'Yep, the same thought had occurred to us.' Leona added.

'Us?'

'Slip of the tongue. I run everything past my dog.' Leona wasn't yet willing to drop Hugo's name into the equation. If she'd gotten it all wrong then she didn't want to spoil his business relationship with Steve. 'He's a good listener and the last word in discretion. Not that he comes up with any original suggestions, but you can't have everything.'

Molly smiled but when she sent Leona an assessing look, she realised that she'd overplayed her hand and abruptly stopped talking.

'What do you intend to do now that you have free access to Steve's records? Perhaps I can help if I know what you're looking for. I would like to help.'

'It's not your fight, Molly. And you need your job.'

'Like I already said, I've seen how Steve rides roughshod over people's feelings, ruining lives. Annie still pines for him, you know, despite everything. We keep in touch and she always asks after him whenever we speak. It makes me so mad. She's a strong, intelligent woman but mention of Steve's name reduces her to a quivering wreck.'

'It's called toxic charm for a reason.'

'It's pathetic and wrong on so many levels.' Molly again fingered her crucifix. 'It flies in the face of my most dearly held beliefs. And yet I have no choice but to work for such a man, turn a blind eye to his philandering, guard his secrets and pretend not to notice a thing. As I said before, you're the first of his victims to show the backbone, the desire to fight back. I've thought often of looking you up but couldn't take the chance, just in case you were as smitten as Annie.'

'You asked me why I came back.' Leona straightened her shoulders. 'Well, the simple answer is that I want my life back. He's taken up with Stella's situation right now but he will get back to me in time and I will spend the interim looking over my shoulder, wondering when that time will come. I need at the very least to prove to the police that he has been harassing me and I hoped somehow to gain that proof by pretending to be back on his side. Perhaps record what he says to me on the phone or... well, something.' She threw up her hands. 'Vague, I know, but I'm depending upon his arrogance to work in my favour and if I go in with a set agenda, he'll smell a rat. He's nobody's fool so I have to tread carefully.'

Molly nodded. 'It won't be easy.'

'I realise that. Stella's situation won't deter him for long, no matter how it turns out. But while he is preoccupied with her, busy playing the part of the devastated husband, I thought it might be a good opportunity to catch him off guard.'

'And to find evidence that he orchestrated Stella's attack?'

'Yes, that too,' Leona replied sombrely. 'Ambitious, I know, but worth a try.'

'You're aware that he has several offshore accounts that he thinks no one knows about?'

Leona nodded.

'If he paid someone to kill Stella then that's where the funds will have come from but I don't have the access codes.'

A slow smile spread across Leona's face. 'I think I do, to at least one of them. I was in his office late one night. He took a call, got very agitated with whoever he was speaking with and said something about making it happen. Payment was discussed and as soon as he ended the call he went into an app on his phone.'

'If it's on his phone...'

'I've seen the same bank saved under "favourites" on his desktop. He needed access codes and you know as well as I do that he's incapable of remembering passwords, or codes, and writes them all down. He took them from that small, locked drawer in the centre of his desk.' She smiled across at Molly. 'Do you happen to have a spare key?'

Molly returned Leona's smile. 'It just so happens that I do,' she said.

* * *

Steve, showered and refreshed, examined his appearance in his full-length mirror, admiring what he saw. Leona would find him irresistible and he would finally get what he wanted from her. He ought to look gaunt, he supposed, given that his wife was clinging so precariously to life, but hopefully Leona would be too pleased to see him to make the connection.

Life was good.

More than good. It was panning out just the way that Steve had hoped it would, with the added and unexpected bonus of Leona willingly being back in it. There was never any question of the two of them not getting around to unfinished business. Steve simply hadn't counted on her making it so easy for him.

He spent half an hour on the phone, arranging for more rumours about Bizham's precarious financial situation to be planted in the press from a different source, and then made his way back to the hospital.

There was no change in Stella's condition, which was annoying. He'd hoped for a deterioration. But still, he couldn't have everything. He thanked the nurses, squared his shoulders, schooled his features in a sombre expression and joined Stella's family in the waiting area. They were all there, along with Bizham's lawyer, who was in close and quiet conversation with his client.

'Did I miss something?' Steve asked.

All heads turned in his direction.

'We are making arrangements to announce the reward,' Bizham replied curtly. 'Khan here will handle that side of things.'

Steve nodded. 'I am more concerned with speaking to Stella's doctors. They must have some idea about her chances by now.'

'No one has said anything to us,' Tariq replied, an edge to his voice.

'Whereas they will to her husband,' Steve replied, meeting Tariq's gaze and holding it. The other man eventually looked away first but Steve felt disturbed by the open distrust in his expression. Then again, his sister had been brutally attacked with a weapon that an insider would find easier to filch than an opportunist ever would. The police would assume that if anyone within the family wanted to harm Stella, they would hardly bring suspicion upon themselves by using a weapon that they had easy access to: a weapon that was highly individual and easily identified.

Its use had simply been a ruse to distract Bizham from his business affairs whilst Steve set about ruining his company and casting doubts over his reputation. Always easier to do when the subject of an attack had taken his eye off the ball.

It stood to reason, Steve supposed, that the brothers might suspect him, especially given that the directorship had gone so publicly to the man with whom Stella was intimately involved, a situation that none of her family would approve of and which they might even have taken steps to brutally rectify. That, Steve hoped, would be the way the police were thinking.

Tariq was Stella's favourite brother. They spent a lot of time together and Steve suspected that his wife confided in him about their open marriage, despite the fact that she always denied doing so.

'Excuse me,' Steve said. 'I'll see what I can find out.'

He went in search of a doctor who could give him an update on Stella's condition. He eventually tracked down someone in the know, delighted when he told Steve not to get his hopes up.

'Her internal injuries have been patched up but there's nothing we can do about the massive blow to the head and that's what's giving us cause for concern. If she does survive, there could well be brain damage; you need to prepare yourself for that.' The doctor touched Steve's shoulder. 'I'm sorry not to be the bearer of better news.'

Steve swallowed and thanked the man. He returned to the waiting area and conveyed what he'd just learned to Stella's nearest and dearest. Bizham visibly paled. Tariq, who had stood up, fell back into his chair and ran a hand through his hair.

'Fuck!' he muttered.

'Go home, all of you,' Steve said, waving a hand. 'I'll take this shift by myself. I need time alone to come to terms with what's happened. I am sure you have things to do.'

'Nothing more important than our sister's welfare,' Depan said.

'You are all over the papers,' Khan, the lawyer, told Bizham.

'Front pages and the financial section. The things being said about your company have had an adverse effect upon your share price. You might want to turn your attention to damage limitation. A strong performance from you right now will help to calm the jitters.'

Bizham nodded, almost as though he no longer gave a shit. Steve knew that couldn't be true. His father-in-law had worked too hard to establish himself as a force to be reckoned with to lose sight of his ambitions now. Even so, he was delightfully distracted and therefore no match for Steve's underhand cunning.

'Very well. Come on, boys. We will be back in a few hours, Steve. Call me at once if there's any news.'

'Of course.

Tariq was the last to leave the room. He gave Steve a long, lingering look over his shoulder. Steve met it with equanimity but found it highly disturbing. He was relieved when the door finally closed softly behind Tariq and he found himself alone.

Steve slumped in the same despised chair, closed his eyes and assessed his position. He wished that he could shake his feeling of unease regarding Tariq but after a moment's reflection was able to reassure himself. The man might have his suspicions but Steve had covered his tracks to perfection. Tariq could turn over as many rocks as he liked but he would never find anything that led him back to Steve.

Steve applied his mind to business and flipped through his emails on his phone. There were dozens of condolence messages which he speed read with disinterest, including one from Hugo. Why was it that just the sound of his old friend's name still had the ability to rile him? Steve reminded himself that he was ten times the success that Hugo would ever be.

He smiled when he saw a couple of emails from Leona, updating him on a few of his more important contacts with whom he hoped to do lucrative business. He had to hand it to her; she hadn't let the grass grow and had honed straight in on the contracts that were in danger of slipping from Steve's grasp. She'd hold the hands of his would-be clients and have them playing ball in no time flat.

Steve closed his eyes, thinking of the types of games he would very soon be playing with his highly desirable assistant. With Stella out of the way, he could have his cake and eat it too. Despite the fact that she'd caused him so much trouble, or perhaps because of it, he wanted Leona with an urgency that had grown stronger the more she fought against him. Her return to the fold indicated that her attitude had mellowed and for his part, Steve would forgive her.

Eventually.

They were a great team professionally and could be in other ways too. Who knew, if she played her cards right, perhaps he'd keep her around as a permanent fixture in his life.

His eyes flew open again when his phone pinged, indicating a message from his bank. A very distinctive ping, peculiar to his offshore account: the one no one knew anything about.

'Shit!' He shook his phone, convinced that it had to be an error. Someone had accessed the account from his desktop. 'The fucking bitch!' he yelled as the pieces fell into place.

17

Hugo's research was at a vital stage but he found it impossible to concentrate that morning with his usual single-minded clarity. Commitments had prevented him from seeing Leona after her first day back at the coal face and a long telephone conversation had failed to convince him that she had acted with caution. He was relieved to know that Steve hadn't shown his face but also knew that situation wouldn't last for long.

His distracted state concerned him since he was well aware that lack of concentration led to errors being made. Even so, his thoughts dwelt upon Leona's situation and not the latest glitch in the production of a pathfinding new computer chip that meant so much to him.

Leona hadn't told him much on the phone, other than that she was bonding with Molly. Steve's staff were known for their loyalty. If any of them suspected Leona's motives then the boss would hear all about it and Molly was the most likely to snitch on her. Leona knew that but if she got on the trail of anything significant then the chances were that she wouldn't let it stop her.

'Foolish woman!' he muttered.

God help her if her delving threw up evidence of Steve's involvement in Stella's attack. Hugo's blood ran cold at the very thought. Was that her real purpose in throwing herself into the fray? She had mentioned the possibility in an offhand sort of way but Hugo knew it would be an effective way of getting Steve off her back, *if* she could get the proof to the police before Steve got to her.

'Of all the headstrong, stubborn, reckless...'

Hugo threw up his hands, unable to say why he felt so hell-bent on protecting her. He thought of his sister and his lovely, young nephew and knew precisely why. Things had turned out well for Jess but only because she'd seen Steve for what he was when still little more than a child herself. It could so easily have ended badly.

Hugo's musings were interrupted by his PA telling his that a Cleo Addison insisted upon seeing him.

'She doesn't have an appointment, Hugo, but she says it's important and that you'll know what it's about. She's in quite a state.'

'Okay, Diane, send her in.'

Hugo pushed his papers aside, put his computer back to screen-saver mode and stood up when Cleo walked into the room. He was shocked by her dishevelled appearance. Her eyes were bloodshot, her makeup smudged and it was obvious that she'd been crying.

'Can I get you anything?' Diane asked, clearly bursting with curiosity.

Hugo looked at Cleo, who was very agitated, but she shook her head. 'Thanks, Diane,' he said. 'Make sure we're not disturbed.'

'Of course.'

'Sit down before you fall down and tell me what's wrong, Cleo,' Hugo said as the door closed behind Diane.

'It's James.'

'I rather thought that it might be.'

'Bizham rang him this morning. I was in the next room but the door was open and James didn't bother to close it. He seems to think that I don't exist, or that I don't have a brain in my head if I do overhear what he's saying. Anyway, he addressed Bizham by name, which is how I knew who he was talking to, and there was a full-on argument. I only heard James's side, of course, but it was clear that Bizham was berating him for his affair with his precious daughter.'

'Since they took little trouble to conceal it, I assumed he must already have known.'

'Well, Bizham has threatened to withdraw the directorship.'

Hugo flexed a brow. 'Can he do that?'

'James told him he couldn't but I think Bizham must have pointed out that it wasn't legally binding yet. He blames James for what happened to Stella, you see. If she hadn't been leaving the Randolph after meeting him then she couldn't have been attacked. James told him that was ridiculous. If someone wanted to attack her, they only had to follow her and await their opportunity.'

Hugo nodded. 'The reasoning of a deluded man who's grieving. Even so, Cleo, I don't see why this has brought you running to my door.'

'Because there was talk of a consignment. I jotted down what I heard.' She pulled a crumpled piece of paper from her pocket and handed it to Hugo. 'Coming into Tilbury next week.' She paused, her eyes wide and wary. 'James said that trust was a two-way street and if he didn't honour the directorship then Bizham's share of the consignment would find its way into James's hands.' She leaned forward and grasped Hugo's arm. 'You have got to stop them, Hugo! If James is mixed up with something illegal and gets caught then he'll go to jail. Then what will happen to me?' she wailed.

'Calm down, Cleo.' Hugo patted her hand, then stood to pour her a glass of water from the bottle on his credenza. 'Drink this and take a breath.'

She took the glass from Hugo and swallowed inelegantly.

'Has James got financial problems?' he asked.

'He's always complaining that funds are tight.' Cleo sniffed. 'But he's been more upbeat recently, since he started seeing Stella, in fact, now that I think about it.'

'How do you know when their affair started?'

'I always know when he's seeing someone else, but it never usually lasts so I turn a blind eye.' A tear slid down her cheek. 'It's different this time.'

'Do you have any idea what could be in the shipment coming into Tilbury?'

Cleo shook her head. 'None whatsoever.'

'Not to worry. Go home and leave this with me, Cleo.'

'You will stop him though, won't you?' she wailed. 'There's no one else I can ask. I can't bear any of this. Stella's at death's door and James is moping around the place like a wet weekend in August. Everything went wrong when that woman came into his life. She's toxic and James is too blind to see it.'

Hugo was careful not to offer any reassurances, wondering how Cleo supposed he could stop a shipment that was already on its way. Or how he could stop it even if it wasn't, for that matter. Bizham and Farmer had clearly joined forces in order to improve their respective finances. But what was so lucrative? Drugs? Precious stones? People?

Hugo's money was on people. It was highly profitable, the cargo expendable. Dozens could be hidden away in the hold of a big ship. Hugo's first inclination was to let the cargo reach shore and follow it to Farmer's warehouse, before common sense kicked in.

What the hell had he been thinking? Leona's gung-ho attitude must be catching. He was not equipped to do anything like that and had no particular desire to. It wasn't as though he had a death wish. Better to drop an anonymous tip to the border authorities that illegals were hidden on that ship. If Hugo had got it wrong then no harm would have been done and his name would be kept out of things.

He probably had got it wrong, he conceded, slumping in his chair to think it through after a subdued Cleo had left him. Would Bizham really risk his political ambitions, to say nothing of the reputation that meant so much to him? His freedom would be in jeopardy too if he got mixed up in such a tawdry business. If he had done so then he really must be desperate. How long had James Farmer been a people smuggler, if that was what he was into? He'd heard that for the people at the top of the chain, it was highly lucrative, but even so...

'This is above my paygrade,' he muttered, putting Cleo's piece of paper in a drawer. He needed to give the matter some thought rather than acting impulsively and living to regret decisions hastily made.

Or worse, not living at all.

He tried to return to his work but it was complex, vital to get it right, and his head was all over the place. On a whim, he picked up his phone and called Leona's mobile.

'Hey,' he said, relieved when she answered immediately. 'How's it going? No, don't answer that. You can tell me in person. It'll be lunchtime soon and I'm coming over to feed you.'

'No need.'

'You've got to eat.'

'You'll be seen and recognised. It will get back to Steve. He'll think we're dating.'

'A little competition is healthy.'

He was gratified when she didn't put up too many more objections and agreed that he should pick her up from Steve's offices.

'See you in an hour,' she said. 'I'll let them know on reception to expect you.'

This time, when Hugo attempted to return to his work, he found that his brain was actually in gear.

* * *

'Fuck! Fuck! Fuck!' Steve paced the length of the waiting room, attempting and failing to remain calm. It could only have been Leona who'd accessed his account but how the hell had she known about it? 'Think, think, think!'

He'd let his guard down a bit in front of her, he realised now. She would know where he kept his passwords and perhaps he had dropped the odd remark about having funds squirrelled away for a rainy day. He'd wanted to impress her, have her look up to him with admiration, especially when he'd sensed that she was no longer falling for his line. She'd seemed indifferent to his success, which is why he'd been less discreet than ordinarily would be the case.

He needed to be at the office and he needed to be there now, to stop her before she uncovered anything incriminating. Although it was too late for that and it was now a question of damage limitation. She would have seen the large sum he'd shelled out to pay for Stella's attack and if she passed it on to the police then the game would be up.

His problem was that he couldn't leave the dying wife about whose welfare he was supposed to be bereft. If he did, it would start alarm bells ringing with Bizham and Steve feared his retribution a damned sight more than he worried about being the subject of the bumbling police investigation.

Having calmed down a little, he realised that Leona had obtained sight of his records illegally. Surely a decent brief could have them dismissed from the investigation, or he could come up with a plausible reason for having a secret account and using the funds? Better to be in trouble with the taxman than facing suspicion of arranging Stella's attack.

Bizham was another matter, though. If word got back to him, he wouldn't care about the legality of the find. He would only have to convince himself that Steve was responsible for Stella's situation – he wouldn't bother about actual proof – and Steve's life wouldn't be worth diddly squat.

Was there anything more incriminating than that withdrawal for Leona to find? Steve attempted to calm down and think the matter through. If anyone tried to trace that payment, they would be led round in circles but it would still set alarm bells ringing and Steve would have awkward questions to answer.

'I really need to get out of here.'

As though in answer to his prayers, alarms sounded, followed by the sound of feet running. Curious, Steve stepped into the corridor and saw that the activity was centred around his wife's room. Several people were working desperately on her. Steve watched impassively from the other side of the window.

'Do us all a favour and die,' he muttered. To anyone watching, it would look as though he was praying, which he was, but not for the outcome that most people were likely to imagine.

Eventually, Stella appeared to be stable and Steve again cursed. Those attending her stepped away from her bed. A nurse fiddled with the tubes to which she was attached.

'She had a minor stroke. We were concerned that she might.' A doctor emerged from the room and informed Steve. 'We've managed to stabilise her. She's tough and hanging in there.' He slapped Steve's shoulder. 'Don't give up hope.'

'Thank God,' Steve said with feeling.

But he was actually giving thanks for the opportunity that had been created. He rang Bizham to update him and naturally he wanted to be there.

The moment he arrived, this time without any of his sons in tow, he insisted that Steve take a break.

'You look terrible,' he said. Steve knew that he did. He'd just dropped a little liquid soap in his eyes for that very reason. 'Get some rest. Go for a walk. Do something. I'll stay here.'

'No, I can't. I need to—'

'I'll call you if the situation changes. Just go!'

'Well, all right. I need to call in at the office. I'll go for a couple of hours but call me at once if... if anything happens. Anything at all.' Steve shook his head, his soapy eyes leaking realistic tears. 'I really thought it was the end. What if she doesn't come out of this, Bizham? What are we going to do? How can I cope without her?'

'Don't think that way.' Bizham squeezed Steve's forearm. 'The power of positive thinking will get her through. You just see if I'm not right.'

You usually are, or think you are, you arsehole.

'Let's hope so.' Steve picked up his discarded jacket and ensured that his phone was in the pocket. 'Okay, I'll be back soon. Keep in touch.'

'Depend upon it.'

Steve left the hospital, jumped in his car and turned the radio up loud to an oldies station. He sang along out of tune with a Stones number, feeling anxious and yet in control once again. Whatever it was that Leona thought she'd found, he'd soon put her right. It was a shame that she hadn't come back simply because she wanted to re-establish their relationship. It was a bit of a blow to the old ego, that one. Damn it, why did she have to be so fucking stubborn?

How to deal with her? Steve would have to tread carefully. He'd chosen his inner circle of staff carefully, purchasing their loyalty with salaries above the going rate. As far as they were concerned, he walked on water and it wouldn't be wise to do anything with

Leona that would dispel that notion. He needed them to have his back if the shit hit the fan, either over Stella's attack or with the Leona business.

By the time he slid his car into his reserved space, he'd come up with an idea. It was almost lunchtime. He'd insist upon taking Leona out for a working lunch and let things develop from there.

He schooled his features into a sombre expression, glad that his eyes were still bloodshot following the soap trick, even if they did sting like buggery. It was a small price to pay to look the part of the grieving husband.

'Hey, boss,' the security man on duty said, looking surprised. 'Didn't expect to see you today. How's your wife?'

'Hanging in there but it's touch and go. I... I needed to get away for a while, to do something normal.'

The man nodded. 'Understandable. We're all rooting for her. And for you.'

'Thanks. Much appreciated.'

He conducted similar conversations as he made his way through the offices. Molly smiled at him when he reached his own bolthole, her face wreathed with concern. Good old Molly. She'd been with him for years and was as solid as they came.

'What can I get you?' she asked.

'I'm good, Molly, thanks. Just need a distraction for a while.' He paused. 'Is Leona here?'

'In her old office.'

Not still in mine then. 'Okay, I need to catch up with her. Anything urgent I should know about?'

'Everything's under control, Steve. You just need to concentrate on Stella.'

Steve nodded and headed for his office. Everything was just as he'd left it. If it hadn't been for that alarm, he never would have known that anyone had been in there but for the feint aroma of a familiar perfume that lingered. He switched on his computer, fished out his password by using his key to unlock the drawer where they were kept, and accessed the offshore account. He didn't know what he'd been expecting to see. There was no indication that anyone had accessed either it or the drawer that contained the passwords. No tell-tale scratches indicative of lock-picking. No splintered wood or missing contents.

The healthy balance flashed at him from his screen but failed to give him any satisfaction. The last transaction, the payment to the hitman, looked accusatory. He logged out of the account, thinking he should have changed the password, but to do that, he would have to phone the bank and he really couldn't be arsed. This matter would be resolved now, today, and Leona would no longer be a threat.

She'd taken on Steve in some misguided attempt to have the final word, simply because he'd perhaps made more promises to her than he'd had any intention of keeping. Clearly, he'd underestimated Leona but she needed to get over herself and move on. Too late now, she'd crossed a line, become a liability and would have to be silenced.

Permanently.

Shame that, but perhaps they could have a little fun before she breathed her last. After all the trouble she'd caused him, he deserved a reward.

18

'Steve's car has just arrived in the car park.'

A breathless Molly put her head round Steve's door to warn Leona, who was in mid-snoop, wondering what else there was to discover that she might have missed the previous day.

'Thanks.' She swallowed down her anxiety. 'I didn't expect him to show up so soon.'

Molly shook her head. 'Me neither.'

She left Steve's office as she'd found it and returned to her own seconds before she heard him talking to Molly. Her heart palpitated and her hands were unsteady. If Molly hadn't warned her, she'd have been caught in the act of rifling through Steve's personal stuff. A close call and evidence that Molly really was on her side. Be that as it may, now that the time had come, she felt unready to face Steve and needed to get her emotions under better control first.

She hoped he'd give it a few minutes before he came in to see her but knew that if he'd left Stella and come straight here then he'd done so for a reason. A reason that probably involved her. Was he on to her? How had she given herself away? Had Molly tipped him the wink after all?

Random thoughts percolated through her addled mind. Frightened of what he would be capable of now that she had probable proof that he'd arranged Stella's attack, she wondered if she'd bitten off more than she could chew. The desire to call Hugo and ask him to help her was overwhelming, but what could he do? If Steve wanted to get to her then he would find a way. Besides, Hugo was coming to take her out to lunch. What would Steve think when he saw him arrive? Would there be safety in numbers?

She'd held out on Hugo when they'd spoken the night before. She had wanted to tell him about her discovery and ask him what he thought she should do about it but knew he'd take her to task for her reckless snooping and so had kept it to herself. She decided now that her reticence had been misplaced. If Steve was on to her then someone else needed to know what she'd discovered. She glanced at her phone, at the pictures she'd taken of his offshore account showing the highly suspicious and very large amount that had gone out the day before Stella's attack. As a precaution, she sent it through to Hugo. He would know what he was looking at and understand the implications as well as she did.

Feeling that she'd done all she could to cover the bases and slightly more in control of herself as a consequence, she heard Steve's office door open, then close again. She picked up her phone to call a client seconds before a tap on her own door preceded it opening. She turned with her phone to her ear, smiled at Steve despite the fact that her heart lurched with fear at the sight of him, and indicated the chair in front of her desk as she conducted her conversation. Smiling at the man who'd spitefully wrecked her life was one of the hardest things she'd ever done. All she really wanted to do was pummel him with her bare fists for what he'd put her through.

Her conversation with the client came to an end and Leona had no further excuse to prevaricate.

'Steve,' she said. 'What are you doing here? How's Stella? I expect you're tired of answering that question.'

'She's hanging in there but we've been told to prepare for the worst.' He dashed at his eyes with the back of his hand. They were bloodshot but Leona still wasn't convinced that his grief was genuine. 'I needed to get away for a few hours. To do something normal. I'm just in the way at the hospital. She's sedated so...'

'Well, you don't need to worry about anything here. I've got this lot more or less under control.' She indicated the pile of files on her desk with one hand.

'I never doubted that for a moment.' He paused. 'Have a working lunch with me and you can update me on your progress.'

Panic welled inside of her. She hadn't expected that. 'Too soon, Steve. I haven't got myself up to speed with everything yet.'

'Even so, I need a distraction.' He sent her a winsome smile that would once have melted her heart. Now it just worried her. She was being played again and it infuriated her that he seemed to think she'd still be taken in by his performance. Be that as it may, how did you say no to a man whose wife was at death's door without seeming like a heartless bitch? The fact that the man in question shouldn't be issuing pseudo-social invitations under such circumstances was not something she could remind him about. 'Please.'

She fixed him with a look of regretful determination. 'Remember the terms under which I agreed to come back,' she said.

'Surely you don't think that I want to...' He ran a hand through his hair, looking disgusted. 'Christ, Leona, whatever do you think I am?'

Trust me, you don't want to know. She wasn't fooled by his performance; in fact she thought he'd overdone it. 'I knew this was a mistake,' she said, gathering up her bag. 'No good deed goes unpunished. I think it would be best if I left.'

* * *

Steve hadn't expected her to stand so firm and knew that he'd overplayed his hand. He wondered if she had actually come back because she really did want to help out and not because she wanted a second chance at him. Fuck, that would be a blow to the old ego, if he really believed it possible and if he let it get to him.

Not happening!

Christ, but he wanted her! He felt his cock hardening as he continued to watch her. It was such a shame that she was so determined to shaft him, and not in the sense that he'd hoped for. Her phone rang and she snatched it up, looking grateful for the interruption. The conversation was a brief one and as soon as it was over, she reached for her jacket. She really did seem intent upon walking out on him.

Again.

Steve simply couldn't allow that to happen, particularly since she was clearly on to him. He'd just checked the log on his computer and that bank account had been accessed from his office the previous day. There could be no further doubt. He felt anger welling up inside of him but squelched it down. It was always dangerous to make decisions when worked up, he knew from experience gained during his formative years.

Steve prided himself on keeping a cool head, no matter what the circumstances. It helped that he didn't have a conscience to trouble him and didn't have much time for people who were guided by theirs. In this dog-eat-dog world, a ruthless and single-minded attitude was the only way to get ahead. As far as he was concerned, he'd been put on this earth to look out for number one. Anyone who got in his way, even if they were as attractive and desirable as Leona, had only themselves to blame for the consequences if they crossed him.

Committing murder, he now knew, was a doddle. Not that Stella was dead yet, but she might just as well be. Perhaps it would be better, a more suitable punishment, if she didn't actually die. The doctors had warned him that if she pulled through, there was likely to be substantial brain damage.

He returned his thoughts to the subject of murder. As far as knocking people off was concerned, he reckoned that it would get easier and he would become more proficient with practise. Only this time, he would do the job himself rather than depending upon others to cock it up for him.

'I'm sorry,' he forced himself to say. 'I didn't mean to push you but we do need to talk about a few of the clients you're now dealing with. You can't guide them in the right direction if you don't know what it is that I have in mind for them; how much leeway I'm prepared to give in the negotiations.'

She nodded, hung her jacket back up and resumed her seat, seeming more comfortable when there was the barrier of a desk between them. 'Okay,' she said, picking up her pen. 'Fire away.'

Steve worked through her pile of files, forcing himself to concentrate. Leona took copious notes and asked intelligent questions. He thought again that it was such a pity she had to go. They'd make a formidable team.

'Remember, the Frobisher account is the one that I really want.'

'I gathered that. I put in a call this morning, asking for an appointment with Mr Frobisher. I'm waiting to hear back.'

'Well, good luck. He's proven to be annoyingly elusive of late.'

'I can be tenacious. Besides, I'd spoken to him a few times before I left and we got along well. Hopefully, he will remember that and return my call.'

He sat back when they'd almost reached the bottom of the pile.

'Is it okay with you if I ask Molly to send in coffee and sandwiches?' he forced himself to ask contritely.

'Er yes, I guess, but if we're finished here, aren't you anxious to get back to the hospital?'

He shook his head. 'Nothing will have changed. Bizham would have phoned if it had. She'll still be unconscious and it's too depressing to observe her being monitored by all that beeping machinery. Anyway, I need to stay away for a bit longer. Is that cowardly?'

'Understandable, I would imagine. Everyone has a different way of coping under such circumstances. There's no right or wrong way.'

'Excuse me.' He got up. 'I'll ask Molly to organise our lunch, then use the facilities.'

Steve made sure the men's room was empty, locked himself in a cubicle and made a quick call. Satisfied that his orders would be obeyed to the letter, he returned to Leona's room, sat back in his chair and enjoyed the view. He also enjoyed Leona's nervous discomfort that she disguised quite well. But not well enough to deceive Steve.

Good!

He enjoyed the chase, the cat and mouse, taunting her and keeping her guessing. He figured that part of her would still want to believe that she'd gotten him all wrong and that he was one of the good guys, if only because no one liked to be taken in. Oh yeah, he enjoyed the game almost as much as he'd enjoy having her and then strangling the life out of her.

'We need to talk about before,' he said into the ensuing silence.

'Why?' She looked genuinely surprised by the suggestion. 'That's water under the bridge and I don't want to revisit it. You didn't behave well, Steve, but you don't need me to tell you that. You lied to me and then got all aggressive when I called you on it. But what's done is done. We both need to move on and I'm only here helping out because you have a family crisis. If you think otherwise, and I don't see how even you could reach that conclusion at such a time, then think again.'

'Wow! You really do have a low opinion of me.'

Fuming at her audacity, Steve was relieved when the tension was broken by Molly's arrival with their lunch.

'Thanks, Molly,' Leona said, smiling at the older woman. 'My lunch engagement will be here soon. Do you mind telling him that I'm tied up and can't get away?'

Molly nodded. 'Of course. Is there anything else you need?'

Molly addressed the question to Steve. He smiled and shook his head. 'Thanks, Molly. You've thought of everything.'

She sent Leona a lingering look as she quit the office, closing the door quietly behind her, almost as though assuring herself that Leona was okay. Not you too, Molly, Steve thought, suppressing a sigh. Of all his employees, Molly had always been the most reliable and dedicated: his number one devotee. She fucking well should be, given the amount he paid her, effectively buying her loyalty. But now, with one look, she'd given Steve cause to doubt that loyalty.

'Who's the lucky man you were supposed to lunch with? You should have said that you already had plans. I would have understood.'

'You didn't give me an opportunity,' she replied, not obliging with the man's name.

Her reaction was a timely reminder for Steve. He no longer knew who was significant in her life; she no longer hung on his every word. Clearly, she really hadn't come back because she missed him and saw an opportunity for... well, a second opportunity.

It wouldn't do to assume that she was still a loner, he now knew, with no one who would miss her for several days. He needed her out of the way, and out of the way fast now that she'd seen his bank account and that telling withdrawal, but he also needed to box clever.

He had no idea if someone else had put her up to snooping into his private finances and if that was the case, she'd probably already reported back with her findings. For that reason, doing away with her himself was sadly no longer an option. He'd need an alibi, to be somewhere in public view when the deed was done, but how could he pull it off? His mind went into overdrive. If someone else connected to him met with an accident, even the dense plod would smell a rat. He thought of Sergeant Potter's remarks about his association with Leona and cursed inside his head.

The alternative was to move the funds from that account. He had others in places where banking regulations were considered to be optional and no questions would be asked if large influxes of cash hit those accounts. He urgently needed to know if Leona had copied down the relevant facts from the account that she'd accessed or worse, taken pictures on her phone. He needed to get hold of the phone in question and satisfy himself on that score. If she had taken pictures and sent them on elsewhere then he was screwed.

No! He shook his head decisively, belatedly recalling that Leona could see him when she sent him an odd look. Christ, but he was losing the plot! *Get a grip!*

'Sorry,' he said, 'my mind's all over the place and I appear to have developed a habit of conducting conversations with myself inside my head. I keep wondering what I will do if Stella... well, you know.'

She nodded in sympathy. 'Let's hope it doesn't come to that. They can work miracles nowadays.'

If she had sent the pictures on, he reasoned, then he would have to scarper. Fortunately, he had enough funds squirreled away to ensure that he'd still be able to live in luxury and start again somewhere else. Even so, he was nowhere near ready to leave the UK yet. If it became necessary then it would no longer matter if Leona met a tragic end and he *would* personally ensure that she did so before getting out. She was entirely responsible for his current dilemma so he'd make damned sure that she paid the ultimate price and also ensure that she suffered before the lights went out.

Steve finished his sandwich, drained his coffee cup and stood up. 'Thanks for keeping me company,' he said, 'and welcome back. You've been missed.' Well, that much was true. 'I suppose I'd better get back to the hospital but do text me if there's any movement on the Armitage bid. We need that one to stay solvent.'

She raised a brow. 'I wasn't aware that there are cash flow problems.'

He winked at her. 'Occupational hazard but don't worry. We're not about to go under.'

'That's good to know,' she said, switching her computer back on and immersing herself with whatever was on the screen.

So much for my compelling charm, Steve thought with annoyance as he left the office. There was a time not so long ago when she couldn't look anywhere other than him when they were in the same room.

Steve sauntered down to reception, keen to know who Leona had had a lunch date with. He chatted to the receptionist as he glanced at the sign in form and his heart stuttered.

Hugo? Fucking hell!

Steve went out to his car a worried man. He'd never completely trusted Hugo ever since the business with that silly bitch at uni. Then there was Jess, Hugo's sweet little sister: too sweet and tempting to resist. He'd always thought that Hugo blamed him for screwing with both women's lives and that was one of the reasons why Steve still did business with his old friend, even though he could get the components that Hugo supplied cheaper elsewhere.

Even though, he'd long since thought of Hugo as anything other than a friend. He was the one man who didn't seem to fall for Steve's bullshit, looking at him in a superior way that got Steve's goat.

Whilst Steve had nothing to berate himself about when it came to the two women in question, there were other aspects of his life that Hugo knew a bit too much about and which wouldn't stand up to public scrutiny. More women who'd behaved irrationally when Steve ended their affairs. Taken as a whole, the evidence could hurt Steve if it was made public and especially if Bizham got to hear about it. Not that Bizham would be a force to be reckoned with in Steve's life for much longer. His dying daughter and terminal share price would keep him well and truly occupied.

Keep your enemies close, and all that, he reminded himself, returning his thoughts to the saintly Hugo.

Steve did look upon Hugo as an enemy, and a rival. His standards irked Steve, who felt that Hugo looked down on him simply because he preferred to make money rather than invent the next big something. It wasn't as if Hugo's precious computer chips would find a way to secure world peace or eradicate poverty. It was just another way of making a name and reputation for himself, to say nothing of money. They were the same in that respect but Hugo would insist upon flashing his intellect and adopting the moral high ground.

It was galling.

Leona and Hugo appeared to have joined forces and, since Hugo had called at the offices to pick Leona up rather than meeting her somewhere, he clearly wanted Steve to be aware of the fact. And that was worrying. Even so, Steve was more than a match for the pair of them, if they were daft enough to take him on.

Okay, buddy, point made.

Steve drove away but stopped about a mile down the road,

where he pulled into a layby. Using a burner phone and a programme that disguised his voice, he called his offices, identified himself as Frobisher and asked to be put through to Molly. When she answered he told her that a Leona Carson was keen to meet with him and had left several messages.

'I'm at the Clarendon Hotel not far from you,' he said. 'My next meeting has cancelled. If Miss Carson can get here within half an hour, I can spare her a few minutes.'

Molly assured him that she would pass on the message and was equally sure that it wouldn't be a problem.

No, Steve thought, hanging up, pleased with his ploy. He was pretty sure that it wouldn't be either. He drove to the hotel, hid his distinctive car from view behind the building and paid cash for a room in the name of Frobisher.

'Now we wait,' he said to himself as he settled into the room and helped himself from the minibar.

19

Hugo was deeply disturbed. He'd arrived to collect Leona for their lunch date, only to see Steve's car in the parking lot.

'He's here already,' he said aloud, stating the obvious.

Unsure what to do, his mobile rang. It was Molly, cancelling their lunch. He thanked her and hung up again. By that point, he'd signed in at reception and was at a loss to know what to do. Should he go upstairs and confront Steve and Leona? To what purpose? Drawing attention to his friendship with her would set alarm bells ringing with Steve.

'Whoops.' Hugo smiled at the receptionist. 'Seems I've been stood up.'

The receptionist sent him a surprised smile. 'That's a pity,' she said.

Hugo returned to his car, thinking matters over. He pulled up the picture of Steve's offshore account that Leona had just sent to him. That massive payment rang equally massive alarm bells. The police would be interested, very interested indeed. But Hugo wasn't about to involve them until he was assured of Leona's safety. If Steve's back was against the wall, then a misogynist of his stature would never go down without taking the woman responsible for his downfall with him.

Leona's wellbeing was his first priority.

He sat where he was, with Steve's car in his sights. If he took Leona off somewhere then he would follow. But the chances were he would have to return to the hospital soon. It would look suspicious if he didn't, which is why Hugo decided to wait and see how things played out.

Sure enough, fifteen minutes later, his patience was rewarded. Steve strode from the building and climbed into his car, not taking any notice of the other cars in the lot. Not that Hugo's would have stood out anyway. He didn't think Steve even knew what make and model he drove.

He watched Steve drive away, alone. Now was the time to call Leona and make sure she was okay but before he could do so, his phone rang with an urgent query from his laboratory. It took ten frustrating minutes to resolve the problem. He'd only just hung up when Leona emerged from the building, climbed into her car and drove away. He called to her and flashed his lights repeatedly but she seemed preoccupied and obviously didn't see him. He wondered where she could be going. He called her but her line was engaged, so he did the only other thing he could do and followed her.

He called repeatedly as he did so, flashing his lights once again when he got close to her but she either didn't look in her rear-view mirror or else thought he was some sort of boy racer keen to get past her on the single lane road. He lost distance when she jumped an amber light and he was forced to stop at the red. He continued to call her phone but she didn't pick up.

Perhaps she was ignoring him for reasons Hugo couldn't fathom.

By the time he caught up with her, she'd already pulled into the

Clarendon Hotel's car park and was striding towards the entrance. She barely glanced in his direction when he sounded his horn but did quicken her stride. Hugo cursed and thumped his steering wheel in frustration.

With no other option available to him, he wasted valuable time finding a spot in the crowded car park. By the time he'd done so, Leona had disappeared from sight. He entered the hotel himself but there was no sign of her. If she was here to meet a client then that meeting wasn't taking place in the bar, which he discovered to be virtually empty when he put his head round the door. What to do? A pretty young girl was manning reception. Hugo walked up to her and flashed his most engaging smile. He'd seen Steve pull the same trick and it usually guaranteed him the complete attention and cooperation of its recipient. The girl returned his smile and Hugo hoped that he would have equal success.

'How can I help you, sir?' she asked brightly.

'I'm embarrassed,' he said, leaning towards her and attempting to look sheepish. 'I have a meeting arranged with my colleague Miss Carson, who arrived a few minutes ago, and I can't remember the room number.' And he assumed that the irresponsible woman must have headed for a room. Why she would do something so rash, he had yet to decide. 'Can you help me out and save my blushes please?' He fixed her with his full attention. 'I've tried calling her but she's not picking up. She's probably already put her phone on silent in preparation for the meeting.'

'Well, I probably shouldn't...'

'Please, Sylvie.' He read her name tag and flashed another smile. It appeared to sway her.

'Well, I don't suppose it's a state secret.' The girl checked her computer. 'She's meeting Mr Frobisher in room 427.'

'You might just have saved my life.' He winked at her and turned towards the lifts. 'Thank you.'

Hugo rode up to the fourth floor, wondering who the mysterious Mr Frobisher could be. One of Steve's potential clients perhaps but if that was the case, why the hell had Leona agreed to meet a man she didn't know in a private hotel room? The bar or one of the conference rooms he could live with at a push, but this? He rolled his eyes, feeling disturbed. Something about the situation just didn't feel right.

He shook his head as he left the lift at the fourth floor and looked down the anonymous corridor with doors on either side as far as the eye could see and a patterned carpet that made him feel dizzy. It was deadly quiet, not a soul in sight. He checked the signs and walked in the direction of room 427, wondering what the hell he should do now. He tried Leona's mobile again. It went straight to voicemail. If he barged in on a private and genuine business meeting, he'd feel like a right prick. But better that than Leona finding herself facing some mad axeman.

There had been no sign of Steve's car in the car park. Even if he'd discovered that Leona had been snooping into his private finances, Hugo reasoned, he hadn't had time to arrange for her to meet with an accident. That thought was comforting, to a degree, but still Hugo's anxiety prevailed. Any paid assassin worth his salt wouldn't kill someone in a hotel room, would he? Hugo had no way of knowing for sure but he had noticed cameras in the foyer, the lift and this corridor. How could a person intent upon committing murder be sure that he wouldn't be caught on one of those cameras?

Partially reassured, he loitered outside the room in question and could hear voices coming from within: a man's and a woman's. The door was too thick for him to identify them. For now, he would wait but at the first sign of distress on Leona's part, or the least indication of a struggle, he would intervene.

* * *

Leona was annoyed by the boy racer who kept flashing his lights at her. She was driving faster than was safe for the road she was on. What was his problem? Preoccupied as she relived her meeting with Steve, she knew she should call Hugo and discuss the contents of that bank statement but she couldn't because she was driving and didn't have the hands-free facility in her old car. Besides, despite everything, her professional pride made her want to pull off this deal with Frobisher. Her stand-in had been trying for weeks, to no avail, and she couldn't help feeling just a little vindicated to have procured a meeting with the man on her second day back on the job.

She had met him a couple of times before she'd walked out on Steve. They'd gotten on well and she wondered now if her return was responsible for this sudden opportunity. An opportunity that she would do her best to exploit for Steve, as well as restoring her own tarnished reputation, even if she fully intended to bring him down, now that she had proof of his involvement in Stella's attack. That being the case, it hardly made sense that she wanted to pull the deal off, she reasoned as she drove into the hotel's car park and took one of the last spaces. She was annoyed to see Mr Road Rage pull in a little behind her and without looking at him, she quickened her pace and headed for the safety of the hotel's entrance.

'What is his problem?' she muttered again, feeling distinctly uneasy.

Her phone rang. It was Hugo but she didn't have time to talk to him now. Frobisher had been specific. Turn up immediately or he would be gone from there. Not only did she want to secure the deal but she had a more specific reason for wanting to impress Frobisher. He had a thriving business and if he approved of her methods then perhaps there would be a vacancy worthy of her talents in his establishment. Leona wanted Steve permanently off her back so she'd have her life back but she also wanted to resume her career at the level she had worked so hard to reach.

She felt uneasy when the receptionist told her that Mr Frobisher was expecting her in room 427. She had assumed he'd be ensconced in the conference facilities. Even so, she was here now. She transferred her can of illegal mace, acquired when Steve had started harassing her, from her bag to her coat pocket and headed for the lifts. She brought Hugo's number up on her phone, put the phone itself onto vibrate and slipped it into her other pocket without actually connecting the call. If it became necessary then she would be able to do so at a glance.

She arrived at room 427, rehearsing in her head all the benefits she needed to spell out regarding Steve's offer in order to convince Frobisher to invest. She knocked at the door. It was pulled open immediately and she gasped when a hand grasped her upper arm in a vicelike grip.

'What kept you?'

Leona almost fainted when she looked up into Steve's angry features. She tried to break away from him but his hold was too strong. She was dragged into the room. The door closed behind them and she heard Steve lock it. Then he pushed her hard and she landed on her back on the bed, winded and very afraid. In a trice, her hand found her phone and without pulling it fully from her pocket, she pressed the button that would call Hugo's number.

'Did you really think I wouldn't know what you were up to?' Steve asked, looming over her like an angry, avenging devil.

'I have no idea what you mean, Steve.' It was important, vital, if Hugo was actually listening, that he knew she was in trouble. He wouldn't know where she was but perhaps there was a way for him to trace her phone. She'd been a fool and was now obliged to fall back on tenuous hopes. 'I genuinely wanted to help you but it seems my good intentions have been misinterpreted.'

'Leona, you're out of your depth. You always have been. It will take more than a silly little girl to get the better of me. But don't feel bad; you won't be the first of your sex to underestimate me.'

'Why have you been harassing me?' she asked.

'Isn't it obvious?' He shrugged and carried on talking before she could formulate a reply. 'You walked out on me, reneged on our agreement.'

'I think you'll find it was you who did the reneging. You assured me that your marriage was over.'

He gave a manic little chuckle. Seeing the look on his face, Leona wondered now if he was slightly unbalanced mentally. It would explain a lot. 'Well, darling, it is now,' he said cheerfully. 'If Stella survives, she will definitely be a few sandwiches short of a picnic, which is less than she deserves, given that she cheated on me so publicly with Farmer.'

Leona shook her head. 'You're despicable.'

'I don't take betrayal well, as you yourself are now aware.' He leered at her as she remained on the bed, supporting herself on one elbow but disinclined to get up. She wanted to give him the impression of being weaker than she actually was. A woman-hater of his stature would find it easy to believe that she was intimidated, frightened and completely at his mercy. She wanted to give Hugo time to find her and ride to the rescue as well, tenuous though that hope was. But still, he worked with technology, didn't he? Surely tracing a phone for a man with his background would be a doddle. She had to believe it, otherwise she would lose all hope. 'You should not have taken me on, Leona, then none of this would have been necessary. You brought it all on yourself; you must see that.'

All Leona could see was the reasoning of a warped mind but it would probably be wiser not to say so.

'What do you want of me? Why am I here?'

Steve chuckled. 'As if you didn't know. But if you want to play it that way, I'll go along with you.' His amusement gave way in the blink of an eye to a granite expression that scared Leona. He was definitely unhinged, boxed into a corner and highly unpredictable. 'What did you do with the information you took from my computer?'

How the hell...

Her mind raced. He knew that she'd been in so there seemed little point in denying it. 'The money you spent to have your wife attacked?' she asked, sitting up fully and meeting his glare with one of her own. 'It set you back a pretty penny,' she added, hoping like hell that her phone wouldn't run out of battery life at such a vital moment. She knew it was dangerous to taunt him but what other choice did she have? She was backed into a corner and hell, it felt good to fight back! 'Assassins don't come cheap.'

His responding grin was more terrifying than the blaze of anger it replaced. 'But worth every penny to get rid of the cheating bitch. And you, my sweet, had you been a good girl, could have taken her place.'

'And been your next victim.' Leona shook her head. 'No thanks.'

'We seem to have drifted from the point. I'll ask you once again, and bear in mind that I don't like repeating myself, what did you do with the information you took from my computer? Who did you send it to?'

'Sergeant Potter,' she replied without hesitation. 'He will be wanting a word with you.'

Steve looked momentarily afraid. 'How do you know Potter?'

'He responded when I reported you for your latest attempt at intimidation,' she replied with a sweet smile.

'Ah yes, the dog shit. I was rather pleased with that one. It seemed relevant, given that you've gotten yourself a dog. And I had friends, some of them mutual, I believe, willing to give me an alibi.'

Leona's heart froze and her expression clearly gave her away since Steve chuckled. 'That's right. I know all about your cosy little arrangement with that prick Hugo.'

'Potter will know that I was right about you by now. You can't afford to hang around in the UK now that he knows your grubby little secret. In fact, he's probably looking for you as we speak. You don't have much time and shouldn't be wasting it with me. Besides, if anything happens to me, your name will be well and truly in the frame.'

'Give me your phone.' He held out his hand, waggling his fingers.

'Why?'

'You really are the most aggravating female. Why must you question everything?'

'It's a gift.'

'Phone,' he said for a second time, his voice hardening. 'Don't make me search you for it. Although, upon reflection...'

Without warning, he dove towards her, pinning her to the bed, a manic, determined look gracing his features. She screamed and tried to bite him but couldn't sink her teeth effectively through his clothing. She managed to bring a knee up into his groin and he groaned, momentarily releasing his hold on her, but not for long. She reached for the bedside table, hoping to find something, anything to clout him with, but even the telephone was secured in place. There was nothing.

Steve rummaged in her pocket and gave a little cry of triumph when he found her phone. His triumph quickly turned to an outraged string of oaths when he saw that she was connected to Hugo.

'So clever,' he muttered, ending the call. He scrolled through her pictures and again cursed when he came to the picture of his secret bank account.

'Well, darling, you've got what's coming to you. You shouldn't have run to my wife with exaggerated tales of our plans to elope together.'

Leona blinked. 'Is that what you think I did?'

'Why else would she have taken up with Farmer and arranged for me to be so publicly humiliated? Stella was jealous. She thought I'd actually fallen for you. Despite everything, she loves me and couldn't bear to think of me taking up permanently with someone else.'

Leona laughed in his face. 'That might well be the case but I have never had a private conversation with your wife, so if you're wondering why she turned against you, you'll have to look elsewhere.'

Steve sent her a hard, assessing look. 'I don't believe you.' His hands slipped around her neck and he started to squeeze.

'Surely you're not going to kill me here,' she gasped. 'You'll be on CCTV checking in, and it won't take the police five minutes to join the dots.'

'Oh no, darling. We'll be going for a little ride in a moment. We'll have some long-overdue fun and then see what's what. But first things first.'

He eased the pressure of the weight pinning her down as he looked through her phone, which was Leona's opportunity. The only one she was likely to get. In one desperate movement, she reached into her other pocket, belatedly recalling the presence of the mace. She got hold of the can, withdrew it and pressed the button down, firing it directly into his face.

At the same moment, what sounded like a battering ram caused the room's door to shudder. The lock broke and it sprang open.

Leona almost fainted with relief when she saw Hugo's musculature filling the opening. Steve turned to face him, his vision blurred by the mace, tears pouring down his face. But it was clear that he was far from down and out.

'Well, well,' he said, 'if it isn't Mr Virtuous.'

Steve swung a punch towards Hugo but it was ungainly and easily countered. Hugo responded by knocking him to the floor with one massive blow. Blood spurted from a broken nose. Profanities spilled from Steve's cut lips.

'It's over,' Hugo said, pulling Leona to her feet and taking her shaking body in his arms. 'The cavalry's on the way.'

'How did you know where to find me?' Leona shook her head, then rested her forehead against Hugo's shoulder.

'It's okay,' he assured her. 'I'll tell you everything in a moment.'

He smoothed her hair with sweeps of his hands as the room swarmed with hotel personnel.

Potter arrived remarkably quickly. He took possession of Leona's phone. Hugo handed his over too. He had recorded the entire conversation that Leona had conducted with Steve and they listened now to the maniac boasting as Steve condemned himself with his own words.

'Now do you believe me?' Leona demanded of the detective, finally feeling vindicated.

'I never disbelieved you,' Potter replied. 'But we can't act without direct evidence. I kept telling you that.'

'He'll have more than stalking to worry about now,' Hugo said, his tone imbued with a wealth of satisfaction.

Steve was read his rights and carted away in handcuffs.

'Come on,' he said to Leona. 'I'll take you home. You're in no state to drive. We can pick your car up tomorrow.'

'It was you,' she said, blinking at him. 'You're Mr Road Rage.'

Hugo laughed as he opened the passenger door and ushered her into his car. 'I've been called worse,' he said.

20

Two days later, Steve had been formally charged with the attempted murder of his wife and the papers were full of it.

'All thanks to you,' Hugo said as they walked Mulligan through the woods. 'But for God's sake, answer your phone in future.'

'I hope there won't be a future situation like that one,' she replied shuddering. 'But for what it's worth, I really did think that I was meeting Frobisher and wanted to impress him in the hope of getting on his payroll.'

'Surely you smelled a rat. Anyway, you won't have any career problems now. Steve blackening your name will no longer hold any sway. Quite the reverse, in fact. You're the heroine of the hour.'

'I don't feel heroic. Just lucky to be alive. If you hadn't been there, I dread to think what might have happened.'

'You helped yourself by macing him.'

'That wouldn't have stopped him for long. He was desperate and desperate men have superhuman strength.' She looked up at Hugo. 'How did you come to be there, anyway? We've not had a proper chance to talk it through, what with having to make endless statements and avoiding press attention.'

Hugo explained the circumstances. 'Part of me wanted to come charging in but the receptionist told me you were meeting a Mr Frobisher. If it was a genuine business meeting, I didn't want to screw it up for you, even if you were being impossibly irresponsible. Anyway, you at least had the presence of mind to call me so I could hear what was going on. I was right outside, ready to come in at a moment's notice, but given that you'd got him talking, I wanted to hear him condemn himself with his own words first, which he did. A maid happened along with a master key, just when you screamed. But the chain was on the door; I had to break it down.'

'Thank you,' she said with heartfelt sincerity, squeezing his arm.

'My pleasure. I've waited for a long time to get revenge on my sister's behalf, even if she didn't ask me to. Anyway, my sources tell me that Steve's pretending mental frailty.'

'Doesn't surprise me. Will he get away with it?'

'I very much doubt it; the police are arranging for a psychiatric evaluation. But these people have met the Steves of this world many times before. He's unlikely to get away with it.'

'Nawaz must be fuming. He will use his influence to ensure that Steve feels the full force of the law. Or more likely, meets with an accident whilst in prison.'

'He's got other worries. I might have tipped the authorities off about the arrival of a ship with illegal cargo. The cargo in question has turned out to be illegal immigrants. Cleo told me about the ship and that Farmer and Nawaz were the force behind it.'

'She's burned her bridges?'

Hugo chuckled. 'Never underestimate a woman whose future is under threat.'

'I don't understand.' Leona frowned. 'I know it's a lucrative business but surely not lucrative enough to tempt men of their stature. Besides, would they be openly involved?'

'Probably not but their lives are being turned upside down by the serious crime squad. Someone will give them up in order to save their own hides. Potter seems to think, God knows how he found out, that Nawaz recruited some dodgy people in his native country on the way up and was forced to do them a favour in return.'

Leona wrinkled her nose. 'Why am I not surprised?'

'Farmer had made his millions through various questionable schemes, or so Potter seems to think. This is the making of Potter's career and he's all over it, despite the fact that more senior ranks have now taken over. They will find whatever evidence there is to be found.'

'Blimey,' Leona said faintly. "Why would a man with political ambitions get involved with such a tawdry business?'

Hugo nodded. 'Nawaz was in financial doo-doo and had no choice. His share price will hit the floor now, as will Farmer's, so even if the charges don't stick, HMRC will examine both men's finances through a microscope and Nawaz's political connections will drop him like a hot brick. They're finished.'

'Good!' Leona imbued the one word with considerable satisfaction. 'I hate human exploitation. Anyway, how's Stella?'

'Still clinging to life but it's not looking good. Nawaz's assets will be seized whilst his affairs are investigated so there won't be the luxury care available that Nawaz probably intended for her.'

'Why did she openly consort with Farmer, I wonder? She must have known that Steve's retribution would be brutal, although I doubt that even she realised quite how brutal.'

'I'm guessing that she'd had enough of dancing to Daddy's tune and putting up with Steve's philandering. I think she actually loved him and knew the only way to hold on to him was not to cling. So she played him at his own game. She would have known about your attempts to get a restraining order against Steve and... I don't know, she got jealous, perhaps. Or possessive. Or decided to be less discreet, flaunt Farmer in front of him and force Steve to choose. I guess we'll never know for sure.'

'Unbelievable,' Leona replied, breathing hard as the possibility that she was indirectly responsible for the attack on Stella took root.

'Potter said something about your application for a restraining order. His first contact with Steve was over the phone and, we're guessing here that Stella heard his end of the conversation. That would have been enough to open her eyes. A restraining order against her husband would have infuriated Nawaz and he in turn would have turned the screws on Stella, forcing her to toe the line.'

'For what it's worth, I think she really liked Farmer and saw an opportunity to start again with a man who put her first as well as publicly humiliating the husband who had let her down.'

'Well, I don't suppose we'll ever know for sure but I can't say I feel much sympathy for any of the main players, with the exception of Stella. The others were driven by greed and ambition.'

'And you have your life back.' Hugo took her hand in his and Leona saw no reason to snatch it back again. 'What shall you do now?'

'Take a look at employment opportunities but it will have to be a position that tolerates dogs. I can't leave Mulligan on his own all day.'

'Well,' Hugo replied. 'It just so happens that there's a vacancy at Rossiter Engineering that might well suit your talents. Our research is almost ready for marketing and needs an expert in the PR field to promote it. I happen to know the boss rather well. I'll put in a good word for Mulligan, if you like.'

Leona smiled up at Hugo. 'Why don't you do that,' she replied.

ACKNOWLEDGMENTS

My grateful thanks as always to the wonderful Boldwood team and to my fantastic editor, Emily Ruston, in particular for knocking my efforts into some kind of order.

MORE FROM EVIE HUNTER

We hope you enjoyed reading *The Alibi*. If you did, please leave a review.

If you'd like to gift a copy, this book is also available as an ebook, hardback, large print, digital audio download and audiobook CD.

Sign up to Evie Hunter's mailing list for news, competitions and updates on future books.

https://bit.ly/EvieHunterNewsletter

Explore more gritty revenge thrillers from Evie Hunter...

ABOUT THE AUTHOR

Evie Hunter has written a great many successful regency romances as Wendy Soliman and is now redirecting her talents to produce dark gritty thrillers for Boldwood. For the past twenty years she has lived the life of a nomad, roaming the world on interesting forms of transport, but has now settled back in the UK.

Follow Evie on social media:

THE

Murder

LIST

**THE MURDER LIST IS A NEWSLETTER
DEDICATED TO SPINE-CHILLING FICTION
AND GRIPPING PAGE-TURNERS!**

**SIGN UP TO MAKE SURE YOU'RE ON OUR
HIT LIST FOR EXCLUSIVE DEALS, AUTHOR
CONTENT, AND COMPETITIONS.**

SIGN UP TO OUR
NEWSLETTER

BIT.LY/THEMURDERLISTNEWS

Boldw**oo**d

Boldwood Books is an award-winning fiction publishing company seeking out the best stories from around the world.

Find out more at www.boldwoodbooks.com

Join our reader community for brilliant books, competitions and offers!

Follow us
@BoldwoodBooks
@BookandTonic

Sign up to our weekly
deals newsletter

https://bit.ly/BoldwoodBNewsletter